Rising or ████████████ the
chest. Where v ████████████ w,
a lace shawl, a ████ ██████ continued pulling out her
dear granny's handiwork until she found it. Unwinding a
long, lace table runner, she removed layers of tissue
paper. As the last of the wrappings fell away, she choked
back tears and stared at the face of her farmer, a face she
had known all her life.

The small, framed drawing was one of the few
things of value she possessed. Faded and fragile, it was
a bona fide and precious antique, handed down through
her father's family for generations, placed in her keeping
by her grandfather. It had hung in the great room of the
farmhouse. She'd stood looking up at it so often that
Gramps had finally moved it to her room. She couldn't
have been more than eight years old.

After that, she'd shared every sadness, every
disappointment, and every joy with her farmer. She
gazed at the beloved face.

No one knew who he was, but he'd been the impetus
for her chosen career, the very reason she'd wanted to
study medieval history. In her studies, she'd come across
drawings of medieval farmers guiding their teams of
oxen, but hers stood alone, strong and sure, facing the
artist.

She touched the glass, tracing him with her finger,
feeling that, somehow, he reached through the centuries
to comfort her.

"I wish you were here," she whispered.

Tremors through Time

by

Anastasia Abboud

Tremors through Time

Cover Art by *Kim Mendoza*

The Wild Rose Press, Inc.
PO Box 708
Adams Basin, NY 14410-0708
Visit us at www.thewildrosepress.com

Publishing History
First Edition, 2022
Trade Paperback ISBN 978-1-5092-4000-5
Digital ISBN 978-1-5092-4001-2

Previously Self-published
Published in the United States of America

Dedication

To Colette and Oliver—always choose love.

Acknowledgements

It took me over four years to write this book. I was not always easy to live with. Family and close friends had to put up with a poor version of me—cantankerous, anxious, nebulous. For good measure, add to that bouts of whining. But they loved me through it and did not give up on me. There are several dear ones who gave me extra special support and whom I'd like to thank.

Team Angel: my husband Joseph, our sons Bashir and Raji, and Julia, Raji's beloved wife and our daughter-in-heart, were uncommonly gracious and patient. They're all generally gracious, anyway, but not one is particularly patient. But they were with this. I've talked about my book a lot. Nowhere near as much as I've thought about it, of course, but they were the ones who got weird and random questions about all sorts of things, at all different hours, while I was writing. They always answered as best they could, even helping me with research at times, and they read through troublesome passages upon request. Four years of this! Joseph, thank you for being my rock of love and support. Bashir, Raji, and Julia—thank you, darlings, for your love and faith in me. And thank you, our littlest angels Colette and Oliver, for your hugs and kisses, which always made even a bad writing day sweet.

My brother Reggie Orchid doesn't read romance, but he offered to read my book. I refused. He offered again. My husband told me, "He's going to buy it and read it once you publish it, just to support you. If you want honest feedback, you know he'll give it to you." And he did. Thank you, Reggie, for taking the time to read, for giving me honest, helpful feedback, and for your love and support.

Micheline Abboud, dear sister (in-law and heart), you gave me a woman's perspective just when I needed it most. You rescued the love scenes. Thank you for taking the time to read, comment, and repeat, and for your constant and loving support.

Jessica Abboud, thank you for taking the time to read and for your sweet counsel.

In our hectic lives, it can be hard enough to simply sit and enjoy a book. To be stuck with the same book for three years running would have to be more than strenuous. Elyce de Reefe, thank you for being a great critique partner, for your encouragement and support. You consistently pushed me to write deeper POV and, in effect, taught me to do so. You told me to back away from the ledge more than once and pointed out the good in my book when I couldn't find any. You made me laugh a lot, and I couldn't be more grateful.

Dr. Alison Chand, PhD, the book would have remained a mess without you. Thank you for that first round of editing.

Danny Nouri, thank you for the original cover for the book, formerly known as Tremors.

During the writing process, I often struggled to find time to write and develop the story. There were many days where a gentle inquiry, a casual question in passing, encouraged me beyond all measure. Rick Abboud, Dunia Chbeeb, Mary Ann Kovach, thank you for showing your love and support by regularly remembering to ask about my writing, for patiently listening to my rants, and for cheering me on. You don't know how many times you lifted my spirits. Aline Bertone Sterling, thank you for staying in touch and for your encouragement.

Also, many thanks to Dr. Nouhad Nassar, PhD, for answering my many questions about teaching at a university and about Scotland, and for basically nagging me to finish the book. You encouraged me and made me laugh.

There are also a few people I'd like to thank for generously helping me with research and information. Rex Mennem, thank you for taking the time to sit down and help me visualize the offshore oil rig scenes and for answering my almost endless questions. Mary Ann, thank you for arranging that immensely helpful meeting with your son-in-law.

Sharron Gunn, thank you for all of those wonderful workshops about medieval Scots and for checking my Gaelic. Your generosity and erudition have been much appreciated.

James Brown, you didn't hesitate to step right in when I had last-minute anxiety about certain historical facts. Thank you for sharing your time and knowledge.

Thanks, too, to Alastair Smyth, of Scotland's Forestry Commission, for providing me with wonderful information on Plodda Falls and Glen Affric. You helped me see the area when I couldn't be there in person.

Last, but not least, many thanks to The Wild Rose Press, especially my editor Eilidh MacKenzie. Eilidh, your patience and guidance, help and insight, and your insistence on excellence have been a revelation to me. Thank you.

And in all things, from beginning to end, I thank God for the life, love, and hope He has given me.

Prologue

Scottish Highlands, 1339

The forest was quiet, the only sound the gurgle of the stream as it flowed over the rocks. Shoving his spade deeper into the sodden earth, Lachlann drew a breath of cool, pine-scented air and glanced at his friend. Sunlight, peeking through the branches of the trees, shimmered on the water and upon Rónán's dark head, bent low as he dug.

"Lachlann, I've found a beauty this time!" Triumphantly, he unearthed a large piece of quartz. Rinsing it in the stream, he held it up. The crystal sparkled in the sunlight.

"Do you think I might trade it for parchment?" he asked, handing it to Lachlann.

Lachlann weighed it in his hand, appraising it. "I think you could. You're right, it's a beauty." He handed the crystal back to Rónán and laughed. There were leaves in his friend's dark hair and mud on his nose, cheeks, and forehead. "But you're not. You have muck all over your face!"

"You chose this spot, not me!"

"Are you sorry?"

"No, I'm not," Rónán quickly replied. He held his treasure out once more. "Really, it should be yours. This was your idea."

Lachlann shook his head. "It's through your own labor that you've found it. But you should ask your father to barter it for you. We're too young for proper trading." He glanced up at the sky. Light still pierced through the dense canopy of pines, but it was clear that the sun had dropped considerably. "We should start for home."

He and Rónán washed their stones in the clear, running stream and shoved them into the small pouches they wore at their waists. They washed their hands and faces and drank a little of the fresh, cold water.

The air was damp and the scent of pine heavy as they sauntered along. A red deer crashed through the brush, darting in front of them. Rónán jumped, bumping Lachlann.

"Are you made of stone?" he asked indignantly.

Lachlann shrugged. "It was just a doe. As I said, it's getting late. The animals are waking."

"What animals?"

"All of them." He tried not to laugh as his friend eyed him suspiciously.

"Liar!" Rónán punched him in the arm.

Lachlann chuckled. "I speak the truth, but you needn't worry. The wood's edge is ahead of us, see? Anyway, what wolf would want a skinny meal like you?"

"I'm not worried about wolves," muttered Rónán. "Not when there's a fat, juicy Norse lad with me." Without warning, he pounced on Lachlann's back.

"Fat?" Holding his legs, Lachlann spun round and round.

"*Sguir dheth!* Stop! Ox!" Rónán shouted, hanging onto his neck as they laughed. "You're going to get dizzy and fall and flatten me!"

"It would serve you right." Lachlann stopped

spinning, but he didn't set his friend down until they reached the edge of the wood.

"Maybe we should bury our treasures," Rónán said as they trudged along.

"I thought you wanted to trade your crystal for parchment."

"I don't want to ask my father to do it for me. If I save it, I can get my own parchment later."

Lachlann was hardly paying attention to the conversation as they crossed the rocky Highland meadow toward the lands of Clan Chisholm. Hills rose in the distance, but, before them, in a broad, green expanse, some boys were playing *camanachd.* Their shouts rose on the wind as, sticks waving, they ran for the ball.

"Lachlann!" When Aonghas called out to him, they all stopped. "Come and play! You can be on our team!"

"We're a man short," argued another. "He'll be on ours."

Lachlann didn't reply as he and Rónán approached.

"*A'Dhaimh,* whose team will you be on?" a third demanded.

"No one's," Lachlann replied.

"Why not? Come on, Lachlann. One game!" sounded a chorus.

"I'm going home for supper."

"You're going the wrong way, then." Aonghas' lip curled. "But you have to make sure the cripple gets home all right, don't you?"

Rónán flushed. Lachlann resumed walking without bothering to reply.

"My *sporan!*"

Aonghas had snatched Rónán's pouch from his

waist, snapping the thin strap, and took off.

"Give it back, Aonghas!" shouted Rónán, breaking into a lopsided run.

Lachlann pressed his friend's shoulder. "Aonghas!" he called. "Give it up!"

"Come and get it!" the bully challenged.

Furious, Lachlann chased after him. Why always Rónán? Couldn't they leave him alone? The other boys tried to trip him as he ran. He dodged them, drawing closer and closer to Aonghas until he was close enough to launch himself at him.

They fell hard, rolling. Lachlann stretched over Aonghas as they tumbled, trying to grab the sporan. Aonghas punched him in the eye. They rolled again. Lachlann slogged him in the jaw once, twice. The bully's grip on the small, leather pouch loosened for but a moment. It was all Lachlann needed. He grabbed it and was back on his feet.

"You won't be so lucky next time, *A'Dhaimh*!" Aonghas called.

Lachlann didn't spare him a glance. He tossed the sporan to Rónán as they continued walking toward the latter's home.

"Thanks," said Rónán. He peered at him for a moment. "You're going to have a black eye."

Lachlann shrugged.

"It's good to have a Norseman for a friend," continued Rónán. "That's all they want, you know. For you to be their friend."

"Then they need to be better to *my* friend."

"Why do you want a cripple for a friend?"

"What does your being lame have to do with anything?"

"I can't run like the others. I'm not strong."

"You're strong enough to go digging in the forest, aren't you?"

"Of course, but…"

"And you're smarter than all of us put together."

"I'm not smarter than you."

"You are," countered Lachlann. "You know how to read."

"You would, too, if you'd let me teach you."

"I don't have time. Farming takes all day."

"So we know different things," Rónán said. "I know how to read. You know how to grow things. But the others don't know anything."

Lachlann grinned wryly. "They know how to pick on people who are different from them. They used to call me a dumb ox because of my accent. You were the only one who didn't make fun of me."

"That's not why they call you 'ox' now. One day, when I'm a famous bard and you're the best farmer in the Highlands, they'll show respect."

"I don't care what they think, and neither should you," Lachlann said firmly.

"I don't. But I don't trust them. I think we should bury our crystals in our secret cave. I don't want anyone finding them. Can we go tomorrow?"

"I have work to do in the morning."

"So do I. But if we start early and work hard and fast, we should be done by lunch."

"I won't be."

Rónán didn't answer. Lachlann glanced at his dark, bowed head and relented.

"Maybe if we promise to bring trout for supper, our parents will excuse us."

They were approaching Rónán's home. His father was outside, skinning a rabbit. Rónán's small brothers and sister were laughing and playing. They shouted when they saw the two older boys. In an instant, they were all over Lachlann. He pretended to be a bull, stamping and running with the children on his back.

"Good evening," called Rónán's mother from the doorway. She was a sweet woman with dark, curly hair and rosy cheeks. She smiled at them until she noticed Lachlann's eye. "Lachlann, lad, what happened to you this time?" She moved to take hold of his chin, lifting his face to hers.

When Lachlann didn't speak, Rónán answered for him. "He was defending me again."

"You defended yourself," Lachlann murmured. "I just got the black eye."

"Aonghas took my sporan and went running."

His mother frowned. "Can they never leave anyone in peace?"

"That's lads for you," Rónán's father remarked.

"It doesn't hurt," Lachlann assured her.

"Will you share supper with us?"

"No, thank you. My family's expecting me. I should be going." He disentangled himself from the wee ones and nodded toward Rónán's father. "I bid you all a good evening."

"Rise early and pack your lunch!" Rónán grinned cheekily. "I'll be waiting!"

Chapter One

Scottish Highlands, 1351

Shrouded in mist, Loch Nis loomed, dark and foreboding, in the distance. Lachlann pulled the packhorse along swiftly, anxious to be home before nightfall. He needed to see his family, to hold his son. He checked his sporan. The wee leather ball and wooden horse figurine were there, safe. He could hardly wait to watch Iain's little face light up when he gave him the toys.

Allasan should be pleased that he'd found everything on her list. He grinned. They had their differences, but if there was one thing about his wife, she knew what she wanted. She was the most stubborn Gael alive. Despite fever, nausea, and a sick three-year-old to care for, she'd almost pushed him out of the door.

"You have to go," she'd urged, her brown eyes unnaturally bright. "I want the dye and you'll find it in Inbhir Nis. You promised! I didn't work day and night all summer to be disappointed because of a paltry ailment. I have my family and yours all around me if I need anything. Go! You'll only be in my way here!"

He had to admit, she'd been right. The Lùnastal festival in Inbhir Nis was much larger than their local fairs, with a wider variety of merchants in attendance. Not only had he found her purple dye and wax candles, but all sorts of vegetable seeds as well, even Norse favorites such as horseradish and mustard.

Thanks to a bountiful harvest and the cloth that Allasan wove so skillfully, he'd had plenty with which to barter. He'd even been able to choose gifts—Iain's toys, silk ribbons for his wife and sisters-in-law, and iron gall ink for the bard.

He only wished that Allasan and Iain had been able to go with him as planned. He'd worried about them the whole week.

What's wrong with the horse? He tugged lightly on the rope. The beast stalled, its ears flat back. He tugged harder, then smelled it, the foul stench of smoke.

"Come on," he urged the animal. "Someone's just burning something."

But burning what? As he drew closer to the village, he saw black smoke billowing from the mountain. His gut clenched. Something was wrong. He moved faster.

The packhorse resisted.

Damn it! He had to get home. When the animal continued to balk, he tied him to a tree and ran.

By the time he reached the outskirts of his village, his eyes were burning. Smoke was beginning to choke him.

Iain.

He ran faster.

Someone grasped his arms, swinging him to a halt.

"You're going the wrong way! You need to get out of here!"

Gaelic, but the accent was odd. Dimly, through the smoke, he saw a stranger standing before him, his face shrouded by a hood.

"I'm going to my family!"

"They're gone. You need to turn around and head back to Inbhir Nis."

"What do you mean, they're gone?" They must've moved away from the fire. He pushed forward. He'd be able to help.

The stranger stopped him again. "You're the farmer, aren't you? The Norseman they call 'Ox'?"

"I am."

"I'm sorry, friend. Your family is gone. Your entire village was wiped out."

Wiped out?

"Explain yourself!" Lachlann roared, his heart suddenly pounding in his ears.

"They're all dead. The plague...It took your whole village in less than a week. They've been burning everything—bodies, houses, clothing, bedding. There's nothing left."

Lachlann began to run.

"Turn around!" the stranger shouted after him. *"A'Dhaimh, sàbhail thu fhèin!"*

He ran as fast as he could, the fetid smoke filling his nostrils, burning his eyes and throat. He rushed through the village without pause, not slowing until he reached his longhouse. He stopped then, gasping, his heart beating in his ears. The thatch roof was gone, the stone blackened with soot.

"Allasan! Iain!" Racing inside, he found only ashes. He stared. Ashes. Their iron kettle nestled on the floor of the hearth, blackened, smoldering. On shaking legs, he walked the short length of the house. Not a sign, not a hint. Where were they?

"Allasan!"

They had to be all right. Just a week ago, Allasan had been cooking, weaving, arguing. Iain had been playing, laughing. They couldn't be...They must have fled.

Find them.

He stumbled back out. Black smoke whirled around him like fingers of death. Gasping, he ran to his parents' home. The stone structure still stood, blackened, roofless. Heat seemed to radiate from within. He stared at it, unable to move as dark flakes fell around him. Ashes!

The house built by his grandfather's grandfather, the oldest and largest in their village, the home he'd grown up in, was reduced to a blackened pile of stones. A shuffling sound caught his attention. His heart leapt.

"Mother?"

A hen fluttered from behind the house.

Lachlann turned away, tears burning down his cheeks as dread clamped coldly around his heart.

Where was everyone? He glanced wildly about him. They couldn't all be gone, not the whole village.

Castle Chisholm! They would have sought refuge at the castle. Allasan and Iain would surely be there. It had been Allasan's home. He beat the trail up to the castle. The smoke was thinner as he approached the unfinished stone structure. The gates were closed, but he knew the guards.

"My family," he said urgently. "I want to see my family!"

Brian, an old friend, stepped forward, grimacing.

"Lachlann…" He faltered.

"My family!"

The Gael shook his head. "I'm sorry."

"Where are they?"

His friend's hands grasped his shoulders. "They're not here, Lachlann," he said quietly. "They died."

"They can't be dead! I just left them a week ago!"

"It happened quickly. Your whole village was

10

struck."

"My parents, my brothers…"

"To the best of my knowledge, you're the only survivor."

Lachlann's knees buckled. Brian's hands braced him, held him up.

Allasan, Iain, Mother, Father, Ivar, Vali, their wives, their children…

How could they all be dead? It wasn't possible.

"Allasan's parents?" he choked.

"I haven't seen them, but they could be here."

"Can I go and look for them?"

Brian shook his head. "The chief forbids any of the Norse to enter, if there are any left besides you. The sickness started in your village, but we've already lost some of our own people."

"Rónán and his family?"

"Last time I heard, the bard's family was all right. I thought Rónán would be with you."

"With me? Why would you think that?"

"He set off for Inbhir Nis on one of the chief's horses to find you and tell you of your family."

"Rónán went to Inbhir Nis?" He could hardly fathom it. Rónán hated riding.

"That's where he said he was going. He left a few days ago." The Gael held out a flask. "Take this. I'm sorry, Lachlann, but you have to go."

"Where are the bodies?" His own words sounded distant, as if someone else had spoken them.

Brian gazed at him, tears in his dark eyes. They'd shared many a meal through the years.

"I haven't been to the village, but from what I've heard, all were burned."

Lachlann's stomach roiled. "Did the chief order

this?"

The warrior shook his head. "We bury our dead. But with a sickness like this…" He shuddered. "In the end, some of our people helped. The chief might order the same here to stop the disease from spreading." He pushed the flask into Lachlann's hands. "Drink."

Lachlann accepted the flask and tried to swallow. But his throat was clogged with smoke and tears. He gagged. Wordlessly, he handed the flask back to Brian and nodded a farewell.

He had to check all the houses. He would bury any bodies he found. His family, his people…He headed back to the village on legs he no longer felt. Only his mind worked.

Find your dead.

But where? The scant structures all looked the same, scorched and black with soot. Piles of ashes were everywhere, some still smoldering.

He wandered from house to house, looking, listening for signs of life. But there were none.

Silence taunted him, stark and pervasive, broken only by his own shallow breaths. What should he do? His mind felt numb.

"What are you doing here?"

Starting violently, Lachlann turned to see the hooded stranger striding toward him. A cloth covered his nose and mouth.

"Why are you here?" the man asked him.

"I seek my dead."

"I told you, they burned everything. You'll find no bodies."

"Where did they burn them?"

The man stepped closer to place his hands on Lachlann's arms. "In their homes," he replied quietly.

"Mostly in their beds, where they died."

Oh, God. He couldn't see, couldn't breathe. *Iain.* Lachlann fell to his knees, gasping for air, gagging on it. His chest…He couldn't…

"Breathe." The man pressed his shoulders, sounded long, even breaths.

He couldn't.

"Breathe," repeated the voice. "Steady."

Lachlann tried to mimic the rhythmic breathing of the stranger crouched before him.

"That's right. Keep going. Good."

He didn't know how long they knelt there as he struggled for control. But the pressure remained on his shoulders until he stopped shaking.

"There's nothing left for you to do here." The voice, with its strange accent, finally penetrated his consciousness. "You must leave. You could still get sick."

"Where will I go?" Lachlann asked hoarsely. "I should have helped my people."

"There was nothing you could have done."

"Then I should have died with them."

"But you didn't," came the quiet response. "You're obviously not meant to die yet."

Lachlann swayed.

The man shook him slightly. "Go back to Inbhir Nis. Return in spring."

Inbhir Nis. Rónán had gone to Inbhir Nis. He could find him. Slowly, he rose.

The man rose with him. "Go," he urged again.

Nodding, Lachlann turned away. When he reached the edge of the village, he glanced back. The stranger stood watching him, a lone, upright figure swathed in smoke, surrounded by ruin.

13

Lachlann began running, pausing only when he reached his fields. They were cloaked in the same deathly smoke that was choking him. He hurried on until he reached the loch.

Collapsing to his knees, he howled, the sounds of a tortured animal ripping from his chest.

How could they all be dead, and he still lived? He should have been here. He might have helped them.

He might have died with them. Death would have been preferable to this.

Gasping, he yanked at his tunic, ripping it away from his neck.

"*Nei!*" he bellowed.

He sobbed and raged until his throat was raw, until he could hardly breathe.

He was suffocating.

Up. He had to get up or he would die here in the ashes. He had to find Rónán.

His horse—he had almost forgotten. He stumbled back to where he'd left him and found him waiting patiently. Stroking the thick neck, Lachlann untied the rope from the tree. The poor beast didn't resist as he once again pulled him toward the loch, away from home.

He trudged onward, his legs shaking so hard that walking seemed impossible. But he didn't stop. He forced himself to keep moving, one foot in front of the other.

Night fell. The smoke dissipated, then disappeared altogether. Stars twinkled in the dark, clear sky. Tears poured from his burning eyes, down his cheeks, as he pressed on.

His whole family, his whole village…they'd all been dying whilst he bartered for vegetable seeds and ribbons.

Please, Rónán, be alive and well.

The ground suddenly trembled. Lachlann glanced at the loch. The water was rippling, but there was no breeze. He moved away from the water and kept walking. But this wasn't the mild sort of tremor they usually had in the glen. The earth shook violently. Ahead of him, an enormous pine tree uprooted completely.

The packhorse reared. Lachlann pulled at the rope, trying to calm the frightened animal, but he was unable to steady himself. He fell backwards, the rope flying from his hand as the horse bolted into the forest. He would have to find him later. *Voices!* Was someone calling his name? He rose unsteadily to his feet.

"Rónán!" he called urgently.

In the moonlight, cracks appeared in the earth. He heard the ground breaking. All around him, it was breaking! Twisting, turning, Lachlann desperately tried to find safe ground. Suddenly, there was a terrible roar, like a giant screaming in pain.

A crack raced toward him, widening into a chasm beneath his feet. He shouted as he slipped, grasping desperately at the earth. It crumbled beneath his hands.

"*Nei!*"

He tried to climb out. He was sliding.

Falling!

"Lord, have mercy on my soul!"

Chapter Two

Houston area, Texas, 2016

She'd done it.

Deidre stood in the doorway of her new home. It smelled funny. Dead insects dotted the entry, and some of the medium-dark wooden floorboards were washed out and splintered. But the house was hers and hers alone.

Alone.

Instantly, she squashed the annoying, dejected feeling that accompanied the word. She was happy. She'd bought her own house without anyone's help or unwanted advice.

"Congratulations!"

Deidre jumped as Stella joined her in the doorway, a bottle of champagne in one hand, two crystal flutes in the other. Her Realtor beamed at her, her coral lips curved in a wide smile.

Fine. With Stella's help. But no one else's.

"Professor Chisholm, you are the proud owner of a prime golf course property," Stella said in her heavy Bronx accent. "What are you doing just standing in the doorway? Welcome to your new home!"

Deidre smiled. "You do mean prime golf course *project*, don't you? It's going to take me a few years to elevate the house and garden to what might be considered prime condition."

"Garden? Move, woman!" Stella bustled her through the door. "Granted, your swimming pool needs work, but it's mostly cosmetic. Once you've had it re-surfaced, you should be good to go. The yard is fine as it is."

"I said *garden*, not yard," corrected Deidre as the door closed behind them. "I think I've mentioned that I want to grow my own food?" She'd done more than mention it. If she'd said it once, she'd said it a hundred times. Stella was well aware of her intentions.

"Now, Deidre, we've talked about this. There will be a limit to what you can grow next to a golf course."

"The HOA can't stop me from growing tomatoes."

"No one's telling you not to grow a few tomatoes. But isn't there anything else you'd like to do? You know, paint? New kitchen?"

Deidre arched a brow. "Do you mind if I unpack first?"

"It's the first time you've mentioned unpacking." Stella set the champagne and flutes upon the dusty kitchen counter and grinned at her. "You mean you'll do that *before* you start digging?"

"I guess I'll have to." Deidre sighed dramatically. "I'm sure I'll change a lot, eventually. I've just missed it so much—digging, planting, having my own outdoor space."

The agent's expression softened. She'd become a friend, one of Deidre's few, in the months they'd been house-hunting. Like her, Stella had freed herself from an abusive marriage, was estranged from her parents, and had moved across the country to start a new life and prove herself to herself. While she'd lived in Houston longer than Deidre had, they still swapped stories about the differences between their new cities and old, and they both loved Tex-Mex.

"I know you've missed it," Stella said gently. "I'm just teasing. But do keep in mind that the house has potential, too. It has beautiful bones."

"Beautiful bones?" Deidre repeated dubiously.

"C'mon, Deidre! You know you got a bargain! Even I couldn't believe that we found exactly what you wanted within your price range."

"I didn't exactly want a fixer-upper! But you're right," she added hastily before Stella exploded.

"You have a study." Undaunted, Stella began counting on her fingers. "A nice kitchen, a fabulous master bath…"

"Not on my list," Deidre interrupted.

"The bath? Give me a break. Who asks for a 'dignified house?' " She pinned her with a glare. "Anyway, we got the big backyard, the golf course views." She rolled her eyes. "Pine trees."

Deidre laughed. She couldn't help herself. It was a wonder Stella hadn't killed her. She'd been a tough customer. They'd driven all over the greater Houston area searching the exhaustive inventory of properties for sale.

Deidre didn't care about the commute. She didn't particularly care about the house. She wanted, *needed*, surroundings that soothed her soul, a wonderful view from her windows, and space for a vegetable garden. She would never have a farm back home in North Carolina, but she could have a garden and pine trees.

Her Realtor had worked hard and ultimately succeeded in helping her find a home and secure her first real estate investment. The house, abandoned and foreclosed, had been damaged by its previous owners and left to rot. But it was pretty all the same. Stella was right. It had good bones, and the surrounding area was beautiful.

She gave her a hug. "You've been great," she assured her. "I'm just nervous."

"Why aren't you excited? It's a gorgeous house!" Stella made a sweeping gesture worthy of an opera star. "Just look at all the windows, the art niches, the wood floors. Think of the decorating possibilities! How does a medieval history professor decorate, anyway?"

"Shouldn't I repair the floors before I start decorating?"

"Tsk. Where's your imagination? Will you have a suit of armor in your living room?"

"I will not." Deidre wrinkled her nose. "My favorite medieval warriors wore considerably less than armor."

"Do you mean kilts?" Stella asked, working at the cork.

"Not exactly, but that's closer."

"Deidre, did they really…you know." She lowered her voice as if someone was listening.

"Did they what?"

"Did they really wear nothing underneath?"

Deidre winked. "Why do you think they're my favorites?"

Her friend's face lit up, and she laughed. "That's more like it. You're going to be fine." Popping the cork, she poured the bubbly and handed a flute to Deidre before raising her own.

"Happy birthday, you wild woman, and congratulations! Here's to happy times ahead, to your future success, and to the best garden any golf course has ever seen!"

****

A few hours later, still sipping champagne, Deidre

sorted through her old hope chest. *Hope chest.* The irony wasn't lost on her.

Suit of armor, my ass. She snorted. It was a wonder she even had dishes to eat on after the long, expensive divorce. But she would've paid any price to be free and to prevent that asshole from sucking one more penny from her.

Over. It's over, Deidre. After almost five years of subsisting in tiny efficiencies, living out of boxes, five years of scrimping, saving, and tears, the divorce lawyer had been paid in full and she'd been able to save enough for a small down payment on a house. She'd done it. She'd made a new life for herself. She had her own home, a good position at the University of Houston, and she was on track for tenure. She'd be fine.

Fine, fine, fine.

Rising onto her knees, she rifled through the chest. Where was it? A soft quilt, an embroidered pillow, a lace shawl, a tea cozy…She continued pulling out her dear granny's handiwork until she found it. Unwinding a long, lace table runner, she removed layers of tissue paper. As the last of the wrappings fell away, she choked back tears and stared at the face of her farmer, a face she had known all her life.

The small, framed drawing was one of the few things of value she possessed. Faded and fragile, it was a bona fide and precious antique, handed down through her father's family for generations, placed in her keeping by her grandfather. It had hung in the great room of the farmhouse. She'd stood looking up at it so often that Gramps had finally moved it to her room. She couldn't have been more than eight years old.

After that, she'd shared every sadness, every disappointment, and every joy with her farmer. She gazed at the beloved face.

No one knew who he was, but he'd been the impetus for her chosen career, the very reason she'd wanted to study medieval history. In her studies, she'd come across drawings of medieval farmers guiding their teams of oxen, but hers stood alone, strong and sure, facing the artist.

She touched the glass, tracing him with her finger, feeling that, somehow, he reached through the centuries to comfort her.

"I wish you were here," she whispered.

She worked for another hour, until her back ached and her chest hurt from unshed tears. It wasn't quite dusk, but it felt like midnight to her. She needed fresh air.

Stepping out the kitchen door, she walked around her swampy swimming pool to stand looking out at the fifth green. It was a warm summer's night, but a breeze was blowing. She loved the view. Too bad she had no one to share it with.

She'd always believed she would have a family by the time she was thirty. But here she was, thirty-two and completely alone. Alone on her birthday, alone in a house she had purchased as a gift for herself. She blinked back tears and focused on the golf course.

The green looked almost endless. Small hills rose here and there, framing her view. There was a pond in the distance and, beyond it, a copse of pine trees. It was beautiful, the main reason she had chosen this property. It reminded her of home.

She thought longingly of the peaceful summer days she'd spent following her grandfather around on the family farm while her parents worked in Durham. They'd shared countless happy hours sowing seeds and harvesting together. He was gone now, and she missed him terribly.

She would plant a vegetable garden. Gramps would be with her in spirit.

The sun was dipping beneath the trees when Deidre finally decided to move. Unpacking would be a lot more productive than standing around feeling sorry for herself. Wiping her cheeks, she began to turn toward her house and suddenly realized she wasn't alone.

There was little privacy between the golf course properties. Low, wrought-iron fences and short hedges were the rule.

A man—a huge man—was standing just on the other side of the fence. His face was in shadow. But in the fading light, she could just make out his features. She froze. Her heart began palpitating.

Her farmer! But he couldn't be.

Could he?

Well, of course not, Deidre.

But she would recognize that face anywhere. She'd known it all her life. That face was engraved on her heart.

Wow. She was overly tired, no doubt about it. Maybe it was the champagne. Clearly, she wasn't up to meeting neighbors. With a quick nod in his direction, she hurried back into her house.

Chapter Three

Fall, wonderful fall. It was Deidre's favorite time of year and certainly the herald of good weather for the greater Houston area.

Standing on the small balcony that overlooked her pool and the golf course, Deidre surveyed her backyard. It was prime time to plant fruit trees and vegetables. She could hardly believe that two months had passed and the only thing she'd planted was mint in a pot.

The beginning of a new school year was always busy, and her new position as Director of Medieval Studies made it infinitely more so. The department might be small, but the work was intense.

Her new position and its accompanying pay raise had certainly made it easier for her to purchase her new home. Now, if she could just keep it that way...

Tenure. That's what she needed. It would mean absolute job security. If only she'd had it when she married, her nightmare ex wouldn't have been able to rip her job out from under her when she'd divorced him.

Never again.

Leaning forward, she rested her arms on the wooden railing. Her reputation as an expert in her field was growing. She just needed to publish a few more research papers.

She *would* succeed.

Her shoulders began to tense.

Relax, Deidre.

Today, she was going to plan her vegetable garden. What was the point of having a house and garden if she never enjoyed them?

Too bad she didn't know where to begin. The sandy soil of the area was different from the clay loam of her family's property in North Carolina.

She allowed her gaze to roam over to her neighbor's backyard. As her house was on a corner lot, she only had the one neighbor.

Three men lived there, and two were renters of the third. They were quiet neighbors, offshore oil rig workers who were away two or three weeks at a time. Two of them had stopped by to introduce themselves. Joe, the owner of the house, was an older man, surely nearing retirement. Jackson, who'd accompanied him, seemed barely out of high school. They'd both been polite and respectful and offered their help should she ever need any.

But neither looked like her farmer. Had she imagined him? But no, the others had confirmed there was a third.

Leisurely, she examined their backyard from her perch. Like her, they had a swimming pool. But unlike her plain, smallish oval, theirs was lagoon-shaped with a waterfall. Three tall palms emphasized a tropical look, as did the shiny green leaves of the loquat trees tucked underneath them. There was a bay tree, too, and some sort of citrus in the far corner.

But what held her attention was neither glamorous nor tropical. Planting boxes ran along the fencerow adjoining her property, fronting the standard green hedges. They were vegetable beds, and someone had cleared what was left of some overgrown tomato plants. The soil had been turned and raked, ready for fall planting.

How did those guys manage to grow vegetables? They were never even home!

As she glared, thoroughly jealous, the man she had seen that first night strode out into the yard, moving directly to the planting boxes. Deidre held her breath.

He was as massive as she remembered. Everything about him was thick and muscular, and he was very tall. Sandy blond hair fell loosely to his shoulders. She couldn't see his face, but his skin was bronze, doubtless from his work outdoors. Was his chest as tanned as the rest of him?

He looked up suddenly. Had she said that out loud? His face, strong and clean-shaven, was beautiful in its masculinity. He was…it was him. Her heartbeat quickened, and she fought the urge to run downstairs to check her drawing, to make sure that her plowman hadn't magically escaped. Was she hallucinating?

Squinting in the sun, he smiled at her.

She almost swallowed her tongue. If this was a hallucination, she could live with it.

"Good mor-r-rnin'," he said.

That upward lilt, that rolling "r". Was he…could he possibly be…Scottish?

"Good morning," she replied.

For a moment, they just stared at each other. She wanted to hear him speak again. But what to say…

"Is that a vegetable garden?" *Brilliant.* She tried not to grimace.

"Aye."

"It's a big one."

"Not really." He paused. "You're interested in gardening?"

"Very. It was one of the main reasons I wanted a

house of my own."

"Then you should be planting. It's the best time of year for it."

He spoke slowly, carefully, in a deep, rich, tantalizing lilt, his words heavily accented. Scandinavian? Scottish? Scottish more likely. He'd said *aye*. But his accent…

"I know." She tossed her hair back over her shoulder as she looked down at him. "But I've been setting up house, and I have a full-time job. Give a girl some time, will you?"

"It's not mine to give."

"Time?"

He nodded but didn't pursue the subject.

"What've you planted?" she finally asked when he didn't elaborate.

He shielded his eyes with a very large hand. "You're welcome to come and see for yourself."

"I'll be right down."

Moments later, she stood beside him. She'd lost control of her neck. She kept trying to look at the garden, but her gaze kept returning to him.

He was gorgeous! And huge. She was no small woman, but he loomed over her. She felt deliciously feminine.

He smiled down at her. She blinked. He had a dimple in his cheek.

The garden, Deidre. Look at the garden.

She forced herself to look around. His raised beds ran along the entire side of their boundary and made a short L at the corner hedge that fronted the fifth green.

"This is amazing!" She moved down the row of planter boxes. "But why raised beds? Why not sow directly into the ground?"

"It's easier to control the soil this way and to deter small, destructive animals, of which there are an abundance."

"I see." She needed raised beds. Small mammals had to eat, but they were not welcome to her vegetables. Would she ever get around to planting? She pushed aside the annoying thought and pointed to some red seedlings.

"What's that?"

"Swiss chard," he answered, "and next to it is red Russian kale. It's an international group of vegetables."

She laughed. "It sounds delicious. I hope you'll tell me where you purchased your seeds."

"I have plenty to share."

"Awesome." She was talking like a teenager. She cleared her throat. "You know, I just realized that we haven't even introduced ourselves and here I am begging for vegetable seeds. My name is Deidre, Deidre Chisholm."

His mouth fell open, literally, and he snapped it shut. For a moment, he didn't speak. Did he often go silent or just around her?

"And you are…"

"Lachlann An Damh."

"An damh?" It was her turn to be surprised. "The ox?"

He looked astonished. "You know Gaelic?"

Smiling, she shrugged. "I've studied it. But I've never met anyone with that name before."

"I've met many Chisholms. You're of Scottish background?"

"Yes. You too, right? But yours is more recent, of course."

"Not necessarily."

She chuckled. "Your accent does suggest travel."

He grinned. "Aye, I have traveled," he said slowly. "Tell me, Deidre Chisholm, what do you intend to plant?"

****

Deidre Chisholm. Chisholm! That evening, Lachlann sat at his desk, seeing not his computer but a broad, empty field, the loch sparkling in the distance. His best friend's lyrical brogue sounded crystal clear in his memory.

" 'The sun hung midway between heaven and earth, the great loch silver beneath it, as Lachlann An Damh plowed his field.' That sounds good, don't you think? Must you do that?"

Lachlann stopped in his tracks to glare at Rónán, who sat on a rock, sketching and watching him work. "Must I do what?"

"It would be much more picturesque, and my drawing would look a lot better, if you would guide your oxen like any normal *tuathanach*. But no, you can't be like other farmers. You have to pull the plow yourself, like one of your beasts."

"At the moment, I have more land than beasts," grunted Lachlann, straining as he pulled the heavy, wooden plow over a deep rut. "One day, I'll have more oxen. In the meantime, if you wish to draw a picture of my team, they're in the next field with Fearghus."

"Unfortunately, you're my subject, not the oxen," Rónán murmured as he sketched.

Lachlann sighed. He had too much on his mind for senseless banter.

"I'm to get married," he announced abruptly and continued down the field.

"What? Wait!"

He glanced back, satisfied to see his friend hastily

28

unfolding his long, lean form from the boulder.

"You're getting married?" Rónán questioned as he joined him.

"I am."

"To whom?"

"To your cousin, the chief's niece."

"The chief's...do you mean Allasan?"

Lachlann nodded. "Allasan." He glanced at the bard.

Rónán looked stunned. "But...she's not your type! She's half your size!"

"I know."

"She's not even friendly!"

"You mean that she doesn't like Norsemen. Believe me, I know."

"She doesn't like anyone. Whose idea was this?"

"Your chief's. He and Allasan's father approached my father."

"Are they forcing you?"

Lachlann had to smile. Rónán sounded appalled. He shook his head. "No one's forcing us."

"Then why are you marrying her?"

"It will be another bond between our people." Lachlann paused to adjust the plow. "And I've no one else in mind. Why offend the chief and upset my family?"

"A bond between our people? What about the bond between you and your wife?" Rónán was almost shouting.

"You worry too much, my friend."

"I would wish you happiness."

Happiness...

A movement outside his window snapped Lachlann back to the present. Deidre was in her backyard, setting pots of mums around her small patio. The burnished hues of the flowers complemented the long, rich tresses flowing down her back. She was so natural, so achingly beautiful. She looked like no Chisholm he'd ever known. Those most familiar to him had been dark-haired, and, while Rónán had been on the tall side, most had been shorter, like Allasan.

He'd recognized that first night that Deidre wasn't as thin as so many women were these days. She was tall, big-boned, and well filled out. Bosomy. *Glorious.*

She hadn't noticed him that night when she walked outside to gaze at the golf course, even though they were very nearly standing side by side. She had just stood, still as a magnificent statue, except for the explosion of fiery red curls blowing over her shoulders, away from her face.

She had fine, sweet features and a fair complexion. Even in the fading light, he'd noticed the sprinkle of freckles across her nose, and he'd realized she was crying. It had surprised a pang in his heart. For the first time in years, a pang for someone other than himself.

Deidre fussed over the mums, pinching off spent blooms. If he'd married someone like her back in the fourteenth century, they might've been happy together.

Happiness…Once he and Allasan were wed, he'd not even thought of it. It simply hadn't been part of the equation. Nonetheless, their marriage had been a strong one. They had known what to expect, had grown to trust and respect each other. And they had both loved Iain.

Focusing on the computer screen, he clutched the mouse and…damn it! He ran a hand through his hair. What was he supposed to type?

Deidre spoke Gaelic—wonder of wonders— although he hadn't ascertained how well yet. Maybe she would be able to translate a few words for him, words that might help him with his research. She might even know something about the history of Clan Chisholm.

Was Chisholm a common name in America? C-H-I-Z-U-M. He clicked the mouse and tried to ignore the familiar throbbing in his head. It was one of the countless names and words for which the spelling made no sense, as if he wasn't having enough trouble learning to read.

C-H-I-Z-O-M.

Chapter Four

The next day, Lachlann showed up at her garden gate with vegetable seeds. Deidre was thrilled. Her forehead bumped his as they bent over the packets, spread out on her small patio table. She smiled at him.

"I want at least one of everything we can grow in the fall."

His mouth crooked up at the corner as he shook his head. "Don't say 'fall.' Seasons are different in different places."

"What do you mean?"

"For example, fall in Texas is warm. Fall in Scotland is much cooler."

"True." Why hadn't she thought of that? "What do I say, then?"

"I think…" He paused, frowning slightly. "I think the seed packets say warm season and cool season."

"No hot and cold?" She turned one over.

"I don't think so."

"So, is October cool or warm season?"

He shook his head, laughing. "Don't…Don't comp…complicate matters."

"I'm not!"

Grinning, he held up two fingers. "Two seasons. Would you say the next few months are warmer or cooler?"

The dimple was back in his cheek. Oh, swoon! The man was perfection.

"Deidre?"

She jerked back to earth. "Sorry! Yes?"

"The next few months, warmer or cooler?"

He spoke slowly, his deep voice like velvet, his rolling Rs long and rich. He spoke with the strongest, strangest accent she'd ever heard.

She forced herself to engage in the conversation. "Cooler?"

He nodded.

"Okay, I get it. So, greens are cool season veggies?"

"Greens?"

"Kale, Swiss chard…"

"Aye."

"What else?"

"I…" He hesitated.

Deidre stared at him for a moment, comprehension dawning. She could hardly believe it had taken her so long to understand. Lachlann didn't just speak English with a different accent. He spoke broken English.

"Lachlann…" She laid her hand on his forearm. "Can I ask you a question?"

"Sure."

"You didn't speak English growing up, did you?"

His eyes widened. He looked at her for a long moment, then slowly shook his head.

"You told me you're from Scotland. Did you not grow up there?"

"I did."

"But you didn't speak English at home?"

"No."

"What language did you speak?"

"I…" He hesitated. "Gaelic?"

"You spoke Gaelic at home?"

"Aye."

"But English is taught in school in Scotland."

"I was taught at home."

Deidre was astonished. She hardly knew what to think, much less say. English was the official language of Scotland. How could he have grown up there without speaking it?

Clearly, he'd had a strange upbringing. But she couldn't keep asking him personal questions. She leveled her gaze at him and tried a different approach. "*A bheil gàidhlig agad?*" Do you speak Gaelic?

He grinned.

"*A bheil gàidhlig agad?*" she asked again.

He nodded. "*Tha gàidhlig agam. A bheil i agadsa?*" I speak Gaelic. But you?

"I know it's surprising," she answered, in the same language. "I studied it in college and also in Scotland."

He winced.

"Is my accent bad?" she asked anxiously.

He shook his head. "Not bad, but different from mine."

"You can say that again!"

They began experimenting. For all her studies abroad—she'd lived two years in Scotland—she'd never heard an accent like his.

"Where in Scotland is your family from?" she finally asked.

"Orkney."

Well, that might explain a few things. She'd visited Orkney a couple of times, but she hadn't spent a great deal of time there.

"Let's make a deal," she said in English.

He just looked at her.

"If you'll help me with your brand of Gaelic, I'll help you with English."

He didn't answer.

"Oh, c'mon! We'll start with vegetables!"

His expression relaxed, and he chuckled. "Professor Chisholm, you have a deal."

****

One Week Later...

What had he been thinking? Lachlann maneuvered the dozen cedar planks through Deidre's garden gate. What had she been thinking, taking him up on his offer?

The answers weren't hard to discern. Short of leaving town or lopping his head off, he couldn't stay away from her. Beautiful, modest, funny, she was magnet to his metal. She liked gardening. She spoke Gaelic.

For her part, she obviously needed some muscle and he had offered his help—and not only help. He'd gone out of his way to make suggestions.

She could see that he was strong and experienced. Why would she refuse? He felt his chest swell and a stirring farther down that he'd not experienced since...in years.

Nei.

He wasn't becoming involved with her. He couldn't. But this undertaking wasn't mere socializing. He was learning more English with her than he had since he'd arrived in this century. They were communicating with relative ease, speaking a combination of English and Gaelic. The Gaelic she spoke was very different from his ancient, twisted version, but they were figuring out the discrepancies.

He wished he could share with Rónán that he was teaching someone Norse-accented Gaelic. His old friend would have appreciated the humor of the situation. But he couldn't tell Deidre that he'd spoken Norroena at home and that Gaelic had been a second language. No one spoke Norroena anymore.

In any case, the more he conversed with her, the more comfortable he felt speaking English. The better his English became, the easier his research would be. And maybe, just maybe, if he researched enough, he could find out what the hell had happened to him and figure out how to go back.

If he went back to a time before he'd left for Inverness, he might be able to save his loved ones, at the very least Iain—or die trying. If only...

"I can't believe this is happening." Deidre's sultry voice returned him abruptly to the present. "Can we really finish this weekend?"

When she said "I," it was more an "aw" sound. His accent in English was going to be as skewed as hers was in Gaelic. Unexpectedly, he snorted with laughter.

"What?" she asked.

He glanced at her walking beside him. Her shining red hair flowed loosely past her shoulders, glinting in the sunlight. A maroon T-shirt emphasized her fair skin and soft, pink lips. Faded jeans stretched over shapely hips and long legs.

Best of all, she carried four heavy boards on her shoulders. She wasn't small or fragile. He didn't feel like a hulking brute around her. She was strong, sturdy, and every inch woman. He wanted...

She bumped him. "What's so funny?"

"We're ruining each other's accents."

Her brows knit together for a moment before her lips twitched. "There's nothing wrong with my accent!"

He grinned. "There's nothing wrong with 'mah aksint,' either."

She burst out laughing.

"I do believe you might be right," she finally gasped as they set down their boards. She wiped her eyes on her wrists and her hands on her jeans. "Well, at least we'll understand each other."

"There is that," he agreed.

Their eyes met. He wanted to pull her close, needed to. He forced himself to glance away.

"To answer your question," he continued, "yes, we'll finish this weekend. Cutting the wood will take the most time. Once that's done, assembly will be easy."

"I wish I could've persuaded you to have them cut it at the home improvement center. I hate that you're working so hard on my account."

"I prefer to do it myself," he assured her. "I'm old-fashioned. I like my work to be my own."

"I respect that, and I thank you."

They worked together for the rest of the afternoon, hauling the wood, laying out the areas for the beds. She was willing and able. His admiration for her increased tenfold. They were a good team, falling into an easy rhythm with few words or explanations. It had been a long while since Lachlann had experienced such a pure sense of peace, of rightness.

They agreed that her boxes should mirror his. It was the most practical, natural conclusion. The arrangement worked well with the layout of their backyards and would make their two separate gardens seem almost like one large one.

As Deidre pointed out, they'd be able to compare and share as they worked. If he could get past staring at her. For him, this was something more and completely different from practical.

She's not for you.

The fall days were short, and they'd started late.

Decisions, measurements, and the trip to the home improvement center had all taken time. Darkness was falling by the time they had laid out all the beds with stakes and strings.

Deidre felt her stomach rumble.

"Lachlann, are you hungry?" she asked as they tidied up. "I know I am. Does pizza sound good to you or do you have other plans for the evening?"

"Pizza sounds great," he replied.

"Any special requests?"

He set some boards down and looked at her. Their eyes met.

"Special requests?" he repeated softly.

His gaze was heated, questioning. She suddenly felt like fanning herself.

"For the pizza," she managed to puff.

With a little smile, he shook his head. "Whatever you like. Thanks."

He returned to stacking wood along the perimeters of the beds. She stood watching him for a moment, bemused, before reminding herself to make the call.

Special requests. Oooh, yes. She could think of a few.

Dinner for three wasn't one of them, but at least the company was amiable. Joe, Lachlann's landlord, had just returned from his two-week hitch and joined them for dinner. Deidre had ordered two large pizzas, but she served a big salad as well, just to be on the safe side. They all sat outside around her small table in front of the pool.

Joe said a quick prayer of thanks for the meal, then opened three beers from the six-pack he'd brought with him.

"I appreciate you having me, Professor," he said. "I

was in trouble. I don't know what Lachlann eats when I'm not here."

Deidre chuckled. He was an older man with a pronounced Cajun accent and a twinkle in his eyes. She had liked him the moment she'd met him.

It might have surprised her that Lachlann had even noticed her accent, considering that he lived with Joe, but she had to admit that their accents were different. Hers was by far the slower, more Southern drawl.

"What *do* you eat?" she asked Lachlann as they helped themselves to pizza.

"Whatever Joe leaves in the refrigerator," he replied. "When that's gone, well, I'd rather not talk about it."

They all laughed at that.

"Have you two known each other a long time?" she asked.

"About three years," answered Joe. "I met Lachlann while I was in Scotland, recruiting for our rigs in the North Sea. The moment I met him, I knew I wanted him out here. I liked him right away."

"Same here," volunteered Lachlann. "When I first met Joe, I could've sworn I'd seen him before. I felt as though I knew him."

"Were you in Edinburgh?" asked Deidre.

"Inverness," they answered together.

"I hadn't lived there long," continued Lachlann. "I hardly knew anyone. Meeting Joe was one of the best things ever to happen to me. Not only did he give me a job and help me with my paperwork, he gave me his friendship and a place to live."

"Don't you go getting emotional on me." Joe's eyes were suspiciously bright. He looked at Deidre. "He's like a son to me. When I first bought this house, I figured I might lease out a couple of rooms for a while if I could find the right tenants. I wanted my retirement home to be on the golf course, but it's a big place for just me, and half the time I'm not here."

"It does seem a good idea," approved Deidre, "if, as you say, you have good tenants."

"Lachlann's never felt like a tenant. Now, Jackson…" He glanced at Lachlann, and they both chuckled. "He's a wild one, that boy, but he has a good heart. He's a good worker, too, ain't he, Lachlann?"

"He is," Lachlann agreed. "He works hard."

"Looks like you two have been working hard." Joe nodded toward Deidre's new garden layout. "Are those for flowers or food?"

"Food," Deidre answered. "Lots and lots of vegetables."

"Would you consider planting okra this spring?"

"I told you I would," his tenant objected.

"I don't trust you. You won't have the space. Your summer crops get too big." He turned to Deidre. "Did you see his tomato trees? Professor, you're in charge of the okra."

"Yes, sir, as long as you'll cook it."

"That I will, *cher*. Don't you worry about that!"

"You'll need good soil first," Lachlann reminded her. "If we finish tomorrow—and we will—when do you think you will have it delivered?"

"Not until next Saturday, I suppose," Deidre answered. "Will you be here?"

"No, I leave Monday."

"And you'll be gone for two weeks?"

"Aye."

"That's terrible."

Lachlann and Joe laughed.

"For you or for me?" Lachlann asked.

"For both of us?"

"You're seeing his good schedule now," Joe informed her. "Me, I work two weeks and take two off. Some fellas work two and take off three. But Lachlann here, he's the opposite. He usually works three weeks at a time and only takes one off."

"Why?"

She looked aghast. Lachlann fumbled for an answer. The truth was that he usually had no reason to be home, that he'd rather work than be alone with his thoughts. Not a subject he cared to open.

"I'm saving." It's what he'd told Joe.

"He'll have his own business one day," predicted the older man.

"How interesting! What do you have in mind?"

"Nothing concrete, yet. I'm…I'm still exploring my options."

He didn't make plans, couldn't make plans.

"You're still young and strong," Joe continued. "You both are. Don't either of you let anything get in the way of your dreams."

Lachlann shook his head. "I don't think much of dreams."

"Don't you go talking like that," the older man admonished him sharply. "Like I've told you before, just pray to the good Lord and work hard. Anything's possible."

"I agree." More than Joe would ever know. But he knew that his friend worried about him and didn't want to upset him. He raised his beer. "To possibilities."

"Possibilities." The three of them tapped bottles.

He tried not to think of the possibilities that haunted him even in his sleep, tried to ignore the tension that never left him.

"We're talking about good possibilities, damn it!" Joe slapped the table with his hand. "Quit your frowning!"

"Was I frowning?" Hastily, he glanced at Deidre. "Sorry."

She looked at him sympathetically. "Joe's right," she said softly. "It's something I sometimes have trouble with, too. But just look at the site of my future garden. It's full of possibilities, and most of them are good."

"That's true," he admitted, a little surprised. "You're both right. Again..." He raised the bottle once more. "Here's to good possibilities."

"To hope," she amended as they clinked.

Lachlann felt a sudden constriction in his chest. It had been a long time since he'd thought about hope.

Chapter Five

What a difference a day could make. Arranging a platter of po-boys and bottles of ale on a tray, Deidre felt her grin stretch from ear to ear. She couldn't help it. She normally would have refused help of any sort, especially from a man, but, well, she wasn't crazy.

Yesterday morning, she'd been frustrated because she didn't know where to begin with her vegetable garden and because she had yet to meet the man who looked like her farmer drawing. Today, her farmer incarnate was in her backyard building planter boxes.

But, oh, he was changing her lifelong image of her two-dimensional friend. Would it be weird if she moved the framed drawing from her home office to her bedroom?

This morning, to her astonishment, Lachlann had arrived carrying a handsaw. A handsaw! But any concerns she might have had about his time or trouble had disappeared in moments. He was sure, fast, and strong—so strong. Watching him was like a dream, a strange, delicious dream.

Pushing the kitchen door open with her shoulder, she stepped out. "Lunch is...glory!" She almost dropped the tray.

Bronze, damp, male...Lachlann's powerful torso glistened before her, barely covered by a form-fitting, white muscle shirt. He was the most amazing sight she'd ever laid eyes on.

He was still sawing boards on a makeshift sawhorse and had worked up a sweat. His T-shirt was slung over the back of a chair. She watched, fascinated, as he sawed a thick board.

His shoulders were massive; they moved almost like separate entities. His chest was vast, muscular; his abdomen lean, ripped. Deidre's mouth went dry. She was hyper-focusing.

The board split. He looked up, wiping his brow on his forearm, and smiled at her. Deidre didn't smile back. She'd forgotten how to breathe.

Today, he wore his hair bound back in a ponytail, revealing the chiseled perfection of his face. Broad cheekbones, a strong nose, light, slate-gray eyes. His wasn't a pretty face. It was too strong, too masculine, to be pretty. Except for his lips, which were full, sensual. She stared at his mouth. Kissable.

Swoon.

She set the tray down.

"Thank you," he was saying. "I'm hungry. I'll just go and wash up."

He walked to the side of the house where she'd arranged a small basket with hand soap, a scrub brush, and a couple of hand towels near a hose. The day before, he'd set his bar of soap on a brick and dried his hands on his jeans. The least she could do was offer small conveniences.

"It's hot!" he said, returning to the patio. He grabbed his T-shirt. "I thought it was supposed to be cooler in October."

"Cooler, yes, but not yet cool," she replied as they sat down. "And you're working hard. I can't believe how fast you are. You really don't like power tools?"

"I told you I'm old-fashioned." He helped himself

to a sandwich. "But in all truth, I haven't had much need of any up till now, and it's not as though I have my own workshop. Joe wouldn't begrudge me the space, but his garage is full as it is."

"I understand. Don't get me wrong. It's just that I've never seen anyone so fast with a saw. You're…" She stopped and felt herself blushing.

"I'm what?" he questioned, frowning slightly.

"You're strong," she answered and hurriedly continued, striving to cover her embarrassment. "Do you work out?"

He looked confused. "Outside?"

"No. I mean, do you work out in a gym?"

"Ah, work out. No, I hate gyms. I understand training for warriors…"

"Warriors?" she interrupted.

"Soldiers," he said quickly. "I can understand training for the military, or policemen, and others who protect people, and for certain other jobs. But otherwise, I believe that people's daily lives and work should keep their bodies strong enough to suit their needs."

"But what if, like me, a person's job largely involves sitting?"

"You sit when you teach?'

"No, not usually. But I do have a desk. Lots of people sit at desks all day."

"They shouldn't, no matter what their job. But if they earn their livelihoods sitting, why do they need to be muscular?"

"Because it's healthy?" Deidre sputtered.

"It's all about health, then?"

"Yes! No!" She blew out a breath. "All right, some of it has to do with vanity, but not all of it. I walk. Do you consider walking a vain pursuit?"

"Walking is a normal activity. You're an active person. When you're at home, you're outside a lot, working, moving. I live next door, remember? You take care of your garden, you work on your pool. You don't just sit."

"Well, I'm from the country. I like being outside and working in my garden. But you're awfully hard on people who are just trying to look good and be healthy."

"Am I?" He shrugged. "I don't mean to be. It's their time, not mine. I feel sorry for them. It seems unnatural, not using one's body enough to sustain a healthy life."

"I can agree with that," she conceded. "Not everyone does, though, and not everyone looks like you." She almost gasped. Never mind that it was the vastest understatement in the history of understatements. Was she losing her mind?

"Me?" He grinned broadly. "How do I look? Do you like it?"

Wasn't it supposed to be cooler in October? Deidre fanned herself with her napkin. She had to get hold of herself and this conversation which, she knew only too well, she had started. She forced a laugh.

"How am I supposed to answer that?" she teased. "If I say no, you might stop working. If I say yes, your head might become too big for such menial labor."

"Honesty is the best policy," he quoted pompously.

Smiling, she put a hand to her chin and pretended to assess him, giving herself a moment to think. Good thing he wasn't a mind reader. She wasn't any good at flirting. But could she be honest? It seemed easy enough. Never, not even for a moment, had he seemed anything but supremely unaware of his appeal.

"All right, I'll spoil you with the truth just this once." She held up her ale. "Here's to the world's most handsome gardener."

His eyes widened. Unbelievable! His grin stretched like a kid's from ear to ear.

"And to the world's most beautiful gardener."

They clinked their bottles, and she hoped he would attribute her blush to the heat. Her whole face was burning! He'd flipped tables on her.

She could count on one hand the number of men who had ever called her beautiful.

Chapter Six

Lachlann shifted on a boulder, uncomfortable, awkward. He stared out at Loch Nis for a long moment before glancing at the small figure sitting primly beside him.

"Our families want us to marry."

Allasan Chisholm looked down at her hands, folded in her lap, and nodded. "I know."

"Would that be agreeable to you?"

She didn't answer.

"Is there someone you prefer?"

She shook her head. "There's no one else. I just…"

"Just what?"

She looked up at him, a small frown creasing her smooth brow. "I always thought I would marry a Chisholm, not one of the *Gall Gàidheil.*"

He drew a breath, surprised. *Gall Gàidheil.* Foreigner-Gael. She was prejudiced.

Before he could think of a reply, she spoke again. "If we marry, all of this land will be yours, even this rock we're sitting on."

He shrugged. "There's no shortage of land."

"Do you want to marry me?"

"When I marry, I will be respected in my own home, by my wife."

"Of course." She paused. "I was just being honest. I'll be a good wife. You're the best farmer in the Highlands. I want a good life, Lachlann An Damh."

"That will be up to both of us."

"Do you think I'm pretty?"

"You're very pretty."

It wasn't a lie. With her large brown eyes, mane of thick, shiny brown hair, and dimples, Allasan was probably one of the prettiest young women in her clan. She just wasn't his type. Fine-boned and slim, on the short side of average, she'd obviously inherited her looks from some French ancestor of the Chisholms. So very small…

He'd always admired tall, bosomy women, had imagined marrying someone with whom he could lose himself, whose body fit his completely. Someone like Deidre.

Deidre! She was holding open her gate, and he was just standing there, gaping. He blinked at her, and she grinned.

"Earth to Lachlann," she teased. "Where were you just now?"

He shook his head to clear it. "You wouldn't believe me if I told you."

She chuckled. "It must be the manure. The aroma is getting to you."

He smiled. "Probably. Where do you want it?"

"Wherever you want it," she answered as he walked past her with a hundred-pound bag of composted horse manure on his shoulder. "Please make it as easy for yourself as possible."

He carried in two more bags, setting them near the beds. "That should be enough, don't you think?" he asked.

"More than enough." She rolled up her sleeves and retrieved her shovel from where it leaned against the side of the house. "Where do we start?"

He fought back a smile. "There's no reason for both of us to be up to our elbows in dung. Let's leave this job to me."

"No." She shook her head.

"Pardon?"

"Absolutely not. You've gone through so much work and trouble on my behalf. I never would have thought to go to the neighborhood equestrian center to get composted horse manure for my beds, much less from horses whose feed is organic." She wrinkled her nose. "Even if I did, I wouldn't have had a way to transport it. I'm not going to leave you to spread it alone. I can't thank you enough as it is."

"You can thank me by working on something else while I do this."

"No."

They stared at each other.

"Deidre…"

She raised her small, firm chin. "It's my garden. I'm going to help."

Hopefully, she'd change her mind after a few minutes. He shrugged. "If you insist…"

"Thank you. I also intend to serve you supper this evening. In no way will it equal hauling manure from stables to truck to backyard, but it's the best I can offer for now."

"I appreciate the thought, but it's not necessary. We can order a pizza."

"I have a pot roast simmering in the slow cooker as we speak. We'll both need sustenance by the time we're finished. Please say yes?"

She was such a sweet, bonnie lass, and she smelled heavenly with her earthy, womanly scent of citrus, flowers, and perspiration. Lachlann wondered what she would say if he told her he'd like to have *her* for supper...

"Yes, thank you," he confirmed. "It sounds great. If you have to quit early to work on dinner, don't hesitate."

"Don't worry. I'm used to hard work," she assured him, "although it's been a while since I worked with manure. I grew up on a farm in North Carolina and gardened with my grandfather from the moment I could walk until I left for university."

"Did you like it?" Lachlann asked, his heart somersaulting as he tore open one of the bags.

"Like what?" she asked, smiling slightly as she stepped back, waving her hand in front of her face.

He laughed. "Not the manure, the farm. Did you like growing up on a farm?"

"I loved it. I've always thought that if I ever have children, I want them to enjoy the same privilege. I wish all children could."

His heart thudded in his chest. It was all he'd ever known, ever wanted. "I feel the same," he agreed. "But is it possible these days?"

"What? To have a family farm?"

He nodded.

She leaned on her shovel, looking thoughtful. "It's possible," she replied. "It's true that the most profitable farms are enormous commercial ones. They rely almost as much on chemicals and technology as they do on individuals, soil, and weather. But the demand for organic and homegrown food now is opening up new opportunities, and there have always been options like specialty farms."

"Does your family still have a farm?"

"Yes, my parents do. The farm's been in our family for over two hundred years. But it's smaller than it used to be, and it's not their main source of income anymore."

"They have jobs besides farming?"

"Yes, my father is an engineer, and my mother is a teacher."

"What do they grow?"

"In my grandfather's and great-grandfather's time, it was a very profitable tobacco farm. But now, my father grows mostly soybeans and corn."

"Is that all?"

"He grows a little cotton as well."

"No vegetables?"

"My grandparents kept a large kitchen garden near the house. I honestly don't know if my parents maintain it anymore, but I hope they do. It was my grandfather's passion. Even though he was a tobacco farmer, he always insisted that we grow our own food, that that was what farming was really about."

"I would agree with him."

She smiled. "So would I."

He stared at her sweetly curved lips. He wanted to kiss her.

"Shall we?" she asked, gesturing at the beds.

Get a hold of yourself, man.

Lifting the open bag, he held it over one of the beds and shook it. "Once we've topped this bed, we can mix it into the soil."

"Perfect." She set her shovel aside to pull on dainty, flowered gardening gloves.

Aye, she was perfect. He could hardly believe that someone so beautiful and refined was willing to work with muck.

He'd brought a garden fork. She had a shovel. They set to work.

"You know a lot about planting, Lachlann," she

murmured, struggling to turn the manure into the soil. "Have you gardened a lot?"

"Like you, I grew up on a farm," he answered. "When I was old enough, I had my own."

She stopped and looked at him. "You had your own farm?"

"Aye."

"Do you mean as a hobby or as a means to support yourself?"

"As you would say, it was my full-time job, my source of income."

"Where? In Scotland?"

He nodded. "In Scotland."

"What crops did you grow?"

"Mostly oats, kale, and flax. I also had an experimental vegetable garden."

"That sounds amazing. I've never met anyone who grew flax." She resumed her work. "What happened?" she asked in a quiet, more serious tone. "Did you change your mind?"

For a long moment, he wrestled with an answer. "There was an accident. I…I had to give it up."

"I'm sorry, so very sorry. That must have been heartbreaking."

"It was."

Silence. When Deidre spoke again, her voice was low and a little unsteady. "Well, I'm glad you haven't given up on planting crops altogether. We'll be feasting this winter and spring."

She hadn't pressed him for more information. Lachlann released the breath he'd been holding and felt a weight lift from his chest. "That we will," he agreed. "But for now, I'm more excited about this evening's feast."

Chapter Seven

Lachlann stared at the small, round table decorated prettily with a tablecloth, a small vase of herbs, and a candle. Deidre had done this for him. He was probably making more of it than she intended, but it made him feel special.

Joe cooked. In fact, he cooked a lot when he was home, and he sometimes took requests. Allasan, of course, had cooked almost daily. Her meals had been nutritious, filling, and uninspired. Lachlann knew that it wasn't only that she was still something of a novice, but that she wasn't particularly interested in the activity. He'd never blamed her. She was busy with their home and their son and much more interested in her cloth-making.

This…the savory aroma of beef, onions, and herbs assailed him as he entered Deidre's kitchen. This was different.

"It smells great," he said, smiling at her. "What can I do to help?"

She was taking a tray of rolls from the oven. She smiled back, her face flushed, an apron stretching over her full breasts. On second thought, who needed food?

"I have two mugs in the freezer, and the ale's in the fridge. Would you do the honors?"

"Gladly."

A few minutes later, they were seated cozily at the table, plates of roast beef and root vegetables steaming in front of them.

The golf course was in darkness, but Deidre's swimming pool was lit, a small, luminescent oval, and she had strung lights around the covered area where they sat. The wax candle, a luxury where he came from, cast a golden glow on the table and upon Deidre, lending a fiery gleam to her curls.

It was intimate, the two of them on an island of light in the growing darkness.

"I was a little worried about the smell of, um, our day's work being too strong for us to want to sit outside this evening," she told him. "But the breeze must be blowing it away from us. I can hardly smell it. What about you?"

"It wouldn't bother me either way. But good compost is usually tolerable, and I think you're right about the breeze."

She smiled at him. "Thank you for all of your help with my garden. I can hardly believe that you would give up your free weekends or that I would be so lucky as to move next door to a farmer."

"It's my pleasure. It's the sort of work I enjoy."

"The building or the planting?" she asked as she laid her napkin over her lap.

"It's all necessary, all part of the same work."

"You consider gardening work?"

"Why do people nowadays seem to think of work as a bad word?"

She shot him a grin. "You're right. In fact, there's no better word for our activities today. I think it's because people equate the word 'job' with 'work,' and often people don't like their jobs."

"That makes sense."

"Do you like your job?"

He had speared a tender slice of beef with his fork and took a bite before answering. Rich, well-seasoned, it melted in his mouth. "Mmm." He closed his eyes briefly, then smiled at her. "Delicious."

She beamed. "Thank you."

Small red potatoes, thickly sliced carrots, onion chunks, whole cloves of garlic...He ate in blissful silence for a few moments before he realized what he was doing. He looked up to find her watching him with a smile and a twinkle in her blue eyes.

He grinned. "Sorry. This is really good. What were we talking about?"

"I'm glad you like it. I only asked if you like your job."

"My job." He shrugged. "I like it well enough, I suppose. As they say, it pays the bills. It's very different from anything I've done before. Do you like yours?"

"I love my job, but I know that I'm one of the lucky ones."

"Tell me, please, your job title again? Joe kept talking about it the last time he was home."

Deidre laughed. "He did seem surprisingly interested when we talked about it. I'm Director of Medieval Studies at the University of Houston."

Medieval studies...Lachlann struggled for words. He knew what "medieval" meant. If he had one question, he had a thousand. Simple ones would have to do for now.

"What do you like about it?"

"There's so much," she replied. "The ongoing learning, the students...I love teaching."

"Why did you choose medieval studies?"

Deidre opened her mouth as if to speak, then closed it again. Glancing down at her plate, she pushed around a carrot. "I…I've been interested in medieval artwork and history since I was a little girl. It's always fascinated me."

"Why?"

"I…" She paused again, her brow knit, her soft lips twisting a little as she searched for words. "Life was so different back then," she finally said. "People were different, and yet they were still human."

Lachlann blinked. "Well, of course they were human!"

She put a hand up. "Now, hear me out. For all intents and purposes, they lived in a different world from ours. Almost everything they knew was different from what we know. Agreed?"

"Agreed."

"But their humanity was no different from ours. They had the same emotions, the same feelings, the same basic needs."

"How do you know how they felt?"

"They left us art, music, writing, and so much more."

"But their languages were different. How did anyone ever learn to read their writings?"

"Languages changed slowly," she explained, "and one translation led to another."

"But if a group of people died at once, their language would have died with them. Isn't that true? So would their history."

"That would be true in some cases, but not all. Is there a particular language or culture you have in mind?"

Lachlann hesitated, sorting his thoughts, still trying to get past her "yet they were human" remark. What had happened to his own language? Should he mention it? Could it hurt?

"Have you heard of Norroena?"

"Norroena." Her eyes widened. Clasping her hands together, she leaned toward him. "Lachlann, are you talking about Norn?"

"Norn?"

"The language of the islands, of Orkney and Shetland."

"Aye, that's the one." He tried not to show his excitement. She knew of it!

"But the people didn't all die at once. I believe Norn was spoken well into the sixteenth century."

"Was it?"

"Yes, it was."

He thought that over for a moment. "It still died out. But it was spoken on the mainland as well as the islands, wasn't it?"

"Yes, it was." She smiled at him. "It was spoken in Caithness. You know your history."

"Where else?"

She was silent for a moment, that thoughtful little frown forming between her eyes, and then she shook her head. "I haven't seen evidence that it was spoken anywhere else."

But it had been, damn it.

"If it's any consolation," she continued, "Norn lasted longer than many other ancient languages. What's sad is that we're not sure how it sounded, and there are very few examples of written Norn."

He couldn't help her with the written part, but he'd love to surprise her, to speak his language to her.

"That's why history is so important." Deidre's voice drifted off.

"Why?" he asked, glad he had caught that last sentence.

"So that we won't forget."

He felt the familiar constriction in his chest. "You're saying that if the history is lost or no one cares about it, everything happened for nothing."

She looked shocked. "That is most certainly not what I'm saying. It's not true!"

"It is."

"It isn't! Nothing is ever really lost."

He sat back, folded his arms, and forced himself to speak calmly. "I disagree."

"Lachlann…" Reaching over the table, she tucked one of her hands into his, her knuckles pressed against his chest. "Let's take today as an example. Today, you performed an act of kindness. You affected my personal history and even your own."

"Making a garden is hardly history-making."

"Maybe not to you, but there's that ripple effect for every little stone tossed into the water. Those ripples cause more ripples. Every moment affects the next. They're all part of time, part of history. You might not think that what we did today was important, and it's true the world will never know of it. But it is important to me, and I count. My life counts. It means something, and so does yours. So does all life."

She moved her hand from his and started to sit back, but he grabbed hold of it.

"Today was important to me," he said, looking directly into her eyes. "But…"

"If I moved away, if you never saw me again, would you regret your kindness? Would you think it was all for nothing? I hope not. Because to me, it meant everything."

Lachlann wasn't prepared for the stab of pain her words caused him. The thought of never seeing her again almost took his breath away. He stared at her, struggling for an answer, but words failed him.

She squeezed his hand. "I'm so grateful for today. You can't know how much. Thank you again for all of your hard work."

"It was my pleasure." He forced himself to let go of her hand and shrugged. "I know how it feels, to want to grow things."

"Of course you do." Her expression softened as she looked at him. "We gardeners understand each other."

"Aye, we do."

She took a sip of ale and settled back in her chair, her arms loosely folded against her, her curls glinting in the dim light. She wore a soft blue V-neck sweater that hugged her curves and accentuated the deep blue of her eyes.

"And believe me," she continued, "if farmers are hard to meet in the city, medievalists are hard to find anywhere, which reminds me…Are you busy tomorrow?"

"A little. I have some laundry to take care of, not to mention my own garden. I leave early Monday morning for the rig."

"Would you be interested in going with me to the Texas Renaissance Festival? It's not far from here, and the grounds are beautiful."

"A festival?"

"Yes. It's huge. Everyone who works it dresses in period costume and so do a lot of the visitors. It's called 'renaissance,' but it's really more medieval. That's why I go. I like to be able to discuss it in my classes. There are all sorts of entertainment, mostly medieval-themed— shows, exhibitions, games—and plenty of food and drink. It's fun."

Fun...Lachlann hesitated. He wasn't sure how fun a medieval festival would be for him, but one more day with Deidre...Could he? Should he? He was so damned tired of waiting for the next terrible thing to happen, for the next terrible fall. It had been a very, *very* long time since he'd enjoyed a day of true leisure.

Fun. *With Deidre.*

"And the grounds aren't far from here?" he questioned, playing for time.

"They're quite close, actually," she assured him. "I know you probably have a lot to do before you leave, especially since you've spent so much time helping me. But the festival will be over by the time you return."

He made up his mind. "What time do you want to leave?"

Her eyes widened in delight. "Yes?" she asked breathlessly.

"Why not?"

Grinning broadly, she raised her mug. "Here's to a very fine weekend."

He gently tapped his mug of ale against hers. "A very fine weekend."

Chapter Eight

Why had he agreed to go? What was he doing? Lachlann tossed in bed. He would never sleep. He wouldn't have laundry to worry about the next day. He had washed, dried, folded, and packed, and still he didn't feel tired. He probably should have drunk more.

For the past four years, he'd remained apart, a ghost of himself, a man who was somehow, unbelievably, lost in time. Lost! He'd never confided in anyone, not even in Reverend McKinley, the man who'd saved his life and taken it upon himself to see him through his healing. He'd wanted to, had desperately needed to tell someone, but the old reverend hadn't wanted to know about his past. In fact, he'd given him advice to the contrary.

I'm an old man. I've seen many things in my time, and it doesn't matter to me what you've done or where you've been. But most men despise what they fear and what they don't understand. If you have secrets, keep them to yourself.

There was nothing McKinley could have done, anyway; nothing anyone could do. Lachlann stared out of the window at the half moon gleaming in the darkness. So many unanswered questions…

Had he died? But he was living, breathing. Was it a dream? Would he wake and be back in his own century? And if it wasn't a dream, would it happen again?

Was it fair for him to become involved with Deidre when he didn't know how long he would be here?

What if sorcery were involved? What if he had lost his mind and just didn't know it? Would being with him place her in danger?

Fists knotting the bedsheets, he closed his eyes, his chest heaving. He still broke out in a sweat when he thought of it—the earth trembling, opening before him, and then falling. The last thing he remembered about that day was falling, but it wasn't the worst that had happened or the worst that was to come.

His injuries—the physical pain—should have been proof enough that he hadn't died. He'd been hospitalized for over a month and still got headaches from the injury he'd sustained. That he was alive at all was a tribute to modern medicine.

Going to his window, he peered out, inhaling deeply, his exhale a trembling breath. Again. Inhale. Exhale. He forced himself to focus on the view. Their backyard was in darkness, as was the golf course. But Deidre kept a light on, a beacon. That's what she was to him, a blessed beacon in the darkness, in the blindness of his struggle.

He couldn't ignore his attraction to her, couldn't pretend she wasn't there. He didn't want to. He felt good when he was with her, as if he was where he was supposed to be.

How much they talked fairly astonished him. For one thing, they'd worked through their differing pronunciations of Gaelic. Hers was getting better or, he thought wryly, worse, depending upon whom one might ask. His English was certainly improving. He'd learned quite a bit, especially since living in the States, but he hadn't practiced much. He'd been determined to keep himself to himself as much as possible. But now, he was practicing.

Communication had never been a problem for him before. He'd grown up bilingual, speaking Norroena at home and Gaelic with the neighboring Gaels. He also spoke a smattering of Romani as well as a few other languages he'd come across on a regular, if infrequent, basis.

But the language of his own people had died, and the Gaelic he'd spoken in the fourteenth century bore only a vague resemblance to the language of the Gaels now. It wasn't commonly spoken, anyway, although Inverness purportedly had more native speakers than most areas of Scotland.

And then there was English. He'd barely begun to understand Scottish English when he'd left for the US to be faced with a completely different language— American English. After almost three years in the States, he was just beginning to feel comfortable conversing. Much as he detested sitting idle, he was grateful for American television. He had learned from it and probably would have learned more if watching television didn't give him a headache. It was the same with reading. He smiled wryly. Rónán would have fared better in this century. Any bard and many a chieftain would have done better than an illiterate farmer—not that he'd wish this on anyone. And that fall…He shuddered.

Lachlann ran a hand through his hair. He had learned in his own way, survived, and would continue to do so. For him, day-to-day living taught him more than anything else. Most of the men he worked with were from Texas, and he'd got used to their accents and expressions. Joe, of course, didn't speak like the others. He hailed from another state called Louisiana. Lachlann would have found him completely impossible to understand, but Joe was persistent and liked to talk. He was a good man, too. Lachlann had come to like and trust him, even without understanding half of what he said.

Deidre was different. Even though she had a pronounced accent, he found her easier to follow than anyone he'd conversed with thus far. She spoke directly, simply, slowly. She never rushed her words. And her voice…sweet, clear, and a little deep. Sexy. Like everything else about her, it alternately calmed him or roused wild, almost uncontrollable, yearnings within him.

Her mouth, her eyes, her neck…his breath came quicker. Her breasts…*Và*. Her everything. He desired every inch of her.

Returning to bed, he laid an arm across his eyes, forcing them shut even as his thoughts rambled on. She was a farmer's daughter. And she wanted the same for her children.

Children. Iain. He had dreamed so often of his family, his farm. Had they existed? What was real? Stuck as he was, he sometimes wondered if he really was in hell or purgatory. He couldn't imagine what he'd done to warrant hell, but wouldn't there be hope in purgatory?

Suddenly, it seemed there might be. Now, small though it was, there was a flicker of a hope of a dream, or a dream of a hope—that, one day, he might be whole again.

Sleep, man.

How could he sleep when he felt he was just waking, just coming back from the dead?

Chapter Nine

Houston, midtown

Never mind that the project was closed. Someone needed to save the information. The young geophysicist downed his martini and ordered another. He appreciated the warnings he'd received about discretion. He took them seriously. The international ramifications were staggering.

He fingered the flash drive attached to his key chain. He could be discreet. No one had to know what he'd done. But, one day, someone would thank him.

Sipping his second drink more slowly, he congratulated himself on his new career with TransGlobal Research and Investment. It was a researcher's dream job, with a six-figure salary and unheard-of benefits. It came with a price, but one he was willing to pay. He could live without talking about his work.

He could think about it, though. They might have caused a massive earthquake, possibly changed history. He'd deleted photos for hours. He might have saved a few, but his mind recalled every image. There'd been one…blurred and dark as it was, it had shaken him to the bone. The image of a man sliding down into a fissure…He shuddered. God knew how long he'd fallen before he died. And that was just one example. He finished his second drink and ordered a third.

A couple of drinks later, he stumbled out of the mixology bar. Midweek, Bagby Street was quieter, darker than it would be on a weekend. He wouldn't have to worry about traf…

"Don't move."

He tried to turn and felt something hard press into his back.

"Don't fucking move."

The thief drew his keys from his pocket. Damn it!

A sudden, burning sensation knocked him to his knees. Even as he cried out, he felt the barest touch at the base of his skull.

****

Lachlann sauntered across Deidre's driveway just as she was locking her front door. She turned toward him, smiling. He froze. She was wearing a saffron-colored *lèine*, or tunic, underneath a blue, fitted surcoat. He should have known! She was a woman from his own time. His heart and head began to pound as he stared at her.

"Lachlann?" Deidre's voice reached him, soft and hesitant. "Don't you like my costume?"

Costume. Of course, it was a costume. He struggled to regain his voice as his heart rate calmed. "It's great," he managed, giving himself a mental shake. *Fool!*

"Thank you," she replied, her voice still uncertain. She looked at him inquiringly. "I surprised you, didn't I? I'm sorry. I should've warned you. I like to wear something fairly authentic in case I run into some of my students."

"You do look authentic." He managed a wink. "Bonnie as well."

She blushed. "You've probably seen lots of costumes like this in Scotland."

"Not so many, and none in Texas."

It was a wonder to him that he was still standing. Her costume, as she called it, was perfect. She might have fallen through time like himself. It was an even greater wonder that he had not yet carried her off to bed. He'd never wanted anyone as he wanted her.

Now, dressed in such a familiar manner, she suddenly seemed more tangible than ever. She looked magnificent, the clothing emphasizing her generous breasts and hips, her deep red tresses flowing freely down her back.

His mouth went dry as he wondered how he might persuade her to dress like this more often.

Their eyes met. To hell with time.

He stepped toward her.

Chapter Ten

Jousts, schmousts. Deidre allowed herself a good, long look at Lachlann. He was an enigma, a beautiful, spectacular hunk of an enigma. Concentrating on the nonsensical tournament, he sat head and shoulders above everyone else. His lean, powerful physique was marvelously showcased by a simple T-shirt and jeans, while a broad-rimmed baseball cap pulled low partially concealed his face and kept his shoulder-length hair at bay.

A thrill raced from the top of her head to her toes. He was a heart-stopping piece of eye candy, but there was so much more to him than that.

When he'd first seen her in costume this morning, he'd appeared stunned, even shocked, if she were honest. He'd stopped walking, his eyes had widened, and she could swear he'd gone pale. It was as if he'd seen a ghost. But then…

Who knew what might have happened had a passing car not distracted them? Just thinking of the expression on his face made her tremble. Never had anyone looked at her with such hunger, such unguarded desire. Lachlann had seemed ready to consume her.

No question about it, she was going to invest in a few more medieval outfits and find excuses to wear them.

She might even garden in them.

Suddenly, he turned toward her, caught her staring

in a lustful daze. His expression changed. Oh, mercy, it was happening again.

She grabbed hold of his shirt, yanked him closer, and kissed him. He pulled her closer, his hands in her hair.

A burst of applause startled her. Deidre shook herself out of her daydream.

Wake up, woman!

"That was interesting." Lachlann turned toward her. "Are all the shows farces, then?"

Blinking, she forced herself to attention.

"No. The tournaments have become more and more about light-hearted family entertainment, but there's a variety of demonstrations and shows that are both entertaining and educational. I think you'll enjoy many of them, such as the falconry show."

"I'm sure I will," he agreed easily.

"Are you hungry?"

"Always."

She laughed. "Let's go find some food and ale."

The festival was unlike anything Lachlann had ever seen or imagined. He was having a hard time stopping himself from gaping. The grounds were expansive and beautiful with broad green fields, gardens, and numerous arenas and stages. Wide pedestrian thoroughfares were lined by shops and restaurants.

The structures, Deidre explained, were supposed to resemble those of medieval cities or villages. They didn't look much like anything he'd seen, but then, he'd never left the Highlands.

He was rather surprised and certainly appreciative that the area hadn't been cleared of trees. Except for the fields and the jousting arena, pine and other trees offered shade and, to him, a pleasant feeling of naturalness.

Diversions beckoned at every turn. Fire-eaters, jugglers, mimes, and musicians were just a few of the entertainers performing offstage as well as on. Costumed actors strolled through the crowds and many of the festivalgoers were costumed as Deidre was. Faeries, barbarians, medieval royalty, knights, kilted Highlanders, and dragons could be seen in every direction.

Demonstrations of medieval handiwork, only some of which he'd seen firsthand in actual medieval times, were offered along the thoroughfares.

There were rides and games. The sounds of music, laughter, and excited shouts of children filled the air, along with the aromas of roasted meats, corn, and other tempting foods.

A group of young men passed them eating…large drumsticks? He glanced at Deidre with raised brows.

"That was a roasted turkey leg," she explained. "There's a wide variety of food available—gyros, pizza, fish-n-chips, noodle bowls. But the turkey leg is standard. Would you like to try it? I'm sort of partial to sausage-on-a-stick, myself."

"How about one of each?" he requested.

She grinned. "I'll stick with my sausage, but you should try both. We can wash it all down with ale."

They walked while they ate, strolling under the trees amidst the crowds and tents, enjoying the cooler weather and the sights.

"Have you ever ridden a camel?" Deidre asked suddenly.

"A what?"

"A camel." She gestured with her chin to his left.

He stared at the animal. Had he even seen a picture of one? "Can't say that I have."

"Let's!"

He raised his brows. "Let's what?"

"Let's ride!"

He shook his head. "No, thanks."

"Oh, c'mon. It'll be a great souvenir!" She grabbed his hand and began to pull.

"You can't climb onto one of those things with your dress!"

"Of course I can. You're not afraid, are you?" she teased.

He was, in fact, a bit curious. "I'm terrified."

She laughed as she pulled him toward the camels.

It proved to be a short ride, but he got a better look at the beast. It was a pack animal, a strong one. And Deidre was right. Their photo made a fine keepsake.

Afterward, they rounded the fairway, where games of skill beckoned.

"Have you any experience with archery?" Deidre asked him.

It had been a while since he'd caught his dinner. "Some."

"Shall we?"

The bows and arrows weren't high quality, but they worked for a game. The target was close, though, too close, and not moving. He wouldn't miss, not after shooting at food most of his life. He made three bullseyes.

He turned and winked at Deidre.

She arched a brow. "*Some* experience?"

He shrugged and chose a flowered headdress for his prize.

It looked beautiful on her. The flowers were dried rather than plastic, like some he'd noticed, and the blue and rose hues accentuated her fair coloring. She looked like a warrior princess as she took aim, and he had to force his gaze away from her face to the target. She missed her first shot and frowned.

"You're holding your bow the wrong way," he informed her.

"What's the right way, sharpshooter?"

He moved to stand behind her and put his arms around her shoulders. Her hair smelled fresh and sweet. He corrected her hold on the bow, then stood back to position her.

"Now, concentrate," he instructed.

She let the arrow fly. It didn't hit center, but it was closer.

He adjusted her a little more. She stared long and hard at the target.

Bullseye!

"I did it!" Clapping in delight, she turned around and gave him a hug.

Ahh. Her warm, soft body pressed against his, and he closed his eyes. It had been a long time since anyone had held him, and it felt so good. Like home...

Something shook inside him. And then she stepped back, baring him body and soul to the emptiness of his utter loneliness. Almost blindly, he reached for her, and she slipped her hand into his.

Holding onto her tightly, he turned back to the vendor. "Do you sell bows and arrows?"

"We don't, but there's a shop in the artisan demonstration area."

Lachlann glanced at Deidre. "Do you know where that is?"

She nodded. "I do. It's very interesting. Do you want to go?"

"Lead the way."

He probably hadn't had this much fun since childhood. He couldn't help a wry grin. For him, recreation had always been a luxury, and he liked it that way. That's what made festivals, celebrations, and days like this, special.

They wound their way through the crowd, stopping for ale along the way to the craft demonstration. It seemed to him that, whatever the century, a fair was a fair was a fair. There were crowds of people, smiling faces, a variety of foods, merchants, entertainment—something to see and do at every turn.

Glassblowing caught their attention first. Lachlann had never seen it before. Blown glass had not been available in the fourteenth-century Highlands. It was a fascinating process.

Deidre found the potter more interesting than he did, and the forge was mostly a show.

The archery shop, however, was a different matter altogether. The number and assortment of bows were staggering. They spent over an hour in the shop and were glad to leave their packages with the shopkeeper when they set off to see more craft demonstrations.

Lachlann felt more relaxed than he had in years. He smiled at Deidre. "That," he announced, "was fun."

She shook her head and rolled her eyes, smiling. "I can't believe you bought three bows. Three! You didn't have to buy me one. I could've practiced with yours."

"No, you need your own. We'll have to find a place to practice. I don't think they'll like it on the golf course."

She laughed. "You're probably right about that."

They stopped in front of a woodworking exhibition.

"I love the toys," Deidre remarked, pausing at a display. She picked up a small, wooden sword. "I'm sure these aren't as sturdy as they would have been back then, but they're cute."

"They're not…probably not," he agreed.

A number of small, hand-carved wooden figurines were arranged on a table. An elephant, a crow, a cow, a horse…Lachlann's breath caught sharply. He felt as though someone had just punched him in the stomach.

As Deidre picked up a bird, he chose the horse.

Iain.

He still possessed the small horse figurine he'd chosen for his son at the festival in Inverness. It had made it through his fall through time. How was it that the toy had survived and Iain had not? The whole of his little son's life had been three years. Tears blurred Lachlann's vision. Setting down the figure, he turned and walked away.

Chapter Eleven

He moved blindly through the crowd, grief overwhelming him.

"Lachlann?"

Deidre's hand was on his back as she caught up with him, rubbing gently. But he couldn't answer her, couldn't speak.

Her hand slipped into his.

They walked for a long while in silence. It seemed fair to Lachlann that just as he'd allowed a festival to lure him away from his family, one now served to remind him of his mistake. If only he hadn't left, he might have been able to help them, to ease their discomfort.

Had Iain been afraid? He was sure of one thing. His son wouldn't have been afraid in his arms.

A sob escaped him.

Suddenly, a textile display was in front of him. Looms, raw wool, dye…Allasan. He turned abruptly, nightmare images flashing in his mind. He had to get out of here.

"Lachlann!"

He almost ran into her. Deidre had moved in front of him, her voice quiet, urgent, as she clasped his upper arms.

"Lachlann, look at me."

He tried to do as she asked, but bile rose in his throat. He barely made it to the closest trash bin.

When his heaving finally ceased, Deidre handed

him a bottle of water. He rinsed his mouth.

"Are you all right?" she asked gently.

No, damn it! He would never be all right. "Sorry," he murmured, wiping his eyes on his sleeve.

A hawk swooped by, surprisingly low. She took his hand in hers again and pulled him toward the small arena they were passing. "Let's sit for a moment and watch the falconry show."

He didn't want to watch a show. He wanted to leave. But sitting down for a moment was probably a good idea. He was still shaking.

Without waiting for an answer, she released his hand to wrap her arm around his waist. She was nestled against him, their bodies touching. He shut his eyes, absorbing her warmth, comforted by her nearness.

The show captured his interest. Deidre sat close, holding his hand unless she was clapping. As they learned about various birds of prey and watched them do tricks, his shaking subsided. The tightness in his chest slowly eased. The lump in his throat gradually diminished.

They went from the falconer's show to a Gutenberg printing press exhibit to mud wrestling. Lachlann couldn't help but think of Rónán. His friend would have enjoyed every moment.

Deidre never let go of him. His thoughts were in chaos, but he wasn't lost in them. He wasn't lost because Deidre held onto him. Her touch grounded him, sustained him.

Darkness was falling by the time they made their way to the parking area. It comprised rows and rows of long, packed-dirt roads with parking on either side, separated by pine trees.

A cool breeze rushed through the trees as they

walked hand in hand toward her car.

Lachlann gently squeezed Deidre's fingers. "Thank you for today, Deidre."

She glanced up at him searchingly. "Are you sorry you came?"

Was he? He looked down at their hands clasped so tightly together. "No," he answered, surprised at the truth of it. "I'm not sorry about today."

"Do you…" She paused, then continued softly. "Do you want to talk about it?"

"No," he said again. "I just…the toy reminded me of someone I knew once. Someone I loved. Someone I miss."

"A child." The words were barely a whisper.

"Aye."

Her eyes filled with tears. "I'm sorry."

"So am I."

They walked for a few moments in silence. The breeze was refreshing, pine-scented. Stars began to twinkle through the trees.

"What was your favorite thing today?" she asked.

He raised the large bag he carried. "Do you need to ask?"

She laughed. "Besides the archery."

"Hmm. The camel ride?"

"Oh, I liked that, too."

"It's a fine festival," he said.

"I agree. The only thing that bothers me about festivals like this is the overall impression they give to those who are less informed."

"What impression?"

"The main misconception is that the Middle Ages were so much simpler than now."

He thought about that for a moment. It was a

78

misconception, all right. Life these days could be overwhelming, complex, but... Suddenly, her words about medieval people being human made more sense.

"You were right in what you were saying the other day," he told her. "I just didn't understand."

"Of course I was right." She grinned. "But what about, precisely?"

He couldn't help but smile. "People are people, in any century. Life is complicated."

"Always! In medieval times, the problems might have been different, but they revolved around the same issues. A dependable food source, clean water, sufficient housing, and public safety are as much a concern today as they were back then."

"Medicine and technology are incredible," he added, "but people still die."

She nodded. "We might have conquered the plague, but so many other frightening diseases have come along to challenge doctors and scientists. Life has never been simple. Humankind has always struggled, always fought, always will."

"So why bother?"

"Why bother with what?"

"With anything? Why bother with life?"

Her brow furrowed. "But...life is a gift."

"Some gift!"

"I don't know what you've been through," she murmured as they reached her car. "But you can't let it steal your peace."

"It's too late. I lost my peace a long time ago."

"But you're still here, still fighting, just like I am. I've had my share of hurt, too."

"I know."

Her eyes widened. "How do you know?"

"The first time I saw you, that first night when you stood looking out at the golf course, you were crying."

She nodded. "I didn't give up. I won't, and neither should you."

"I have no intention of giving up."

"But aren't you glad for the opportunity? To be alive? Every moment is precious."

"No." Anger rose to the surface, making it hard for him to speak calmly. "Not *every* moment is precious. I could do without the bad ones, thanks."

Her expression changed. She looked stricken. "I apologize," she said quietly. "You're right. Some moments are just plain shitty."

He blinked. Had she just said...

"You're right," she said again. "But Lachlann, don't you see? We survived."

"So is that the point of it all, what life's all about? Survival?"

"No." She shook her head. "Although sometimes it feels that way."

"What is the point, then?"

Sighing, she leaned back against her car. "I'm no expert," she said softly. "I don't have a lot of experience or success to draw from. But I can tell you what I've observed in my studies."

Moving beside her, he leaned back and crossed his arms. "Go on."

"It seems that all through the centuries, since the very beginning, the universal desire, what people live for..." She paused. "It sounds cliché, but..."

He waited.

She glanced at him. "It's love."

"Love?" He almost rolled his eyes. "That's what you've learned from your studies?"

"Yes!"

He thought about it, about himself back in the fourteenth century. Farming had been his greatest pleasure. It's what he'd lived for. He shook his head. "I disagree. In fact, I would say it depends on the individual. But most people want and need a lot more than romance."

"I'm not talking only about romantic love. Love is more than romance. There's love for children, family, friends, too, and love of God. It moves and motivates, gives us joy, hope. You might say that a warlord lives for war, for dominance, but that's twisted. Most parents—even some of those warlords—would say that their greatest joy comes from their children. That makes more sense, don't you think?"

Yes, it made more sense. He shut his eyes as pain shot through him like lightning, took a breath, and looked at her. "So love in all its forms…"

"Love, hope, joy—those are the moments we live for."

"A few moments hardly seem worth it."

She turned toward him fully. Her blue eyes shone dark and deep in the moonlight. Her soft, pink lips were trembling as she looked up at him. "A lot can happen in a moment. Everything can change."

He knew that well enough. And then he realized…this was one of those moments. A tremor…Did she feel it, too?

Everything disappeared as they stood there, the people around them, the sounds of cars, conversations, and crickets, the odd, mixed aroma of pine and exhaust. All gone. It was just him and Deidre. He could hear her breathing, could almost hear her heartbeat and his.

Irresistibly, he bent his head, lightly touching his

lips to hers, and a shudder ran through him. The dam burst. He crushed her against him, his lips on hers.

If he could make her part of himself, he would. A multitude of emotions, long suppressed, threatened to overwhelm him. He had no choice but to hold her tightly; he was shaking.

Deidre wrapped her arms around his neck, pressing closer in a full embrace. As he felt her warm, soft body against his, he shut his eyes.

A sudden cough and some uncomfortable giggles brought them back to earth. He pulled away but didn't release her. He thought he might fall if he did. His chest was heaving, his breathing sharp. He felt as though he'd just run up a mountain. Once again, he felt like a man who had just come back from the dead.

Back to life…

Chapter Twelve

"Professor Chisholm! Good morning, ma'am!"

Deidre, bent over Lachlann's lettuce box, turned to smile at Joe, who stood waving at her from his patio.

"Good morning, Joe. Am I out here too early for you?"

"Course not. How about some good Louisiana coffee before you take off for work? Do you have time?"

"Joe, you know I love your coffee, but I'm afraid I don't have much time."

"I'll bring it to you. How's that sound?"

"That sounds wonderful."

She meant it. Joe's chicory coffee was thoroughly New Orleans—strong, creamy, and sweet.

He returned a few moments later, a mug in each hand. "Here you go. How's our crop of greens looking?"

"Splendid, as you can see," she replied, indicating the healthy young plants, "and much better than mine."

He moved closer to the fence and peered over at her planter boxes. "Yours are babies yet. They'll get there. Lachlann will make sure of it."

"No doubt." She sipped her coffee. "Thank you, Joe. It's perfect, as always."

"It's a pleasure to have such lovely company so early in the morn," he replied, his eyes twinkling.

She chuckled. "Silver-tongued devil…"

"I mean every word."

"Thank you."

He was a typical, old-Southern charmer, and she could not be uncomfortable around him. Of average height, with a trim physique, he was a nice-looking man, although surely nearing retirement age. He was clean-shaven, with a dark, slightly wrinkled complexion and deep brown eyes. Silver strands ran through his dark, curly hair, which showed signs of thinning on top.

He was neat as a pin and, if he wasn't talking or whistling, he was smiling. He was also absolutely Cajun in his speech, his attitude toward life, and his cooking. He loved people, good times, and good food, the last of which he was generous at serving up himself.

He'd lost his first wife, mother to his son and daughter, to cancer many years ago, when his children were still young. He'd told her that he'd tried marriage again, once, for his children's sake, but found that his second wife didn't really want to be a wife at all, much less a mother. All she'd wanted was a free ride, giving nothing in return.

Once he'd finally managed to divorce her, he'd decided there and then that he wouldn't marry again. That wasn't to say that he didn't enjoy the company of women, but life was too short to beg for trouble. He'd been fortunate enough to marry his high school sweetheart, and though the Lord had seen fit to take her early, he'd had a good life.

A geologist by education, he'd worked on the rigs for a long time, learning and advancing through the years. He made a comfortable living, had a solid nest egg, and a good relationship with his children.

That was Joe's life according to Joe. He might be a little rough around the edges and certainly nosy, but he was also a warm, caring person. His story of his second marriage had prompted her to share a little of her own story. She could relate. But she hadn't gone into details. She still had raw patches.

Now he watched her, uncharacteristically quiet, as she watered the last planter box, a jungle of hot peppers that refused to yield to cooler weather. There hadn't been a hard freeze yet; the serrano peppers were happy as could be and so was Joe.

"He's magic in the garden, Lachlann," he said, helping himself to some peppers. "You know he had a farm?"

"Yes, sir, he told me."

"What did he tell you?"

"He told me that he had a farm and that he lost it."

Joe looked at her expectantly. When she didn't continue, his gaze became searching. "You two have a lot in common, don't you?"

"It seems we do."

"You both grew up on farms and like gardening, you share an interest in history, and you're both of Scottish descent. Quite a coincidence, don't you think?"

"It's pretty amazing," she agreed, dousing one last plant. Was Joe playing matchmaker?

"And you never saw him before you moved here?"

Strange question. She turned her head to glance at him. Was that a suspicious expression on his face?

"No. Where would I have seen him?"

"How about Scotland?"

"Scotland? Joe, what are you talking about?"

Did he think she was a stalker? He definitely looked suspicious and more intense by the moment.

"You care for Lachlann, ma'am? Truly care for him?"

She dropped the hose, sending water spraying wildly, and struggled to recover it before they were both soaked. Joe hastened to turn off the faucet.

He *was* matchmaking! But why did he seem so suspicious?

"I didn't mean to startle you," he said apologetically. "It's just that he's a fine man, and he's been through a lot for his years. I don't want to see him suffer more than he has already."

"He won't suffer because of me," she replied stiffly. "You have nothing to worry about."

"I'm glad to hear it. Pardon the questions, Professor. It's just that I noticed you two dallying in the driveway Sunday night. It didn't look like nothing to me."

"Oh, Joe!" She blushed furiously.

He chuckled. "Don't be embarrassed. But I'd feel better knowing that you know what you're getting into."

"What do you mean?"

"Have you noticed how Lachlann talks?"

She glanced at him sharply. "Are you referring to his accent?"

Between indignation, mortification, and curiosity, she allowed herself to be steered toward his patio. Where was he going with this?

"Not just his accent," he said as they sat down at a wrought-iron table. "Sometimes, he seems to not understand, to not remember words. Although I must admit that he's gotten a lot better since he met you."

"Are you sure it's not just your Cajun-speak he has trouble understanding?"

"No doubt that's part of it," he answered, completely unoffended, as she knew he would be. "But it's more than that."

"You needn't worry, Joe. Lachlann told me he was home-schooled in Gaelic."

"He told me the same, but he would still have had to

86

pass standardized tests. I've worked with enough Scots. They don't talk like Lachlann does. I think he was hurt in the accident."

"Accident?"

"If he hasn't told you about the accident, then it's not for me to tell you. He'll confide in you when he's ready. Suffice to say that he lost more, much more, than his farm. I don't know if that's where his mind goes or if it's the head injury or both."

Head injury? What else didn't she know?

"There's nothing wrong with Lachlann's head," she retorted, more sharply than she'd intended. "I'm sorry, Joe, but you're upsetting me. Lachlann's fine. He works on an oil rig, for goodness' sake. He speaks clearly enough, considering his brogue, and he understands everything perfectly."

"You sure about that? I love the man, Professor. You won't find a better one. I just want you to understand what you might be undertaking. At the very least, he struggles with post-traumatic stress."

Deidre felt as though her heart was being squeezed. "You're telling me that Lachlann has PTSD?"

"That's exactly what I'm telling you. I'm no doctor. I don't know if he was ever tested for it. But I've lived with him these past few years. Without a doubt, I can tell you he's suffering. Don't you be playing games with him. I won't have it."

Deidre stared at Joe in astonishment. He was deadly serious, his deep brown eyes firmly meeting hers. She wanted to be annoyed, but all she could feel was gratitude. Reaching across the table, she placed one of her hands on his arm. "I don't play games, Joe. Can you keep a secret?"

"Old Joe can keep a secret with the best of them."

She had every doubt, and yet she trusted him. "I care more than I ever wanted to, and it's scaring the hell out of me."

Chapter Thirteen

Why was she always the last one to know?

Deidre stared at her bedroom ceiling. She should have stayed home today for all the good she'd done at the university. After her conversation with Joe, she'd moved through the day in a daze, unable to stop thinking of Lachlann.

Here she was, struggling over her feelings for him, only to find out that she hardly knew him. If nothing else, her chat with Joe had taught her that.

Just as she'd known nothing about Professor James Stanfield or his true intentions.

Shuddering, Deidre curled around a pillow as memories came flooding back. There she sat, on her supposed wedding night, in the middle of the bed, clutching the bedsheets against herself, aching, ashamed, unable to control her weeping.

"Why the hell are *you* crying?" her husband had asked harshly as he yanked on a robe. "I'm the one who should be upset. What a hell of a wedding night!"

How could he speak to her like that, as though he were berating one of his students?

"You hurt me," she sobbed. "I told you that I'd never…"

"I didn't believe you," he slurred. "But I do now. It's no wonder! Look at you! Hell, I could hardly see what I was doing past your thighs!"

He reeked of alcohol. She'd never seen him like this.

He'd always seemed so sophisticated, so very charming and thoughtful. He'd said over and over again how much he wanted her, needed her.

Lies! But why? What did he have to gain?

He ran a hand through his dark, graying hair—she had thought him so distinguished—and turned toward the door. "You're disgusting. I'm going to spend the rest of the night with a nice bottle of gin."

Her cellphone rang, thankfully bringing her back to the present. Swiping her cheeks with a shaky hand, she retrieved the phone from her nightstand to glance at the name on the screen.

Stella. Were they supposed to have dinner together tonight?

"Hello?" Too late, she realized that she should have blown her nose.

"What's wrong?" came the immediate reply.

"Nothing." Deidre sniffled, groping for a tissue.

"Don't give me that crap. You're crying."

"I'm not..." She sighed. "Okay, yes, I'm crying. I was just remembering...you know."

"Why? What's happened, honey?"

It was more sympathy than she could bear. She couldn't answer. Tears clogged her throat.

"I'm on my way."

"No, it's okay," she managed. "Really."

"The hell it is. I'll be there in half an hour."

Deidre nodded, as if her friend could see her. "Okay."

Forty-five minutes later, she and Stella were dunking tortilla chips into salsa and chile con queso that Stella had brought from the restaurant where they'd planned to meet. They were also drinking margaritas— strong, homemade margaritas—Stella's specialty.

"All right, so why did you go *there*? Why the *hell* did you go *there*?" Stella asked her. "I thought you finally put that bullshit behind you."

Deidre sighed as she scooped up some queso. "I was. I am." At Stella's snort, she looked up. "I am, really. Like I told you, I don't even count it as a real marriage or wedding night. The whole thing was a nightmare. A farce."

Stella's green eyes searched hers. "Then why?" she asked gently.

As they crunched and sipped, Deidre recounted her conversation with Joe, almost word for word. Her friend listened without comment.

"I thought about it all day, and the more I thought, the more I realized that Joe is probably right." She placed her hand on her forehead as she looked at her friend. "I don't know about the PTSD, but Lachlann is definitely suffering."

"What makes you think so?" It was the first time Stella had spoken since Deidre had begun her recounting. She was an excellent listener.

"I told you about the Renaissance Festival."

She nodded. "Yeah—the kiss."

"Well, there was something else before that. He got upset, really upset."

Stella stiffened. "At you? Why didn't you tell me?"

"No, not at me. A…it was a toy that upset him."

"A toy?"

Deidre nodded. "He said it reminded him of someone he loved, someone he missed. And this morning, Joe told me that Lachlann had lost more than his farm in the fire—much more."

An expression of horror crossed Stella's face. "Do you think…"

"That he lost a child?" Deidre was fighting back tears. "It makes sense and…Oh, God." She gasped as a thought struck her. She grabbed Stella's arm, almost causing her to spill her margarita.

"What?"

"Where's his wife? Do you think…"

"That's a huge leap." Stella took Deidre's glass and set both drinks down on the coffee table.

"Is it?" For as long as she lived, she wouldn't forget the sight of his tears. He'd looked absolutely haunted. "Stella, I lectured him!"

"*Lectured* him?"

"No, I take that back. I preached. *Preached!*"

"You're not a preachy person."

"Apparently I am. I was all about having a good attitude, appreciating every moment. No wonder he snapped at me."

I could do without the bad moments, he'd told her.

She was such a fool.

Stella was shaking her head. "You couldn't know. You still don't. You're just guessing. He hasn't told you anything."

It was true. She was just guessing. Lachlann hadn't told her a thing. And Deidre didn't have time for guessing games. She had a paper to write, students to teach, a department to run.

And right now, none of it mattered.

What she thought she'd felt for James Stanfield the day they'd married had nothing on this. Leave it to her to fall…No!

Stella was watching her. "Wow. You've got it bad for this guy."

No, no, no.

She shook her head vigorously. "I can't."

92

"Can't you?"

She could not, did not…Nope. She wasn't going there. She cared about Lachlann, desired him. Who wouldn't? She could admit that. "Lust," she said aloud. "It's just lust."

Stella laughed. "Lust, huh?"

"It can't be more. I can't…"

"Do you think he feels the same way?"

Stella had a way of cutting to the chase.

She thought over the question. Lachlann wanted her, too. Didn't he? Could she have imagined the longing, the desperation that she sensed matched her own? And—breaking news—she'd never known passion until he kissed her.

She closed her eyes against the knowing, green gaze, unable—unwilling—to answer. And then her friend's arms were around her, holding her close.

"Oh, Stella."

Chapter Fourteen

Lachlann sat on deck, a book in his lap, staring out over the water at the orange horizon. Behind him, some men were talking in Spanish, laughing while they worked. He knew that they spoke English well enough, but he couldn't blame them for preferring to speak in their own language. He would if he could.

Maybe he could teach Deidre at least a few words and phrases. He ached to hear her speak Norroena, yearned to hear his language on her lips. She was a fast learner. Her Gaelic had improved beyond all imagining, as had his English. But he wasn't prepared to explain how he was fluent in a language that was no longer spoken.

For now, there were other things he wanted from her soft, pink lips. One more day…one more day and he would see her, hold her in his arms and feel again.

He hadn't known what to expect of the Renaissance Festival, and he hadn't been prepared. His emotions, long stifled, had overwhelmed him. Much of the festival was grossly inauthentic, but not all. At times, it had seemed as if the two ages were merging, as if in some sort of time warp. At other moments, the simple fun had calmed his conflicting emotions.

It wasn't until he saw stark reminders of a different life, *his* different life, that his head and stomach gave in. It was then that a true miracle happened. Deidre's touch had brought him back from the abyss.

He closed his eyes and drew a deep breath of damp, salty air. Her touch had been a revelation. She'd had no idea of the rising panic she had calmed. And then he'd kissed her.

Every time he thought of it, of her response to him and his to her, he found himself struggling with an erection. He had thought that part of him dead—literally, physically dead—ascribing it to injury or some sort of trauma. God knew he'd survived much. But now his cock was not only proving him wrong, it was back with a vengeance, and that had everything to do with Deidre. He wanted her in ways he could hardly fathom.

He'd never felt so drawn to anyone. He'd grown to care for Allasan, but there had never been much passion between them. Their wedding night had been just short of a disaster. Allasan had been so skittish that she'd almost broken his nose. He could see it like yesterday, although he'd not dwelled on it often.

She'd been waiting in bed for him, pretty and delicate-looking in a soft woolen gown with yellow flowers embroidered at the neck. Her dark hair hung in a braid down her back, her brown eyes huge in her small face.

"Allasan, are you afraid?" he'd asked.

"A little," she admitted.

"Don't be. We'll take it slowly."

Still wearing his mantle, he sat beside her on the bed and gently kissed her cheek. She was soft, fresh, and trembling as she stared down at her hands in her lap. He lifted her face to his. "Don't be afraid," he whispered.

Slowly, he put one arm around her. It was a wonder that it didn't wrap around her twice, she was so small and slight. Her back was stiff, her mouth tight as his lips touched hers. He held back a sigh. "We don't have to do anything tonight."

"Of course we do! It's our wedding night!"

"Since it's ours, isn't it up to us what we do?"

"They might check."

"I don't think so."

"You don't want me?"

"I do, but you don't want me."

"I do!"

"Prove it."

"I married you."

He shrugged.

She tried to glare at him and grinned instead. Scooting a little closer, she shyly kissed his cheek.

He didn't move.

More boldly, she placed her arms on his shoulders and gave him a peck on the lips. When he still didn't move, she slapped his arm. "Lachlann, I don't know what to do."

He put his arms around her again and pressed his lips to hers. This time, she kissed him back. Making himself more comfortable, he pulled her down beside him, trying to ignore his sudden need. His hands and lips caressed her, lightly skimming over her breasts, her stomach, her hips. Her eyes were closed, and she lay very still, but she finally relaxed. When he began to tug at her nightgown, she made no objection but allowed him to pull it over her head.

He didn't have much experience with women, but he had enough to know that it would be more enjoyable for them both if she were aroused as well. He kissed her gently. When her mouth softened beneath his, he deepened the kiss as his hand slid down one of her thighs.

Bam!

Lachlann saw stars as blood poured from his nose.

96

Allasan had bolted to a sitting position, her head smashing into his face as she did so.

"No!" she cried. "Oh, Lachlann!"

"A cloth…"

After a moment's scramble, she pressed her balled-up nightgown to his nose. She was crying.

She was crying?

"Lachlann, I'm so sorry!" she gasped. "I didn't mean to hurt you. I just don't feel comfortable with you touching me down there."

"You might have just said so," he grumbled, his voice muffled under the fabric.

"I was surprised."

"I only meant to get you ready for me."

"I am ready."

"Somehow, I don't think so."

They both laughed a little at that.

"I am," she insisted. "Has it stopped?"

He removed the gown from his nose, and blood trickled down.

"Almost." His eyes were watering.

Finally, the downpour ceased. He pinched his nose to make sure it wasn't broken. Allasan took the nightgown. Dipping it in a bowl of water at their bedside, she wiped his face and climbed out of bed.

"I'm getting you some ale. You'll need to rinse your mouth and then drink."

She was right. He'd bitten his tongue, too, could taste the blood. Damn it!

The next few minutes passed like hours, but they finally settled together under the covers.

"I'm ready when you are," she whispered.

They were both naked, skin to skin, and Lachlann reveled in the sensation. Suddenly, he was as ready as ever.

But she wasn't. Despite her words, she was nervous again. He kissed her gently, whispering encouraging words in her ear. He took her slowly. She hardly even cried. Of course, it was over almost as soon as it began. Duty done, she fell asleep moments after, while he lay beside her, wishing for more.

Remembering the long, uncomfortable night, Lachlann grinned wryly. It had been a sign of things to come. Allasan had been a fine young woman, God rest her soul. He would never know what might have come of their marriage, but he believed that it would have remained strong despite their disparate ambitions and views of life. They'd come to share a mutual respect and friendship. But she'd never warmed to bed play.

He realized now, with unquestionable clarity, that he'd never known passion until Deidre. Never had he experienced the intense desire and interest he felt for her.

A flock of brown pelicans passed overhead. He watched them fly into the darkness. It was never really quiet on the rig, never dark. The darkness had been within him. Now, there was a faint light of hope.

But hope for what? Would Deidre want him if he told her the truth about himself, especially if he had no answers?

If she knew he had every intention of going back?

He didn't want to hurt her.

He glanced down at the book in his lap, *Clans of Scotland*. He needed answers. He had to find out what had happened to him, what it all meant. Sure, he was hoping that with her knowledge of history, Deidre might be able to help him. But could he bring himself to ask?

The wind picked up, cool, relaxing. Leaning back against some pipes, Lachlann closed his eyes and saw her sweet face. Every time he closed his eyes, he saw her. He drifted off, right there on the deck, dreaming he was in Deidre's arms.

Chapter Fifteen

Home—finally! Lachlann pulled onto Joe's driveway and parked. A two-week hitch had never felt so long. The moment he stepped out of his truck, he smelled it. The piquant aroma of Cajun spices filled the air. Had Joe started Thanksgiving prep or was that dinner? He hoped it was dinner.

But it wasn't food he'd been looking forward to so eagerly. He pulled his bag from the back seat of his truck and closed the door. He wanted—needed—to see Deidre.

"Lachlann!"

She almost knocked him over. Suddenly, his things were on the ground, his arms filled with Deidre, her arms around his neck in a tight embrace. She kissed his cheek again and again.

"Welcome home! I thought you'd never get here."

Speechless, he clutched her against him, closing his eyes as he buried his face in her hair. For a long moment, he simply held her, overcome by her greeting, and then became keenly aware of her body against his. His lips sought hers.

Her mouth was soft and sweet beneath his as she pressed herself closer. She felt so right. Ahhh. A fierce shudder almost split his chest as his entire being roared to life. His arms tightened around her.

"Lachlann, is that you?"

They both jumped. Raising his head, Lachlann

looked over the top of his truck and saw Joe standing in his doorway. "Hey, Joe!" he managed to croak.

He could feel Deidre trembling all over as she pressed her face to his chest. She was laughing!

"Y'all get in here! You're late, and supper's on the table!"

"Yes, sir!" He was laughing, too.

The front door closed. He pressed his forehead against hers, his heart pounding in his chest.

"I missed you," she said quietly.

"I missed you, too." God knew how much.

Retrieving his bag, he wrapped his arm around her shoulders, and they walked into Joe's house together.

****

With a smile, Deidre watched Lachlann examine the beds of leafy greens, winter squash, and root vegetables. She loved that he took his gardening seriously.

As if he could hear her thoughts, he glanced at her. "Everything looks great. Thanks for taking such good care of it all."

"No thanks necessary. I enjoyed it, and Joe treated me to coffee every chance he got."

"And conversation, no doubt."

"Of course."

They laughed together. The sound of his laughter was still new to her, and it was beautiful, intoxicating. He'd been so serious since they'd met. Of course, now she knew why. At least, she thought she did.

It had been terribly hard leaving him the night before, but it had been the only decent thing to do. She'd left with barely a kiss and today everyone had been busy. But this evening...things would be different if she had anything to do with it.

He continued his inspection, pinching off anything

that didn't please him, pulling out a weed here and there. His hands were huge and yet so gentle. She stared at them, her mouth suddenly dry. She wanted his hands on her.

Ever since her conversation with Joe, she had told herself that all she wanted was to hold Lachlann in her arms and comfort him. But whenever they touched, different thoughts and feelings took over.

Lachlann turned and caught her staring at him—as usual. His eyes widened briefly, then darkened with intensity. He took a step toward her. "Deidre, I…"

"Lachlann!"

They both jumped at Jackson's shout.

"Lachlann! Deidre! Hurry! Joe's been hurt!"

****

Lachlann stood with Deidre and Jackson beside the hospital bed and stared down at his friend and landlord, fighting panic. The doctor had assured them that he would be all right.

A kitchen fire…Joe had been trying to cook too many things at once, preparing for Thanksgiving dinner, plus cooking up a big batch of fried chicken for lunch. Somehow, he'd hit the handle of the frying pan, catapulting boiling oil all over his shirt and, if that wasn't bad enough, he had been close enough to the gas stove for his shirt to catch fire. He had first and second degree burns on his stomach, chest, right arm, and right hand.

"I've ruined Thanksgiving," he groaned as the three of them stood there.

"Nonsense, Joe," Deidre said briskly. "As long as you're all right, we'll have plenty to be thankful for."

"I'm going home for Thanksgiving. Ain't none of us going to spend it here in this hospital. But what are we going to eat?"

"Don't worry, Joe. We'll manage," Lachlann assured him. His voice sounded shaky, even to himself.

"We'll be fine," Jackson agreed.

"It's a holiday," Joe persisted.

"I'll cook," Deidre said, "using your recipes. Rest now, *cher*, because I'll be bothering you tomorrow."

Jackson agreed to go home and clean while Lachlann and Deidre stayed with Joe through the night. Lachlann was more grateful than he could express for her calming presence.

Fire. Just thinking about it made his insides coil. He pulled a chair close to the bed while Deidre sat nearby on the sofa.

"Lachlann, Joe's going to be all right," she said quietly. "He has some bad burns. He'll be in pain for a while. But it could've been much worse. Joe's tough. He'll be okay."

"What about infection?"

She shook her head. "They've given him antibiotics, and his burns have been cleaned and covered with antibacterial cream. When he goes home, we'll make sure they stay that way until his skin is healed."

He nodded, silently reminding himself that it was the twenty-first century. Deidre rubbed his arm soothingly. He covered her hand with his own.

"Until you…" His voice shook and he stopped. "Joe is family to me. He gave me work, a home, food, advice when I needed it."

"None of us are going anywhere," she said firmly.

It was a long, miserable night. He dozed in a chair, his feet propped on another. Suddenly, Allasan was in front of him, angry. "Lachlann, go to Inbhir Nis! I want the dye! You'll only be in my way here!"

Her face loomed close to his. As he stared at her, it

became covered with boils.

"Och," he murmured. "I'm sorry. I'm sorry, Allasan."

She didn't answer, only looked at him accusingly. Fire lit her hair and began searing her face.

He shouted.

A soothing voice, a calming touch dispelled the image. He shifted uncomfortably and kept dreaming.

Deidre gave up trying to sleep. Nurses came and went. Joe tossed a bit and moaned as if in pain, but his vitals remained strong. She was just as worried about Lachlann. Every time he dozed, he had nightmares.

"Joe? I don't understand. I can't understand!"

Even as she moved to wake him, he quieted again, but only for a moment. When he spoke again, it wasn't in English. Was it Gaelic? He spoke in a low, desperate tone. She could swear it was a language she'd never heard before.

Another time he shouted in Gaelic, waking all three of them.

"*A'dhia, cuidich mi!*" God! God, help!

"Lachlann! Wake up, son! You're all right. It's Joe," Joe groaned.

"Lachlann, wake up." Deidre shook him gently, her eyes suddenly burning with tears.

"*Tha mi duilich,*" he whispered. "*Tha mi duilich.*"

"He's apologizing," Joe murmured drowsily.

Deidre had understood the simple words, but she was surprised that Joe did.

"You speak Gaelic?" she asked incredulously.

"He's taught me some."

Both men fell into fitful sleep. Just as Deidre began to doze again, Joe's voice startled her.

"You need to get out of here," he muttered, his head

moving restlessly. "Everything's burned. I'm sorry."

"It's okay, Joe," Deidre soothed, moving to stand at his bedside and pat his shoulder.

"*Sàbhail thu fhèin! Tionndaidh gu taobh Inbhir Nis!*" Save yourself! Go back to Inverness!

He was speaking in Gaelic!

Lachlann woke. "Joe?"

"He's okay," she assured him, "just dreaming. Joe, everything is all right."

The injured man moaned.

Lachlann rose stiffly. "I'll go and get the nurse."

"I can buzz for her."

"It'll be faster if I go," he said, "and I need the walk."

He was right on both counts. As Lachlann left the room, she stared at Joe. What was he dreaming? The night was growing stranger by the moment.

"*A 'Dhaimh,*" Joe whispered, startling her, "*sàbhail thu fhèin.*"

Save yourself.

Chapter Sixteen

Deidre woke to sunlight streaming through the large windows. She was exhausted and as stiff as a board. Near her, Lachlann dozed in the chair. He had to be even stiffer than she was. Pushing herself to a sitting position on the small sofa, she glanced toward Joe. He was watching her.

"Y'all didn't have to spend the night."

She hurried to his bedside. "Good morning, Joe. You probably would've slept better without us. You're lucky you didn't have three of us staying, but someone had to go home and tend to the mess you made. Jackson will be here later. Would you like some water? The nurse said I could give you some if you asked."

"Sounds good," he croaked. "Lachlann okay?"

"He's been worried about you."

Joe nodded. "Lachlann and me, we've been through some things together. I might be a nightmare, but his didn't start with me. I told you he's been through a lot."

Deidre held his head as he gulped down a few sips of water, then buzzed for the nurse. She could tell that he was uncomfortable. "I'm glad he had you."

"We've had each other. He's like a son to me," he rasped as he lay back against the pillows.

At that moment, Lachlann woke with a start. "How are you feeling, Joe?" he asked, rising slowly.

"Like hell," Joe answered.

"The nurse should be here any minute," Deidre

106

assured him.

She and Lachlann stayed with Joe until midday, not leaving until the doctor had been in to examine him. He gave them good news. The burns were looking better already. Joe might be able to go home tomorrow or the day after, which would be the day before Thanksgiving.

They ran into Jackson on their way out. He'd already told them that the damage to the kitchen was minimal. There'd been a mess, to be sure, but most of the harm had been to Joe. Deidre liked the young man. Short and wiry and not long out of high school, it was obvious that he had a bit of a wild streak. But he also had a kind heart and a good head on his shoulders.

When they returned to the house, they found Jackson's assessment accurate. He had cleaned up most of the mess, but the room was still greasy in places and the whole place smelled of smoke. Deidre insisted on helping Lachlann scrub what Jackson had missed. He worked quietly, not speaking, his expression pensive.

When they finished, she took him by the hand. "Let's rest."

He looked stricken. "You're leaving?"

"Won't you come with me? You can shower and rest at my house while we air out this one. It's still smoky in here."

"It is," he agreed, relief evident in his face, "and I hate the smell of smoke. I'll grab a change of clothes."

When they got to her house, Deidre showed him to the guest room, which boasted a small, attached bath, and made sure he had fresh towels, soap, and shampoo. She then hurried to shower herself. It wouldn't be easy, but she wanted to be finished when he was. She had seen the bleak look in his eyes while they were cleaning and didn't want him to be alone.

Her hair was still wet, but she met him on the landing. He was standing at the top of the stairs. She knew it! He'd had no intention of sleeping, even though he was obviously in desperate need of it.

She took one of his hands in both of hers.

"Come," she said firmly. "Let's rest together. I'm in serious need of a nap, but I don't want to be alone right now. We can just lie on top of my bed."

He stared at her for a moment, his gray eyes intense.

"Please?" she added.

Sighing deeply, he nodded.

Still holding his hand, she led him to her room.

A vague impression of cream and light registered in Lachlann's exhausted mind. He felt too tired and anxious to relax, much less sleep. He didn't even want to let go of Deidre's hand.

They climbed onto opposite sides of the bed. He stretched himself out on his back, careful to stay on his side, his throat tight as he covered his eyes with his arm.

It took Deidre one moment longer to settle. Without a word, she cuddled against him, stretching one arm across his waist.

It was just what he needed, but the comfort of her touch was almost more than he could bear. Choking back tears, Lachlann put his arms around her and held her close. She felt so right in his arms. The full, womanly curves of her body fit his perfectly. *She* fit him perfectly.

Her breathing became slower, more rhythmic. So did his. With Deidre tucked warmly against him, he felt himself begin to drift off.

Creamy walls faded to a field of oats, to another time and place.

He and Rónán stood side by side on a hill, staring down at his farm. Deep green stalks swayed gently in the breeze.

"Magnificent," proclaimed Rónán. "You shall have a bountiful harvest."

"I hope so. I'd like to take my family to the harvest fair in Inbhir Nis this year."

"During Lùnastal? Allasan and Iain will love it."

There was a long, low rumble as the ground trembled.

"We've been having a lot of those lately," Rónán said thoughtfully as they turned to walk up the hill toward their homes. "It's been different around the glen. Have you noticed any strangers around?"

"No." Lachlann glanced at him. "Troublemakers?"

"I'm not sure. They seem to be just passing through. They're not Gaels."

Suddenly, they heard shouting.

"Lachlann! Help! Lachlann An Damh, we need your help!"

Chisholm clansmen were running toward them.

"*A'Dhaimh*, we need you!"

"What's happened?"

"It's Aonghas! A boulder fell on him! We can't move it!"

Lachlann started to run.

"We were near the crag when the tremors started," explained a clansman. "We should've stopped excavating, but we only needed a few more boulders for the section of wall we've been working on. Aonghas wanted to push on."

Grimacing, Lachlann ran faster. He heard his old friend's bellow long before they reached him.

"Leave me be! Where's An Damh?"

"Aonghas! I'm here!" Lachlann called. He pushed through the crowd, his gut clenching. Aonghas was prostrate beneath a rocky outcrop, a huge boulder pinning his leg just below his hip.

"*A'Dhaimh*," Aonghas grunted, "would you get this damned rock off me? Every time they try to move it, they make it worse!"

Stepping closer, Lachlann assessed the situation. The boulder was half as large as himself, maybe less. Another tremor sent small rocks flying over them. He had to hurry.

He tried pushing the solid stone. It didn't budge. Drawing a deep breath, he tried again. He had to move it. Aonghas was counting on him. He repositioned himself so that one leg was behind him, his knee bent in front. Holding the boulder from the bottom, he shoved hard and felt it give. There was no stopping now. Push! Muscles contracting, veins bulging, he heaved the boulder off his friend with a roar.

Aonghas passed out, and Lachlann choked on a gasp. The man's bare leg was wide open, covered in blood, pieces of bone sticking up and out.

"Has someone gone for the healer?" he asked, although he knew there would be no healing for the leg.

"He should be on his way." Rónán stood beside him.

There was another tremor.

"Rónán, watch out!" Lachlann covered Aonghas' body with his own as rocks went flying off the mountainside. A small boulder hit him in the back. Sand and gravel rained over them.

Aonghas let out an ear-piercing scream. Lachlann hovered over him, trying to protect his injured leg without touching it. The shaking finally subsided, and he was able to look up. Through the dust, he saw Rónán crouched against the side of the mountain.

The injured man thrashed beneath him, moaning.

Lachlann grasped his arms, pinning him down, and heard a shout of anguish. Aonghas' brother had arrived with the healer.

Hours later, sad and weary, he and Rónán left Aonghas' cottage.

"God help him," muttered Lachlann under his breath. He wiped his cheeks on his sleeve.

"You did all that you could," Rónán said.

"I held a man down while they sawed off his leg."

"You and his own brother held him down. I don't think there was much sawing needed. His bones were crushed."

Lachlann shuddered. "I'll hear Aonghas' screams for as long as I live."

"So will I."

"How will they manage?"

"The clan will help."

"What if he dies?" questioned Lachlann. "What happens to his family then?"

Rónán glanced at him searchingly. "Muireall and the children won't go hungry, if that's what you mean. You know that." He sighed. "But it won't be easy for them."

Lachlann was shaken to the bone. Aonghas was the last person he would have expected this to happen to. He'd always been so bold, so strong, and so damn stubborn. He and Muireall had married young. They had three children and another on the way. He was a man who knew who he was, what he wanted from life, and how to get it. How could this have happened to him? Why?

"Do you ever wonder what's the point of it all?" he asked Rónán. "I tell myself that if I plan carefully, if I plow, sow, harvest on time, everything will be all right.

But that's not true. I can't control the weather. I can't predict infestations."

"Of course you can't."

"I couldn't help Aonghas," Lachlann continued desperately. "I can't help you."

"Help me?"

He shouldn't have mentioned it. Rónán never spoke of his damaged foot or the pain it caused him. But it was there, evident in his thinness, his quickly subdued grimaces, and, worst of all, the occasional expression of despair when he thought no one was looking.

"I can't ease your suffering," he muttered, "and I hate it."

His friend opened and closed his mouth. They walked on in silence, the stars shining brightly for such a miserable night.

"Lachlann…" Rónán's voice shook and he stopped abruptly. "I'm not sure I'd even be here if it weren't for you."

"Of course you would."

"My childhood was tolerable because of you. You were my only friend. You've done more than ease my pain. You've fought for me all of our lives."

"It's not enough."

"You might be strong as an ox, but you're not God. It's not up to you to heal my foot. It wasn't up to you to save Aonghas' leg. You always do everything you can to help. You never say no to anyone. But there's only so much you can do, only so much any of us can do.

"Then why bother? If we have no control, if we can lose everything in an instant, why even try?"

"Ah. Now who sounds like a bard?" Rónán scoffed gently. "Why try? Why love? Why live in pain? I can't tell you. But…" He turned toward his house. "You might ask your son."

Iain.

"Iain, I'm sorry." Lachlann whispered the words as he wiped the tears trickling down his face. He was awake, then?

He'd been like Aonghas, strong, stubborn, sure of himself. He'd thought himself invincible, and he'd lost everything—everything that mattered.

Yet here he was, alive, centuries after he should have been dead. Why? How?

Deidre moved against him. Deidre! He'd forgotten where he was.

Pulling her closer, he pressed trembling lips to the top of her head and closed his eyes.

Would he lose her, too?

Chapter Seventeen

"More cayenne, Professor. It needs more cayenne."

"Joe, you're driving me crazy," stated Deidre as she obediently added more cayenne pepper to the mirepoix, a sauté of bell peppers, onions, and celery.

She really didn't mind, of course, and she wasn't surprised that he was being so bossy. Thanksgiving was tomorrow, and they had a lot to do. When she'd promised she'd cook Thanksgiving dinner with his recipes, there were a couple of things she hadn't anticipated. One was that Joe would expect her to cook at his house so that he could supervise. Her mistake. The other was that his children would all change their holiday plans. They were expected to arrive late tonight. They wanted to see their father; they were worried about him. It was only natural. One usually reaped what one sowed, and Joe had obviously been a good and loving father. Of course his children would want to make sure he was okay.

They were helping, too. His son and family were bringing a fried turkey and some pies. His daughter was bringing a ham, a green bean casserole, and sweet potatoes. She was beyond grateful that they were bringing everything already cooked. It would be a challenge enough to get everything hot on the table all at once.

It was still up to Deidre to roast another turkey and to make Joe's cornbread dressing, Joe's garlic mashed potatoes, and, to her alarm, his seafood gumbo. She'd never made gumbo before.

Lachlann and Jackson were sent to the grocery store numerous times as Joe remembered things he would need—plenty of beer and a few good bottles of wine, rolls, breakfast items, cans of cranberry sauce, games for his grandchildren. They were also charged with helping Deidre in the kitchen, which only added to the hilarious chaos.

She was glad and grateful that Joe was home and healing well and that they would all be able to celebrate together. Her last several Thanksgivings hadn't been very happy, and they'd all been looking forward to this one. But she'd be enjoying another, extra-special bonus. To make more room for the family, Lachlann would stay in her guest room through the weekend. Joe had a big house, five bedrooms, and he firmly and repeatedly insisted that the kids could sleep anywhere. But it was a compromise that everyone was happy with, especially her.

She was worried about Lachlann. She no longer held a single doubt that Joe was right about everything, including the PTSD. She would never forget the strange and awful night in the hospital.

"Check the cornbread!"

She'd just retrieved an oven mitt to do exactly that.

****

"Lachlann! Deidre! Don't leave! It's still early!"

Deidre smiled as Joe's grandchildren all but tackled Lachlann. He was better than a jungle gym for them, and he'd roughhoused with them all day. He was a natural with children.

"I'm afraid you're stuck with Jackson now," he told them, gently ruffling their hair.

Jackson grinned. "I'm not dealin' with those wild

things!"

"You don't want to stay and finish watching the football game?" asked Joe's son, Charles.

"Thanks. We can finish it at Deidre's. We'll let you settle in for the night."

"Good night, Joe." Deidre bent and kissed her host's cheek. "Happy Thanksgiving. Thank you for a wonderful day."

"Thank you, honey," he answered, taking her by the hand. "Our dressing and gumbo turned out nice, didn't they?"

"They sure did," she agreed.

"Everything was perfect," said his daughter Genevieve, Ginny for short. She hurried over to kiss Deidre. "Thank you for all of your help, and thank you, Lachlann, for giving up your room for the kids."

"He can stay with us!" suggested one of the boys.

They all laughed.

"Lachlann will be all right at Miss Deidre's house," said their grandfather.

"I'll see you tomorrow," Lachlann assured them. He rested his hand on Joe's shoulder. "Happy Thanksgiving, Joe, and thank you. I'm glad we could all be together."

"Thank you, son. So am I. Happy Thanksgiving to you. God bless you."

Lachlann and Deidre walked to her house hand in hand.

"They're all so sweet," she murmured. "But I have to admit, I feel rather sorry for Jackson."

Lachlann chuckled. "He'll survive."

"Shall we finish the game?" she asked as they walked into her living room.

He shook his head as he pulled her into his arms. "TV gives me a headache."

She slipped her arms around his neck, her heart hammering in her chest. For a moment, they gazed at each other. The expression in his gray eyes was intense, searching, before his lips claimed hers.

Clinging to each other, they sank onto the sofa.

****

The golden rays of dawn peeked through Deidre's bedroom windows as sounds of Joe's family loading their cars penetrated her consciousness. They had said their good-byes the night before, intending to leave before sunrise so that they could get some driving in while the children still slept. They were obviously running a little late, but if they didn't make too many stops, they should still reach New Orleans by nightfall.

She stretched. The children would have this evening and all of Sunday to rest up for school Monday. God knew that they all needed some rest.

It had been a hectic weekend. Clan Dubois, as Lachlann called them, was a sweet and well-meaning group, but also a demanding one. They'd spent almost every waking hour with them. Last night, to her dismay, she'd fallen asleep before Lachlann had even returned to her house.

As for the other two nights...A thrill ran through her, followed by a deep longing. Both nights, he'd been the one to stop kissing. They'd fallen asleep on the sofa, wrapped in each other's arms, and slept through the night together.

But why had he stopped?

Because he's not really interested, that's why. Something about her turned him off. What was it? Her red hair? Her freckles? *Her thighs?*

She sighed. It was just as well. She didn't have time for a relationship.

Didn't want one. Didn't need one.

She stared up at the ceiling.

Liar.

She did want. She did need. So much that it terrified her. And she hadn't been so attracted to anyone since…forever.

But Lachlann was battling some sort of trauma. She'd watched the anguish and misery in his eyes lessen with each day Joe improved.

She wished he would trust her enough to confide in her. She glanced out of the window at the brightening sky. Was she willing to do the same, prepared to face his sympathy or scorn? How could she expect him to tell her his deepest, most personal secrets if she was reluctant to divulge her own?

Did it matter? Yes. Trust was important. But did she have to know everything about another person before she could trust? Before she could love?

Love? Was she really going there? What did she know of either love or trust? She'd been wrong about both with James Stanfield. There hadn't been so much as passion between them.

But Lachlann…Lachlann stirred feelings she never knew existed. Closing her eyes, she imagined she was in his arms again, held tightly against him, feeling his labored breathing, knowing he was just as excited as she was.

Clutching one pillow tightly against her, she buried her face in another and screamed a soft, frustrated scream. She wanted to jump his bones then and there.

Deidre stilled. What if she did? What if she seduced him? She was stunned by her own train of thought.

She couldn't. Could she? After all, a woman didn't run into a Lachlann An Damh every day.

But what if he didn't like her body? What if he hated her thighs? She pressed her face deeper into the pillow.

No. She would *not* go there. Lachlann wanted her as much as she wanted him. She wasn't wrong about this.

And he was leaving for the rig tomorrow. She couldn't let him go without trying. Kicking the covers away, she jumped out of bed.

And stopped. Without trying what? Was she actually going to…was she losing her mind?

Deidre dove back under the covers.

Had she lost all sense of morality?

She lay twisted in the sheets, thinking. She'd saved herself for marriage and where had it gotten her? She covered her face with a pillow. She'd been raped on her wedding night, fired from her job, shunned by her parents…Morality was empty without love.

Chucking the pillow, she sat up again. She loved Lachlann. No more lying to herself. She hadn't wanted to love him, to be so vulnerable. But she did. She'd loved him from the moment they'd met and even before. He was the incarnation of her medieval farmer.

But shouldn't she let him make the first move? How many times had he reminded her that he was old-fashioned? She was, too. Despite having been married, she was inexperienced where sex was concerned. She'd never been with anyone but her ex, and then only once. And that had been a lesson in pain and humiliation.

But Lachlann wouldn't hurt her. Of that, she had no doubt.

But does he love me?

And what if his hesitation was the result of a deeper problem? Something emotional, maybe. Or physical? But would he kiss her the way he did if that were so? And she'd felt him hard against her.

Excuses. She was making excuses. Pushing herself to a sitting position, Deidre squared her shoulders.

She was *not* going to allow her fears and insecurities to dictate the rest of her life. She didn't need anyone's permission to act upon her own desires. If she wanted to throw caution to the wind and bare herself to a man—mind, body, and soul; it could be no less—then she would, damn it.

She slipped out of bed. The past was past. She would tell Lachlann just that if need be. Today could be theirs.

Tiptoeing to the french doors, she peeked out. As she suspected, Lachlann was in the garden. Time was wasting! Hurrying to her bathroom, she freshened up and stood before the mirror, studying her reflection critically. Would Lachlann like what he saw?

Her peach-colored, cotton panties were faded. She'd change into something sexier. Would he think it weird that she was almost naked? Would it seem presumptuous? Since she couldn't stand sleeping in nightgowns or pajamas and really didn't like anything in between, she usually just slept in her panties. She lived alone, after all.

Straightening, she sucked in her stomach and pivoted sideways. She'd never been thin, but for most of her life, she'd been in reasonably good shape. When she was young, she'd spent most of her free time outdoors working on the farm.

It was true that she'd gained the "freshman fifteen" during her first year in college, but in the following years of intense study and long walks, she'd lost most of it. And what she'd retained, her farce of a marriage and subsequent divorce had taken care of.

Okay, so maybe she was a little soft around the middle. And yes, she was tall, broad-shouldered, big-boned. But, well, she needed the shoulders to support her boobs. Hopefully, Lachlann was a breast man.

Maybe she should slip on a camisole? But what was the point? She had blankets and, with any luck, if she got him up here, she wouldn't be wearing anything for long.

Oh, mercy! Was this even her?

She tossed her hair behind her shoulders and blinked at her reflection. Yep, it was her, all right. Freckles, red curls…The eyes that stared back at her were wide and shining with excitement, her chest rising and falling in anticipation. She wanted this.

But did he? Would he?

Was she sure?

Her heart began pounding, her breathing suddenly labored. She crawled back into bed. She couldn't do it.

Rejection. Acceptance. Could she bear either?

Condoms! She didn't have any! Of course she didn't. But she didn't need any for birth control. Her ex had insisted she go on the pill. She'd only needed it that one night…

Don't think of him.

But those little pills had regulated her cycle, which was convenient, so she'd continued taking them.

Convenient, indeed.

But what about STDs? She could ask. *Don't be stupid!*

Damn it! She climbed out of bed again. Wrapping her fluffy white quilt around herself, she walked boldly to the door. It might as well have been an electric fence. Deidre backed away, then moved ahead again. Two steps forward, one step back.

Could she survive his rejection?

It was too late to worry about that. She needed to know Lachlann's true feelings. Now was as good a time as any.

Inhaling deeply, Deidre opened the shuttered french door and stepped out.

Chapter Eighteen

Lachlann absently pulled the tiny weeds that seemed to sprout overnight in the vegetable beds.

"Ain't that a radish?" Joe's voice beside him startled him.

Bemused, he looked at his fistful of weeds. He'd pulled a radish.

Joe slapped him on the back, laughing. "I'm going back to finish sleeping. I suggest you do the same."

Sleep? Lachlann stared at Joe's retreating figure. How could he sleep? How could he garden? How could he do anything when he was besieged by white-hot lust?

But it was more than lust. Lachlann groaned inwardly. God knew he needed Deidre in every possible way.

Holding her in his arms all night, her body pressed against his, had been an extraordinary experience of heaven and hell. He'd kissed her until they were both shaking with desire, clutching each other wildly. Just thinking of it made him hard.

Nostrils flaring, he pinched a pansy bloom. It had taken two hours for his cock to back down—two nights in a row!

What the hell was he going to do? Joe had told him she'd suffered a brief, unhappy marriage. She'd been hurt. The last thing he wanted to do was to hurt her.

And if they got involved, he would hurt her. He couldn't make promises. He wasn't going to stay.

Last night, he'd returned to her house to find her asleep atop her bed, fully-dressed. She must have fallen asleep waiting for him. She'd looked like an angel, her fiery hair cloaking her shoulders, her lashes dark against her fair cheeks. Forcing himself to leave her in peace, he'd spent the rest of the night tossing in her guest bed.

He wanted her as he'd never wanted anyone. But it wasn't just desire. It was no use lying to himself. He loved Deidre, and that was the real reason for his hesitation. To get any closer, to entangle them both, could only lead to heartache.

Maybe she wasn't interested, anyway. When they lay on her sofa together, she'd cuddled back against him and slept. In and of itself, the trust was nice. But how she'd managed to fall asleep with a steel rod pressed feverishly to her back, he couldn't fathom, unless she was truly indifferent.

And yet...*nei*. There was nothing indifferent about her response to him. When they kissed, he'd been the one to stop, for her sake.

"Lachlann!"

He pinched another flower.

"Lachlann!"

Deidre?

He looked around, then up, and froze.

She posed above him, a goddess. Fiery red curls fell wildly over...was she wearing only a blanket? Her upper chest and one fair, freckled shoulder peeked out sweetly. But it was the expression on her face that captured him. Hunger, as intense as his own.

"Come up," she mouthed, gesturing to him.

He gestured back. Now? God, he hoped so.

She nodded.

He glanced back at Joe's house and briefly at the

fencerow. He could clear it.

Easy does it.

"Five minutes," he returned silently, holding up one hand.

He washed up and went around through her back gate, to her kitchen door. When she didn't answer his knock, he let himself in and locked the door behind him.

It wasn't until he reached the foot of the stairs that he hesitated.

"Deidre?"

"Up here!" she called.

He took the stairs two at a time.

"I'm in here."

He found himself standing at her bedroom door. She was sitting up in bed, covers to her chin, the mass of curls rioting over her shoulders.

Deidre stared at the man apparently frozen in her bedroom doorway. He was tall, muscular, and unbelievably gorgeous. His golden hair fell loosely to his shoulders, his gray eyes intense as he returned her stare. Her heart was going to jump out of her chest.

"Are you okay?" he finally asked.

She shook her head. No, she was not okay. She was going to hyperventilate. She took a deep breath. "Lachlann…"

"What's wrong?"

"Are you…are you healthy?"

"Healthy?"

"I mean…" She made a gesture between them. "For sex?"

His eyes widened. "Aye. You?"

"Yes." She bit her lip. "I've been married before."

"So have I."

"But I'm not very experienced. I've never felt like

this, never done anything like this before."

"Neither have I."

He stood motionless before her. Deidre forced herself to breathe calmly as they gazed at each other in silence. Her bedside clock ticked. Her heartbeat thumped in her ears.

His eyes…he wanted her. She could not be so mistaken. When had anyone ever looked at her like that? Yet he'd spent three nights in her house and not even tried.

But he was here, now—at her invitation. What was she waiting for?

With a last, deep breath, she let the blankets drop as she opened her arms.

Lachlann's breath caught in his throat. He would never forget the sight of her. Fiery curls brushed Deidre's full, creamy breasts as she held out her arms. To him. She was welcoming *him*. Looking into her eyes, he saw a yearning that matched his own.

In two strides, he was on the edge of her bed, pulling her into his arms. He closed his eyes, burrowing his face in her hair, against her neck. The feel of her, her warmth, her scent…

She smelled so good…like pears, and vanilla, and some warm spice. His arms tightened as he inhaled deeply, inhaled *her*. He had to taste her.

His lips sought hers.

He meant to be gentle, but it was impossible. His desire for her, his pent-up frustration, her naked body pressed against his…The kiss became ravenous. Deidre seemed up for it, kissing him as fiercely as he kissed her.

Her hands fumbled at his waist, grasping the edge of his T-shirt. Rising to her knees, she drew it up over his head and flung it aside.

Lachlann's heart thundered in his chest as he pulled her back to him. Skin to skin. He clenched his teeth as a shudder shook him to his very soul. It felt so right, so necessary, as though a part of him had been missing until now.

Deidre gasped as their bodies touched and he held her closer, wanting, needing to kiss her. Her hands were in his hair, then running up and down his back. Everywhere. And the more she touched, the more he needed. Desire pulsed through him.

He moved to press gentle kisses against her neck, her collarbone. She moaned softly, and a thrill shot through him. She was...she *liked* it, liked his touch. He raised his head to look at her, to make sure. Her eyes were half closed, dark and deep with passion, her breath coming quickly through her soft, parted lips. He stared for a moment, mesmerized.

"You're so beautiful." He hardly recognized his own voice, hoarse, unsteady.

Her eyes searched his. "Do you really think so?"

Her expression was suddenly fragile, vulnerable. His arms tightened around her protectively. She was truly unaware of her own beauty.

"I've never seen anyone so beautiful. Or wanted anyone so much." He touched his forehead to hers. "But it's been a long time, Deidre."

Her lashes swept her cheeks. "For me, too."

"And you're sure?" His hands were trembling as he cradled her sweet face. It was no small thing to want, to *need* someone this much. And then he realized that she was trembling all over. But she answered him.

"Oh, yes," she whispered. Her gaze met his. "I'm sure. I want you, Lachlann."

He kissed her again before moving to ease her down

upon the soft quilt. Her hair fanned out, the deep red a vivid contrast against the white cloud, her blue eyes huge in her small face. As he finished undressing, he took in her smooth skin with its dusting of freckles and her delicious curves.

He could hardly think as he lay down beside her. He wanted to caress her, to feel her against him, to be inside her. He wanted it all.

Deidre turned toward him, her breasts brushing against him. He pulled her closer, his erection almost painful, and willed himself to calm.

Softly, soothingly, he stroked her back—although whether it was Deidre or himself he was trying to soothe, he wasn't sure. He ran his hand down her side, to the curve of her hip. She was so soft, so sweet. A tremor shook him.

He trailed his fingers down to her lower abdomen, watching her. Their faces were close. When he reached her apex and his fingers delved gently into the curls, her lips parted, but she didn't object. He began to caress her, felt her little whoosh of breath as her body responded to his touch.

Slowly. Gently. Exercising every ounce of control he possessed, he brushed his lips across hers.

But her lips parted, beckoning, and he deepened the kiss.

And then she touched him, softly at first, wrapping her hand around his taut cock.

His breath caught. "Deidre…"

She stilled instantly, her expression anxious.

"Be gentle with me," he said in a hoarse whisper. He tried to smile but wasn't sure if he succeeded.

Her expression cleared. With a little squeeze, she lightly slid her hand up and down his length. He clenched his teeth, his jaw tight as pleasure—sharp, agonizing pleasure—shot through him. But it had been too long. He was too excited. He had to stop her, or he would...He grabbed her hand, held her still until the throbbing calmed.

"No more..." was all he could manage. "I want this to last." He pulled her hand down to her side, still holding it, and renewed his efforts on her, keeping his caress gentle but more deliberate.

He kissed and caressed until she was writhing against him.

She broke the kiss on a sob. "Lachlann..."

He didn't stop but captured her lips again as she began to quiver. With a little scream, she wrenched her hand from his and grasped his shoulder. A sudden warmth flooded his fingers as she shuddered against him.

With another kiss, he moved over her. "Deidre..."

She looked up at him, her eyes dark, intense. "Please," she whispered, moving against him.

Slowly. Gently.

He broke out in a sweat as he tried to ease his way in. She was ready for him—hot, moist. And tight, so tight. The instant he was fully inside her, he began throbbing again. Lachlann stilled, closing his eyes as sensations overwhelmed him.

And then she moved. She pressed up against him, just a little, but...he couldn't...

He tried to move slowly, tried to ignore the urgent need of his overwrought body. But when she began to tighten around him, he lost his mind. Need drove him. He thrust into her, and she met him thrust for thrust. He shook violently, a hoarse shout escaping him as spasms racked his body. Deidre clung to him, crying out as she shuddered beneath him.

Lachlann collapsed on top of her and tried to catch his breath. He was still inside her, could feel her heart pounding against his, and wanted to stay that way forever.

But he was squashing her. With a groan, he rolled to the side, pulling her with him. He held her close and pressed his lips to her forehead.

"Deidre." He pressed another kiss. "*Elskan*, did I hurt you?"

She shook her head.

"You're crying." He cradled her face in his hands.

She shook her head again.

"Aye, you are." With his thumbs, he brushed away the tears from the corners of her eyes.

"I'm just happy," she whispered. "It was so right, so perfect."

"Aye." He kissed her gently. "It was."

They cleaned up and tucked back into bed together. Deidre cuddled against him, and he drew her closer, resting his cheek on the top of her head.

Emotions washed over him. He couldn't even name them. He'd never felt this way before.

She stretched her arm across his waist and burrowed still closer. As her breathing grew slower, more rhythmic, so did his.

Just as he was giving in to the warm, irresistible drowsiness, he felt her lips press softly against his chest. His arms tightened around her.

The past dropped away. The future held no power.

There was only this precious woman and him.

Time stood still.

Chapter Nineteen

Lachlann woke with Deidre snuggled against him, aware of a pervading sense of peace and well-being. Opening his eyes, he saw that sunlight no longer filled the room. How long had they been sleeping?

He had never slept during the day, certainly not in the fourteenth century and not in this one. Since his fall into this century, he'd never slept well at all and consistently woke with a headache.

But now, he didn't have a headache, not even a small one. He pressed his lips to the top of her head. Of course he didn't. He held an angel in his arms.

Fulfillment...he'd never known it before. Relief, aye, and a satisfaction that he now realized had been lacking. But nothing like this.

Deidre was soft and warm against him. He gently stroked the sweet curve of her hip. Even her body fit his perfectly. With her, he was whole as he'd never been. She'd brought him back to life, to feelings more vivid than any he'd ever known.

How was it possible that they'd both been married and yet had come to each other as if untouched? Their joining was unlike anything he'd ever experienced. She'd been nervous at first, despite her bold invitation. But she hadn't allowed her anxiety to ruin the moment. She'd received him with an urgency that matched his own, caressing him, kissing him, holding him close.

His lips moved from the top of her head to her

cheeks. To her mouth. He hadn't meant to wake her, hadn't meant to keep kissing her. But he couldn't seem to stop.

Deidre woke to Lachlann's kiss. Joy flooded her. She wrapped her arms around him and squeezed.

"Deidre," he said huskily. He raised his head, then kissed her again, as if he couldn't help himself. He smoothed her hair back from her face. "*Elskan*, are you sure I didn't hurt you?"

She didn't know the word, but she knew it was an endearment. He spoke so tenderly. She shook her head. "You didn't hurt me."

They lay side by side, their hands roaming gently over each other, exploring. Deidre was awed by the hard, strong planes of his bronzed body. He'd told her she was beautiful, but *he* was the beautiful one. She ran her fingers through the golden hair covering his massive chest, then down his muscled abdomen. The muscles contracted, and her gaze darted back to his face. His jaw was clenched. Hunger and tenderness warred across his strong features. She felt herself thrill.

She scooched closer and closer, until she was lying on top of him. His arms went around her, his hands stroking her back. A tremor ran through her. Lachlann made her feel cherished as no one ever had. He made her feel desired.

She wanted him to feel the same. Remembering how he'd kissed her earlier, she decided to try. Tentatively, she pressed her lips to his neck. His quick intake of breath told her what she needed to know. She continued kissing, working her way up along his jawline.

He moaned low in his throat.

So far, so good. She smiled to herself and kept going. When she reached his ear, she considered. Should she…would it tickle? Would he like it? There was only one way to find out. Fighting a grin, she stuck the tip of her tongue in his ear. To her delight, he shivered. She tried again and realized he was hardening right between her legs.

And then it came to her. She would be on top this time. How hard could it be? She planted a kiss on his beautiful, sensuous mouth and rubbed her whole body against his. Groaning, he grabbed her butt and pressed her even closer. Their kiss turned hot.

As his lips, his hands, his body grew more demanding, so did hers. Deidre pulled back, panting. If she was going to do this, now was the time. She pushed herself into a sitting position.

Astride him.

He started to sit up. She hesitated for only a moment. *Do it, Deidre.* Sinking her fingers into his golden chest hair, she pushed him back down against the pillows.

His eyes widened. Her heart skipped a beat as she leaned forward to kiss him. She was doing this!

She straightened, her gaze roaming over him, taking him in, landing, at last, on his face. Now, his eyes were wild.

She might just combust. She was going to do this. Tentatively, she rubbed against him. His sharp intake of breath encouraged her. She moved again. Sensation flooded her. It felt so good.

"Deidre…" Groaning, he grasped her hips.

He was throbbing against her. She sat still for a moment, only running her fingers along his thighs. Breath hissed from between his teeth as he grabbed one of her hands. Okay—got it—they were both on the edge. He took a few deep breaths, then positioned her over him. It was time. With a deep breath of her own, she began to lower herself onto him.

But, oh…He was huge. Her heart started to thud. Maybe this wasn't such a great idea, after all. And then he reached out and touched her in just the right place. Her nerve endings sizzled. She eased down a little farther as ripples of pleasure coursed through her, then began moving almost mindlessly, wanting more. She needed him fully inside her. Had to feel him…

In one quick motion, she sank onto him, embedding him in her to the hilt. They both gasped.

Lachlann's hands were still on either side of her hips. He held her in check. He was pulsing inside her. She took the moment to catch her breath, waiting for the throbbing to cease. But she couldn't stand it for long. She had to move.

She tried an up, down movement. It felt good, so she tried it again. And again, closing her eyes as sensation flooded her.

Lachlann had let go of her hips, but he took hold again and guided her forward.

Her breath caught. Oh, yes. She repeated the action. Yes, yes, yes. She repeated it some more, a little faster each time.

He grasped her hips yet again. "Deidre, wait…I…" He was breathing heavily. "It's going to take a few more times before I can…"

She moved again. She *had* to.

Groaning, he moved with her, thrusting upward as she thrust forward, in a rhythm all their own. She let her head fall back as his hands stroked her body feverishly.

And then he did something, some little something, some little sideways thing. Ecstasy shot through her. Her gaze flew to his face. Their eyes met, and his nostrils flared. They did it again. She thrust, he thrust. Together.

That angle!

She knew she was moaning. She couldn't help it. But what was Lachlann saying? Was that Gaelic? Another language?

Or just her blood pounding in her ears?

She was coming apart. As waves of sensation shook her, Deidre fell forward. Lachlann clutched her against him as they peaked, pressing close again and again until they collapsed into each other's arms.

They lay that way—entangled and quiet except for their heavy breathing and pounding hearts—for a long, long moment. It wasn't until his large hand began stroking her back that she raised her head from the crook of his neck to peek at him.

He was staring at the ceiling.

"Lachlann..." she whispered. She couldn't quite find her voice. "Did you like it?"

"*Like* it?" He glanced down at her, his gray eyes glowing almost silver. "Aye, I liked it." He grinned at her. "Very, very much. Did you?"

He'd liked it!

"Aye." She grinned back. "Very, very much."

"And the first time?"

"Both."

His sexy grin softened into a tender smile. "Me, too." He bent his head and kissed her.

She started to cuddle back against him. An idea struck her, a *brilliant* idea. She was even impressing herself. "Shower?" she asked.

"I suppose we should." He didn't sound very enthusiastic.

Just you wait. When she led him into her bathroom and he saw the large, jetted space and understood that they were to shower together, she almost laughed aloud in pleasure. She hadn't been wrong. His attitude had changed completely.

****

Lachlann couldn't stop looking at Deidre. His mind, body, heart—aye, his very soul—were in turmoil. Splendid, blessed turmoil.

She sat across the table from him, dressed in what she called her farmer clothes. The denim overalls, far from concealing her figure, emphasized her best assets. Less than an hour ago, those assets had been pressed against him, fragrant and soapy, in her enormous shower. His senses reeled.

His heart was going to explode.

The way Deidre responded to him, held him, her eagerness to enjoy him…His whole being responded to her.

She smiled at him, and he realized that he was just sitting there, fork in hand, staring at her like a fool.

"I thought you were hungry," she reminded him.

He glanced down at his plate. They'd made omelets. Filled with bounty from their garden—chives, hot peppers, kale—along with a little diced ham and some farmer's cheese, they were delicious and satisfying.

"I was. I am." He grinned at her. "I'm just a little distracted."

Distracted. After thinking he was as good as a eunuch for four years—or was it seven hundred?—he'd experienced a morning of lovemaking so intense that he'd thought it might kill him. Now, he sat across from the sexiest, sweetest lover in all history. *Distracted!* He snorted with laughter.

"What's wrong with you?" Deidre chuckled. Taking his fork, she cut a bite of omelet and stuffed it into his mouth. "Eat! We have work to do!"

"I'm happy," he told her. Was it the first time he'd ever said that?

Her eyes softened. "So am I, unbelievably so."

They discussed their garden while they ate. Deidre had suggested that they experiment with some cool season herbs. He could hardly wait to get started.

"The cilantro and nasturtium seeds came in," she remarked as they washed up together. She closed the dishwasher. "Do you have time to sow them this afternoon?"

"Sure. Where are they?"

"They're still with the mail in my office."

"Mind if I get them?"

"Of course not."

He dried his hands on a towel and wandered into her home office. He'd never paid much attention to it. It was at the front of the house, near the front door, and he usually came in through the back. Its hues of calming gray and cream suited Deidre. Tall windows looked out onto her front yard and the street. He liked it.

But she needed flowers out there, he decided as he looked out of the window. Roses? Hydrangeas? Something to enjoy when she looked up from her work.

Retrieving the seed packets from her desk, he turned to leave and froze.

"Professor? Lachlann?" Joe's voice moved from the kitchen through the house. Moments later, he appeared at the door of the study. Walking in to stand beside Lachlann, he, too, halted.

"Hell," he muttered.

Deidre joined them, smiling. "So, you've found..."

"Who are you?" Joe's voice rang out sharply.

She started. "What?"

"Where are you from?" he shot at her.

Lachlann stared at him.

"I'm from North Carolina." Deidre looked confused. "You know that."

"Where are your parents from?"

"North Carolina. What…"

"And their parents?"

"North Carolina! Joe, what's wrong with you?"

Deidre couldn't imagine what was happening. Lachlann was as white as a sheet, and Joe both looked and sounded furious. What was going on?

"Where did you get it?" the older man asked harshly, nodding toward her drawing.

"It's been handed down in my family for generations."

"The Chisholm family?" he asked pointedly.

"Yes, my father's family," she replied, trying to be patient. "They brought it with them when they came here from Scotland."

"When was that?" Lachlann's voice was quiet, strained.

"In the early 1800s. But it's older than that. It's an authentic piece of medieval art."

"How old do you think it is?" Lachlann asked in the same strange voice.

"We're not certain. It could date back to the fifteenth, perhaps even the fourteenth century. I don't want to have it tested. I'm afraid it wouldn't survive."

"How do you think it's lasted this long?" Joe sounded suspicious.

But suspicious of what? She gave a little shrug. "I don't know. My grandfather told me that, as far back as he could remember, it was always pressed in a very old family Bible. He framed it before I was born."

"Where is this Bible?" persisted the older man.

"In my parents' house. Joe, why are you so upset?"

"I'm not upset." He took a deep breath, exhaled. "I'm sorry for being short with you, Professor. It shouldn't surprise me, a medieval history professor collecting priceless, medieval artifacts."

She laughed. "Believe me, Joe, I'm no collector. Not unless you count a collection of one."

"But to see Lachlann staring at me from an antique drawing…" Joe continued. "That startled the hell out of me!"

"*You're* startled?" Lachlann drew a breath. "How do you think *I* feel?"

"But it's beautiful." Gently, almost reverently, Deidre caressed the frame. "I probably shouldn't display it, but it's protected, and this wall is north-facing, so sunlight isn't a worry. I just love it so much. I always have. That's why my grandfather gave it to me when I was just a little girl." She smiled at Lachlann. "Although now, I must admit, I rather feel I don't need it anymore."

"You don't!" Both men almost shouted.

She laughed again. "Perhaps he's one of your ancestors, Lachlann?"

"Son, are you going to stand around admiring art all day or are you going to come help me in the attic?" Joe turned to leave. "We need to get the rest of the Christmas decorations down before you go."

"I'm coming." Lachlann glanced at Deidre. "I'll be back to sow the seeds before I go."

"That sounds good." Grinning, she winked at him. "See you later."

****

How was it possible? Lachlann's mind, not to mention his stomach, was churning as he drove toward the coast.

How could Deidre possess one of Rónán's drawings of him? Could it really be a coincidence that she'd moved next door, that her family name was Chisholm? Clearly she was descended from the same clan as his old friend, from the same clan as Allasan. His head and stomach renewed their protests.

But he had no reason to doubt that Deidre was who she said she was. She wasn't trying to hide anything. The drawing was there on her wall for anyone to see. She had told him her name the day they introduced themselves. If she had meant to cause him harm, she would surely be more discreet.

Harm? Their morning together had been the furthest thing from discomfort. She cared for him. He heard it in her voice, felt it in her every caress. He didn't doubt her sincerity and had no desire to question it.

Joe's behavior, on the other hand, had been nothing short of bizarre. For a wild moment, it had seemed as though Joe knew about him, about his history. He'd voiced all the questions that were running through Lachlann's mind.

Despite himself, he chuckled. If Joe had been that flustered by a medieval artifact, as he called it, what would he say if he knew one was alive and living in his house?

Chapter Twenty

Deidre sank onto the concrete bench and dug through her purse. She needed to do the practical thing and finish her grocery list before she went to the store. Closing her eyes, she breathed deeply, opening them to stare at the fountains in front of her. Cullen Family Plaza was her favorite spot on campus. The University of Houston might lack the Gothic opulence of Duke, but it had its good points and boasted lush, green grounds. Now, the plaza was deserted, most students having left for winter break. Even when it was crowded, she found the fountains both refreshing and calming.

She felt anything but calm now, though. Tonight, Lachlann would be home from a long, three-week hitch, and they were going to have almost a month together—alone. Joe spent most of December through the first week of January in Louisiana, enjoying time with his children and grandchildren and visiting extended family and friends. Jackson had left for north Texas to celebrate an early Christmas with his family and then would earn overtime working through the holidays.

It would just be her and Lachlann.

Smiling, she pulled up the list on her phone. She wanted dinner to be perfect, to set just the right tone, and she didn't have a lot of time. Organization was key. Hot Italian turkey sausage, ground turkey, apples…She worked on the list for a few moments and slipped her phone into her purse, satisfied. She was ready to begin her vacation.

"Professor Chisholm?"

She almost closed her eyes in dismay. Turning her head, she saw a stranger in a long brown overcoat approaching her.

"Yes?"

"I'm sorry to disturb you. My name is Edward Dawson. I work with the DEA."

The DEA?

"How can I help you, Mr. Dawson?"

"We're investigating a certain problematic issue occurring with the oil rigs out in the Gulf of Mexico. Your neighbors, Joseph Dubois, Lachlann An Damh, and Jackson Lee work offshore."

"May I see an ID?" she asked stiffly.

"Certainly." Pulling out a wallet, he flipped it open to reveal his badge and federal ID.

Deidre leaned closer to examine it. She was fairly certain she wouldn't know a real badge from a fake one, but at least it didn't look blatantly false. She looked at the man standing in front of her and compared him to the photo. Same face. He was a middle-aged man of average height, with fair skin, brown hair and eyes, and ordinary features. She supposed he looked decent enough.

She sat back.

"There's nothing to be alarmed about," he assured her, pocketing the wallet. "I only have a few questions about Mr. Dubois and Mr. An Damh. We know that they've both worked overseas."

"Is this an international incident?"

"I'm not at liberty to discuss the details of the investigation, ma'am. Just a few questions." He drew a small pad and a pen from his coat. "Have you known Mr. Dubois and Mr. An Damh for long?" He flipped open the pad.

"No, only a few months."

"To the best of your knowledge, have either left the country recently?"

"No, not that I know of."

"Have they entertained foreign visitors?"

"No."

"Have they discussed past trips overseas?"

"No."

"It seems that they were in Scotland at the same time."

Deidre frowned. First, he asked only yes or no questions. Now, the question wasn't even phrased as a question. But he was looking at her expectantly.

"They never mention it," she replied.

"Are you sure about that?"

A stab of irritation pricked her. "Quite sure," she said coolly.

He looked down at his pad. "Have you heard anything strange or unusual about their time offshore?"

"No."

"Have you noticed any sort of unmarked packages delivered to their house? Or deliveries at unusual hours?"

"I have not."

"Would you describe either man as suspicious, dangerous, or dishonest?"

She stiffened. "Certainly not."

"Would you be willing to testify to their good characters in a court of law?"

"I would."

"That's good enough for now." Closing the pad, he reached into his pocket yet again and withdrew a card, which he handed to her. "If anything comes to mind, you can reach me at this number."

"Is it likely that I'll be called to testify?"

"It's very unlikely. This is just standard procedure, covering all bases, so to speak. In fact, if I were you, I wouldn't even mention this to the neighbors."

"Why not?"

"That's just my opinion. No one likes to hear that they're being investigated, especially during the holidays."

"Don't they know about the investigation? Isn't it their right to know?"

"Not necessarily. But like I said, this is just standard procedure. You have nothing to worry about." He gave a little nod. "Thank you for your time, ma'am. Merry Christmas."

Deidre watched him walk away, her thoughts a whirl of confusion. DEA? Could someone be using the offshore rigs for drug trafficking?

A cool breeze moistened her face with a fine mist from the fountains. She stared out at the water, unseeing, thinking of Lachlann's and Joe's strange reactions to her medieval drawing. When Lachlann had returned to sow the herb seeds and say good-bye, she had questioned him about it.

"Your drawing reminded me of my farm," he'd replied as he'd pulled her into his arms. "I'm sorry if I worried you."

"I'm sorry it upset you." She kissed his cheek. "But what's the deal with Joe?"

"I don't know. I asked him that question the moment we left your house."

"And what did he say?"

He shrugged. "He apologized and said it reminded him of a bad time in his life. He wouldn't say any more."

Another mist brought Deidre back to the present.

Maybe Joe's "bad time" was now. Maybe he'd somehow gotten entangled with drug smugglers and was being investigated.

But what did an antique drawing of a farmer have to do with drug smuggling?

A horrible thought struck her. Lachlann's farm! Had he been growing illegal drugs? Was that why he'd lost his farm?

He'd said there'd been an accident. What sort of accident?

Sitting ramrod straight by now, Deidre shook her head. She couldn't bring herself to believe it of either man. She'd meant it when she said she would testify to their good characters. Of course she would.

So what was going on?

Nothing to be concerned about, my ass.

Chapter Twenty-One

"You really do know how to drive a truck," observed Lachlann from the passenger seat of his vehicle.

Deidre smiled. "I grew up on a farm, remember? I also know where we're going and wanted to treat you to a tour. I hope you don't mind."

"On the contrary, I'm enjoying this."

"It's different from driving in Scotland, isn't it?"

"Aye, it is." *Especially fourteenth-century Scotland.* Gazing out of the window, he changed the subject. "This is beautiful land. It reminds me of Scotland."

They were driving through a pine thicket. There were plenty of pine trees where they lived, but they weren't surrounded by them as they were now. The terrain wasn't mountainous or even hilly, but it was rolling and pleasant.

"I'm glad you think so," said Deidre. "I love it out here. The Christmas tree farm is beside a lake. It's usually very peaceful and smells heavenly."

His heart surged. He was overwhelmingly glad that he'd followed her suggestion to match her holiday schedule and take a full month off from work. He hadn't been sure he'd be able to do it. He'd never asked for vacation before. That had turned out to be in his favor, not to mention the fact that plenty of men were eager to earn holiday overtime.

Joe always spent most of December through New

Year's with his children in New Orleans. Jackson had already left to spend Christmas with his family before heading back offshore.

He and Deidre would enjoy rare privacy. *Privacy.*

He rolled down his window, closed his eyes, and inhaled the heavy scent of pine. Last night, when he'd arrived, he'd found that she'd cooked one of his favorite meals, spaghetti with homemade meatballs, fresh garlic bread, and salad with vegetables from their garden. She'd even baked an apple pie for dessert.

He'd planned to take her out for dinner. The semester had just ended, and Deidre had been spending most of her time at the university. She was professor and director, undertaking two demanding roles with enormous responsibilities. She'd even worked yesterday and must surely have been exhausted. Not only had she gone home and cooked, though, she'd also made love to him half the night.

The way she touched him…His breathing hitched. Touch. It had been something he'd yearned for all his life, the feeling changing and strengthening as he grew older. Growing up, his family lived in close quarters. They sat close together when they ate. They'd had to if they were all to fit round the table. He'd often slept with his older brothers, his size becoming an obstacle long before his age. His parents and grandparents had been openly affectionate. He'd been used to touch, but Allasan hadn't. She didn't like it and had expected him to respect her space.

Deidre was always touching him, and it wasn't always sexual. By day, she showered him with frequent, loving gestures of affection. At night, she snuggled against him as close as she possibly could. And as for sex, her hands were all over him constantly.

It grounded him, comforted him, excited him. Her caresses filled a need deep within him.

How could he ever leave her?

How could he stay?

He was going to tell her the truth, ask her to help him with reading and research. What if they discovered how he could go back? *God...*

"I'm glad you were able to get time off," she said suddenly, interrupting his musings. She wrinkled her nose. "The holidays are usually sort of depressing for me." With a little smile, she shot him a sideways glance. "But not this year."

"Why are they depressing?" he asked.

She shrugged. "Lonely, I guess."

"Are you always alone?" Just the thought of her being lonely and depressed bothered him.

"Most of the time. Last year, Stella and I did ring in the New Year together. But usually she goes to New York to visit her grandmother."

Lachlann nodded thoughtfully. He'd met Stella and liked her. She was Deidre's best friend. But they couldn't be expected to spend every holiday together.

"And you never go to North Carolina." It wasn't a question. He knew the answer.

"Never." She darted another quick look at him. "I know that's just one of the things we have to talk about." Her soft lips compressed. "To be honest, I'm nervous."

"*You're* nervous?" He shook his head. "Believe me, nothing you tell me could be as surprising as what I have to say. In fact..." He hesitated.

Lachlann thought he'd been terrified when the earth opened and swallowed him up. He'd been afraid when he'd awoken broken and lost in a strange time and place. But those feelings were nothing compared to the terror that seized him now. What if, when he told her, she rejected him outright? Be it a day or a lifetime, he was going to ruin whatever time they had left together. But he knew that he owed her the truth, especially if he was going to ask for her help.

"I have a few questions before I tell you everything."

She raised her eyebrows. "*Before?*"

"Before."

"I'm listening."

"Okay." He glanced out of his window. A lake shimmered in the distance. "I have a lot to tell you."

"We agreed that we both have a lot to tell each other."

"But what I'm going to tell you, what I have to say…" He faltered. "You won't like it."

Deidre drew a deep breath, her thoughts racing to the DEA agent. Last night, she hadn't told Lachlann about the strange interview. They'd both been tired, and she hadn't wanted to ruin the evening. Was he going to confess?

"Is it that bad?" she asked.

"You might think so. You might think I'm crazy."

Drug smuggling was certainly crazy. Was now the time to tell him about the agent?

Slow down, Deidre.

First, she should be sure where this was going. "Why would I think you're crazy?"

"Sometimes, *I* think I am. Sometimes, it even seems the better option."

She felt her tension ease. He was going to tell her about his PTSD. "You mean clinically?" she asked gently, keeping her focus on the road ahead.

"Yes."

149

She shook her head. "You're not."

"But what if I am?" he persisted.

"I'll take care of you."

There was a moment's silence. "What if I were a fugitive?"

She almost hit the brake in the middle of the road. "Are you?"

"I'm not sure."

"Excuse me?"

"Let's say I am."

"That's sort of huge." She decided to pull off the road before she drove into a pine tree. She parked on the shoulder and turned toward him.

Lachlann didn't speak. He only looked at her. He was waiting for an answer. What *was* her answer? Moments ticked by. She needed more information.

She looked him straight in the eye. "You've done something wrong?"

"What if I have?"

She stared at him a moment longer. Everything about him spoke of honor, of goodness. He wasn't a criminal.

She shook her head. "You haven't."

He tilted his head slightly, watching her carefully. "You're sure about that?"

"As sure as I can be. I trust you."

He drew a deep breath. "I trust you, too."

She laid a hand on his arm. "Lachlann, if you've made a mistake, I'll help you. We'll fix it together. If necessary, we'll fight together."

"You'd fight for me?"

"Of course."

Leaning across the console, he kissed her long and sweetly. Their bodies weren't touching, but Deidre's whole body responded as her mouth clung to his.

He broke the kiss abruptly, smiling as he rested his forehead against hers. "Can we continue this conversation later?" he asked.

"Conversation?" Deidre blinked. What conversation?

He sat back and shrugged. "Like I said, I have a lot to tell you, a whole lot, and none of it's going to change between now and this evening. But we only have so many hours of daylight left, and I've never…"

Oh, *that* conversation. He wanted to delay it. She raised her brows. "Never what?"

He grinned. "I've never chosen a Christmas tree."

He had a point. The dimple in his cheek had nothing to do with anything.

She sighed. "I'm such a sap."

"A what?"

"Never mind." She gave him a peck on the lips and put the truck into drive. "Let's go choose a Christmas tree."

Chapter Twenty-Two

A few minutes later, they turned onto an asphalt road that led to a gravel parking lot. For the second time in less than an hour, an exclamation of pleased surprise escaped Lachlann. In front of them was a long, red wooden building with a wide front porch and a sign that read Welcome to Olsen's Christmas Tree Farm.

The porch ran along the entire storefront. Decorated Christmas trees punctuated both ends and several large wooden rocking chairs, some red, some green, were arranged on either side of the steps. Glancing around, he realized that the whole property was festively decorated with various rustic holiday displays, greenery, and, of course, Christmas trees.

Beyond the building, in the near distance, long rows of trees grew all the way down to the lake. Near the water, picnic tables were set up under the trees.

"What do you think?" Deidre brushed his shoulder with hers.

"This is great."

She smiled. "I have another surprise. See over there?" She pointed out of his window.

At the far end of the parking area was a horse and a deep green carriage. Parked a little way behind the carriage was a wagon filled with hay.

Lachlann wasn't sure which she was pointing at.

"We'll take one to transport our tree?" he guessed.

She shook her head. "No. I thought it might be fun

to take a carriage ride down to the trees. It's a perfect day for it."

It was a perfect day for anything, cold but not uncomfortably so, and sunny. But it wasn't the weather that made it perfect for him. He watched as Deidre drew their picnic basket from the back seat. Her long, fiery hair moved gently in the breeze and her green sweater, the same color as the trees, hugged her figure. She was all the perfection he'd ever want.

Moments later, they were climbing into the carriage. Jacob, the carriage driver, was a tall, middle-aged man with light brown hair and a friendly smile. He looked up at Lachlann.

"*Velkomminn! Hvat segirðu?*" Welcome. How are you?

Lachlann frowned. Norroena? "*Þat er gott, pökk. Talarðu norrænu? Ertu frá Orkneyjum?*" I'm fine, thanks. You speak Norroena? Are you from Orkney?

"Oh, man." Jacob raised his hands in surrender, laughing. "I guess I forgot more than I thought. I've been to Iceland a couple of times and picked up quite a bit of the language. At least, I thought I had. What an amazing country. I knew when I heard your accent that you had to be from there."

"I'm from Scotland." Lachlann glanced at Deidre.

She looked confounded.

"Scotland?" Jacob looked surprised. "I wouldn't have guessed. You speak Icelandic like a native. You sound just like my cousin's husband. Make yourselves comfortable. There's a blanket there on the seat. We'll get going."

He and Deidre settled side by side on the seat. They didn't need the blanket, but they covered themselves anyway. The moment they took off, Deidre turned toward Lachlann.

"You speak Icelandic?" she asked in a low voice.

He shook his head. "No."

"You obviously just did."

"No." He ran a hand through his hair. Where the hell was Iceland? "I wouldn't know Icelandic."

"That wasn't Gaelic."

"No."

"Did I hear you say Norroena?"

He had as many questions as she did. Now wasn't the time. "Didn't we agree to save this conversation for tonight?"

She crossed her arms. "This conversation about you speaking Icelandic?"

"I don't…It's all part of the same. Trust me, if we go into it now, we won't enjoy this." He indicated their surroundings and shrugged. "But I'll talk if you insist. Just remember, you're not going to like what I have to say."

She stared at him a long moment, then sighed. "Fine. We'll wait."

He cupped her chin and kissed her. "Thank you."

They settled closer beneath the blanket and took in the scenery without further conversation. Only Jacob spoke now and then, pointing out different areas of the farm.

Deidre snuggled closer as a bracing wind blew in from the lake that sparkled in the distance. The scent of pine was strong, and Lachlann breathed deeply, filling his lungs with the fresh, fragrant air. He closed his eyes as memories of the Highlands swept over him. Suddenly, he was in Scotland, *his* Scotland.

"Da!" Iain pointed at him, gurgling with laughter, his blue eyes shining with merriment, as he and a slightly older cousin settled excitedly into the small horse cart. Old Nessie, the packhorse, pulled it slowly while Lachlann walked beside them. He could more easily have pulled the cart himself, but Iain loved the farm animals and always wanted to be with them when he was outside. Lachlann was glad to give him the treat. It was a beautiful day, and he'd finished his work early. He smiled at Deidre, who walked on the other side of the cart.

Gasping, Lachlann jerked to the present.

"What's wrong? Are you okay?" Deidre asked.

"I need to get out!" he said wildly, beginning to rise. "We need to talk."

"Lachlann, wait." She laid her hand on his arm. "Jacob," she said more loudly, "is there a place where we could enjoy a more private picnic?"

"Yes, ma'am, there surely is. It's not part of the tour, so you'll have it to yourselves. Do you want to go there now?"

"Yes, please."

Lachlann would have preferred to walk. Actually, he wanted to run, shout, come out of his skin. He took a deep breath and exhaled slowly. He was losing his mind, losing his grip on reality.

"This place reminds me of the tree farms in North Carolina." Deidre spoke smoothly, as if he hadn't almost jumped out of a moving carriage. "The difference is that there, the trees grow down mountainsides and it snows in winter. It's really very beautiful."

"Do you miss it?" he forced himself to ask. His heart and head were pounding.

"I used to." Her hand was still on his arm, rubbing gently, soothingly. "But not anymore. It's amazing what a difference one person can make."

"Aye." He pulled her closer. "I know what you mean."

"Do you miss Scotland?" she asked as she snuggled back against him.

"No." Closing his eyes, he rested his cheek on the top of her head and focused on breathing.

Neither of them moved or spoke again until the carriage stopped.

"Jacob, it's perfect," Deidre called out. "Thank you."

Opening his eyes, he saw that they were right beside the lake. A red metal barn was in front of them, surrounded by pine trees. On the side of it, facing the lake, was a wooden picnic table.

"We eat here when we're working on the trees in summer." Jacob grabbed their picnic basket and carried it to the table as they climbed out. "Nobody comes here much during winter. You shouldn't be disturbed. When you're ready to look at Christmas trees, just follow the path along the lake, that way." He pointed to the right. "Call when you're ready for me to pick you up."

Lachlann nodded. "Thank you."

The carriage disappeared around a bend.

"Would you rather walk or sit?" Deidre asked.

Lachlann held his hand out to her. "Walk."

As she slipped her hand into his, they headed toward the path and turned left, away from the Christmas trees.

"I'm sorry," Lachlann said as they began strolling alongside the water. "I thought I could wait until tonight to tell you my story, but this place has brought up too many memories."

She looked anxious. "I'm sorry, Lachlann. It never occurred to me that it would make you homesick."

"I'm not homesick. If it were up to me, I'd never go

156

back to Scotland."

"So we're back to your being a fugitive?"

"Not exactly."

They strolled for a few moments in silence, the only sound the distant call of a hawk. Lachlann was afraid. He, who had always been fearless, was afraid on so many levels.

Had he, in fact, lost his mind? He'd almost jumped out of a moving carriage. Were his medieval memories figments of his imagination? Dreams? Deidre had told him she would fight for him. But what if she couldn't believe him? Worse, what if she shouldn't?

He stopped walking. Turning to face her, he clasped her other hand. She looked at him expectantly, her expression calm, tender. She was so beautiful to him. Her hair gleamed in the sunlight, the breeze from the lake blowing the length of it sideways. She had to push it away from her face.

He needed her more than he'd ever needed anyone. But he wasn't being fair to her. He had to tell her everything.

Where to begin? If only he could get lost in those blue eyes.

"At the beginning," Deidre said suddenly.

He blinked. Was she reading his mind?

She chuckled. "Don't look so surprised. We're about to have a momentous discussion. Naturally, it's hard to know where to begin."

"Things between us could change after this."

"There's only one way to find out."

"Right." Lachlann drew a deep breath and released one of her hands to begin walking again. The beginning...

"Once upon a time, around the year 1200..."

Chapter Twenty-Three

A chuckle escaped Deidre. Lachlann glanced at her and, despite himself, felt a grin tug at the corner of his mouth.

"You did say to begin at the beginning," he reminded her.

"Yes, I did." She attempted to make a straight face. "I apologize for the interruption."

Easing into his story might work best for both of them.

"Are you going to control yourself?" he asked with mock severity.

"I promise." Her expression grew serious. "Please continue."

"As I was saying..." He winked at her. "Once upon a time, around the year 1200, a brave Norseman called Jon the Strong left Orkney with a small group of followers. He sought a place to live in peace, to farm and raise his family. The group settled in the Scottish Highlands not far from Loch Ness, near modern-day Drumnadrochit."

He glanced at her. "Do you know the area?"

She nodded, her expression serious. "I do."

"The Norse worked the land, keeping to themselves, sheltered by the forests and hills. Marriages often required travel to Orkney and back. The people wanted to preserve their language and traditions. The Gaels and Normans began to arrive shortly after. Clans Chisholm,

Grant, Fraser, Urquhart—all arrived after our people were settled."

Deidre made a small exclamation.

"What?" he questioned.

"*Our* people?"

"Aye."

She cleared her throat. "Please, go on."

"The newcomers arrived in far greater numbers. It was a time of war and upheaval, but the Norse settlers were determined to hold onto their peace. They vowed to aid and protect the clans and to share the bounties in return for their land and freedom. The chiefs, busy building their castles and defending themselves against others, needed friends, not more enemies, especially the Norse sort. One by one, they agreed, and so my family, or clan, as the Gaels called it, came to be known as 'Friends of the Gaels, *Càirdean nan Gaidheal.*' "

"*Càirdean nan Gaidheal,*" Deidre murmured. "I've not heard of that clan."

"They died."

"They couldn't all have died."

"They did, all but one."

"But…"

He gently laid a finger on her lips. "All but one," he repeated, and moved his hand away. "I know the name of the farmer in your drawing."

"What?"

"The farmer in your drawing. I know his name."

"You can't."

"I do."

"You can't know," she repeated, her brow furrowed.

"It should be obvious."

"What's obvious? Lachlann, what are you talking about?"

"Can't you see? You've said it. It's a picture of me."

Her expression changed. She looked astonished, wary. "I beg your pardon?"

"It was drawn by my best friend, Rónán Chisholm."

"Are you saying that it's not authentic?"

"No, it's authentic."

"I don't understand."

Lachlann looked away from her confused expression toward the lake. The water's surface rippled, the wind blowing cold and fresh in their faces.

He was going to lose her.

"Do you want me to continue?"

She released his hand to cross her arms. "Yes. I'm interested to see where this is going."

Was that anger in her voice? Sarcasm? He clenched his jaw. "You can't say I didn't warn you. I told you that you wouldn't like what I have to say."

For a moment, they walked in silence. Then she sighed. "You're right. You did warn me. Please, continue."

"You're sure?"

She nodded.

"You guessed that my first language wasn't English. It isn't Gaelic, either. It's Norroena."

She drew a breath. "Norroena?"

"It was the common language of my people. It wasn't a dead language, as it is now."

"What do you mean?"

"I was born in, roughly, 1325."

Deidre stumbled.

He caught her arm to prevent her from falling and didn't want to let go. He wanted to hold her, hold onto her. But he couldn't—not now, not ever. Releasing her, he forced himself to continue his narrative. Not a word, not a sound escaped her as he told her about his family—his parents, grandparents, siblings. He described Rónán and Clan Chisholm.

"I loved my family. I idolized my older brothers. To me, they were everything that was strong and honorable. But I spent most of my free time with Rónán. We were the same age, outcasts to some degree, and best friends."

He'd never talked so much in his life, but he found it was a relief to speak of those he loved, so long gone. Deidre walked quietly beside him.

The wind sent ripples, tremors, across the lake.

"Allasan made cloth, and she was very skilled at it. She was an artist in her own way, and she worked hard." To his surprise, his throat stopped working. He might not have shared a deep love with his wife, but he'd cared about her. She hadn't deserved to die as she had. If only…

A cool hand slipped into his. Gratefully, he held onto it tightly and continued.

But when he tried to speak of Iain, it was as if a large hand gripped his throat and squeezed. His words came out in a croak.

"He was a strong boy, kind, fearless. He…" Lachlann choked. "He loved animals and playing outdoors with his cousins."

Still not speaking, Deidre led him to a fallen tree. They sat down together, the forest at their backs, a cold wind blowing in from the lake in front of them. Tucking her arm through his, she laced their fingers.

He shut his eyes, breathing deeply as her warmth penetrated the icy hollow within him.

"We can continue this later," she said softly, "if you prefer."

He held onto her tightly and shook his head. "I want

161

to tell you. I…I went to Inverness, to the fall festival, to trade. We'd had a good harvest, and Allasan had worked hard to send some of her cloth with me. There were things she wanted that weren't available in our local villages. She was to go with me, but she got sick. So did Iain. I should've stayed with them. I wanted to, but she wouldn't have it. She wanted supplies for her weaving, things for our home."

He swallowed. "I think the combination of the illness and disappointment made her more upset and anxious than either would have alone. We argued, and I finally gave in. She was, as she told me repeatedly, surrounded by our families."

"What year was this?"

"It was 1351."

Her breath hitched.

He glanced at her. "You know what happened."

She nodded. "I can guess," she replied in a near whisper. "The plague."

"Aye." He sighed. "I have no idea of the circumstances they died in. All I know is that, when I returned to our village, everyone was dead."

Deidre gasped. "Everyone?"

He nodded grimly. "Every single one of our people. Ashes were falling everywhere. To this day, I can smell the stench. Burning human flesh…"

Lachlann stopped as bile rose in his throat. He struggled not to vomit.

As he fought for control, he felt her hand on his back, rubbing slowly, soothingly. His breathing calmed. Finding his voice again, he told her how he was turned away from the castle, described his weary trek to Inverness.

"It was a clear, starry night—and still. Only the loch

was rippling." He gestured to the water beside them. "Just as this lake is now. But there was no wind. Then the earth began to tremble."

"An earthquake?" she asked, her grip on him tightening.

"An earthquake like I'd never experienced. The ground began cracking all around me. Trees were uprooting. I couldn't escape, couldn't run from it."

He could feel the panic beginning. His breathing was shallow now, his chest constricting. The damp sand at his feet began to tremble, to rise up…It would swallow him.

Soft hands squeezed his. Lachlann glanced at their interlocked fingers. *Deidre…Texas.* He was in Texas with Deidre. The knot in his chest loosened. His breathing began to slow.

He began again. "I kept stumbling, falling, trying to avoid the cracks, and then the earth roared. Another crack appeared, a huge one. It ran straight to me. I tried…I couldn't avoid it." He gulped some air as his heart began pounding in his ears. "The ground opened right at my feet and I…I fell. I tried to stop myself, to hold onto the edge, but there was only gravel."

His breathing was harsh, now, his voice hoarse and shaky. But he'd regained his bearings. He was all right. He dared a glance at Deidre.

She was staring at him, her mouth slightly open, a look of shock on her pale face.

"But…" She paused, swallowing. "But you lived. How?"

"I don't know. I was knocked out almost immediately. When I woke up…" He stopped and looked directly into her eyes. "It was the year 2012."

Her eyes widened. For a moment, she just stared at

him. Then, rising abruptly, she opened her mouth as if to speak and closed it again. Folding her arms tightly across her chest, she began walking swiftly along the lake.

Away from him.

Chapter Twenty-Four

Deidre was furious. She wanted to run, screaming, into the forest, away from the damned lake, away from...

He'd lied to her. Repeatedly. She hated liars.

Even worse, he hadn't trusted her enough to tell her the truth until now—not even after they'd slept together. But could she blame him? Had she told him *her* secrets? But this was different. Wasn't it?

Oh, God, she was upset. She hardly knew what to think.

She was going to throw up.

Lachlann called out from behind her. She walked faster.

Deidre thought of herself as a practical romantic. She'd grown up on a farm. She'd been raised to be practical. And she'd been hurt. Hardened, too. She understood what was real, and she wasn't about to be fooled again.

Time travel wasn't real. Was it?

Some romantic part of her wanted to believe it might be, to believe in the seemingly impossible. Her medieval studies had left an indelible mark on her, continued to do so. History was mysterious in so many ways. Despite her extensive studies, perhaps even because of them, she knew there were many things they'd never fully understand. And where written historical accounts were lacking, a wealth of stories and traditions filled in some, though not all, of the gaps. Sometimes, it was impossible to tell truth from legend. So many things could not be explained.

Was she actually believing this?

Deidre huffed out a breath. She believed him, all right. It wasn't just a feeling, or her love, or her faith in him. Lachlann's story made sense to her. She'd had so many clues.

His apparently inherent yet limited understanding of medieval history, his poor English, his strange Gaelic, his aversion to power tools, his behavior in general…

The haunted look she'd often observed, the nightmares, the headaches, and much more…

He wasn't lying. Scratch that. He wasn't lying *now,* and he wasn't delusional, as he seemed to fear, if their conversation in his truck was anything to go by. Why, oh why, had he not told her sooner? Was he alone here? Did Joe know?

"Deidre, wait!"

She neither slowed down nor looked at him when he caught up with her. She wasn't ready. She was still trying to make sense of it all.

"I told you this would change things."

Her initial fury instantly returned. She reeled on him. "Of course this changes things!"

He looked taken aback. "You're angry?"

"Angry? How about furious? Lachlann, how dare you? How *dare* you?"

"I'm telling you the truth. At least, I think it's the truth."

"Of course it's the truth." Fighting back angry tears, she fisted her hands at her hips. "I have more faith in you than you have in yourself, and you don't trust me?"

He looked confused.

She couldn't do this right now. She turned and

continued walking along the shore.

He walked beside her.

"Go away!"

"I can't do that."

"I hate liars," she muttered.

"But you just said it's the truth."

"Exactly."

"Are you saying…you believe me?"

She stopped and glared at him. "I'm Director of Medieval Studies at a major university," she ground out. "My field of specialization is the Celts. I have a drawing…" Her voice broke on a gasp. It was all so overwhelming. "I have a drawing of you hanging in my study at home. I'm in love with you!" She was shouting by the time she finished her list. "Which one of those things would stop me from believing you? Why didn't you tell me sooner?"

He'd suffered so horribly. Why hadn't he trusted her? Outraged, she pushed him in the chest with all her might. "Old-fashioned?" she yelled.

He was staring at her as if she'd lost her mind.

"Well?" she demanded.

Lachlann was having trouble processing. Had she just pushed him? God help him, he started to laugh. He wasn't sure if it was the ridiculousness of the situation or sheer relief. Probably both.

"What's so funny?" she fumed, glaring into his face.

He wasn't crazy after all. *She* was. Something snapped within him. Roughly, he pulled her into his arms, holding her tightly against him and burying his face in her hair.

She believed him. How, he couldn't fathom. He hardly believed himself.

"You're sure?" he questioned urgently. "I thought I

would lose you when I told you my truth."

"You don't trust me," she accused, wriggling free.

He looked down at her. "I do."

"Then why didn't you tell me?"

"It's not an easy story to tell."

She stared at him. "I suppose it's not," she said after a moment.

"But now I've told you—and only you. You really believe me?"

She sighed. "Yes, I believe you. But it's not a question of belief. I don't understand how this has happened to you, but I accept that it did."

"Thank you."

Acceptance. It was the exact opposite of what he had feared and expected. He pulled her back into his arms, closing his eyes as he felt hers wrap around him. He could feel her trembling and realized that he was, too.

A gust of cold air blew in from the lake. Deidre's arms tightened around him, and he drew her closer still. They stood there holding each other, breathing almost as one, until their tremors subsided. A strange feeling washed over Lachlann, something he hadn't experienced since childhood. He told himself that there was no reason for it. But the feeling was too strong to deny, and too good for him to want to ignore. For just a moment—one precious, illusory moment—he let himself bask in it. Wrapped in Deidre's warmth, he felt more than safe. He felt…protected.

"Lachlann, how badly were you hurt?" Her voice was still a little shaky. "That's why you get headaches, isn't it? Because of the fall?"

He touched her chin with his hand, nudging her face up toward his.

"I'm all right now," he assured her, surprised by the

truth of his words.

"How?" she asked in a whisper.

He pressed his lips fervently to her forehead. He couldn't tell her that it was because of her, not yet. He wouldn't force the burden of his welfare upon her shoulders.

"Do you want to hear more?" he asked quietly. "Or is that enough for now?"

Together, they turned and began walking slowly toward the rows of Christmas trees, still a good distance away.

"Can you tell me what happened…" She swallowed. "What happened after you fell?"

"I woke in front of Loch Ness, probably not far from where I fell. It was as if I'd fallen off a cliff. My ribs were broken; I could hardly breathe. My shoulder was dislocated. My head…I kept vomiting, passing out. I think it took me three days to reach Inverness."

Deidre's hand tightened on his. "You suffered a concussion," she murmured, "along with everything else."

"That's what the doctors said, that I'd sustained a severe concussion."

She stared at him, concern and confusion playing across her features. "But why three days? Why didn't someone help you? Surely there were people around who saw you?"

"I've often wondered about that. I don't recall seeing anyone, but it took all my focus just to walk. It could be that between my size, clothes, and condition, my appearance was frightening. But what I really think is that few people noticed me. I traveled mostly at night. My head hurt too much to walk in bright daylight. And I was high up on a hiking trail for much of the time. It's sort of funny. I was in so much pain, so confused, I thought I was hallucinating. Perhaps some of the time, I was. But I was also seeing cars, buses, traffic lights, airplanes…"

"It's not funny," she muttered beneath her breath.

"When I finally reached the church and collapsed in the churchyard, I thought I was going to die and that they would bury me there."

Deidre's steps faltered. She stopped and closed her eyes. When she opened them again, he saw they were sparkling with tears. Wrapping his arm around her shoulders, he drew her close.

The gesture was as much for himself as for her. He needed the contact. He couldn't count the number of times he'd awakened, drenched in sweat, reliving that moment. There'd been many.

They walked in silence for a moment. Sighing, she stretched an arm across his back.

"Which church was it?" she asked quietly.

"St. Stephen's, the Old High Church in Inverness. Even now, I can hardly believe it still stands. Of course, it's very different. An old minister, Reverend James McKinley, found me before dawn. He called for an ambulance, stayed with me, and took care of me afterward."

"Have you kept in touch with him?"

"Aye. He's retired now."

"Does he know?"

"No. He didn't want to know."

"What do you mean?"

"He found me in my old, medieval clothes, or what was left of them, including my sporan. He kept them for me while I was in hospital and then in a rehabilitation facility. He gave me a place to stay until I healed. But he never asked what happened to me, and when I tried to speak of it, he couldn't seem to understand."

"Were you able to converse, then?"

"Not much. He spoke some Gaelic and although it was very different from what I knew, a few words were better than none. And I began picking up words in English. But that wasn't it. I think he was afraid. When I was leaving to come here with Joe, he advised me to let go of the past and not to talk about it with anyone, and I've followed his advice. Who would believe me, anyway?" He glanced at her, his expression softening as he grinned. "Except for a crazy woman, of course?"

"I am crazy." She stretched up and kissed him. "I'm crazy about you, and I don't agree with your reverend. You needed someone to talk to. What do you think he was thinking?"

"No idea."

"You didn't find it odd that he didn't ask questions?"

"Of course I did." Lachlann paused, recalling how desperate he'd been. "I thought it was really odd, and I really wanted to talk. I had questions of my own. But it finally occurred to me that he might be trying to protect us both. I didn't speak English, and it was probably for the best. Who knows how he might've reacted had I been able to tell him?"

"That's true."

"He did his best to help me. He saved my life, and I will always be grateful to him for that."

She squeezed his hand. "So will I. Who knows about you, then?"

"No one."

"You haven't told Joe?"

"No. How would telling him help? It could only

hurt."

She frowned. "You've borne a terrible burden alone."

He shrugged.

"Not anymore," she assured him. "You're not alone anymore."

"I know." He stopped walking to pull her into his arms and gaze down at her. They'd almost reached the Christmas trees. "Thank you, Deidre. Thank you for believing me, for believing *in* me."

"Lachlann…" She drew closer and put her arms around his neck, her eyes seeking his. "I feel that our souls speak to each other. Maybe they always have. Do you believe that?"

He stared into the blue depths, his throat tightening. "I do."

With his whole being. He'd never been so close to anyone. He and Deidre had been born over six hundred fifty years apart, yet he felt she was a part of him and always had been. Holding her tightly, he captured her mouth with his. As she melted against him, he heard children shouting excitedly. He raised his head.

"Shall we choose a Christmas tree?" he asked hoarsely. "I never have, you know."

She smiled tremulously. "We'll have the most beautiful tree you've ever seen."

Hand in hand, they walked toward the rows of evergreens.

Chapter Twenty-Five

Lachlann passed the string of colored lights to Deidre as they wound it around the tree. It was a good thing that her ceilings were tall. It had seemed a sacrilege to him to chop down such a large, beautiful tree for fleeting decoration. Deidre had explained that the trees were grown for that purpose, that the tree farmers sowed seeds every year, and that they grew fairly quickly. She also told him that they charged more for the larger, older trees.

He found it an interesting concept, and he had to admit that the ridiculously large Virginia pine filling a corner of Deidre's living room, the cozy fire in the hearth, and the scents of pine, juniper, and cinnamon were all very appealing.

Had the day been a dream? He still felt strangely withdrawn, almost as if he had observed it—observed his whole life—rather than lived it. Was anything real? His fingers touched Deidre's as they passed the lights, grounding him. *She* was real; of that, he had no doubt. Not only had she been affected by his revelations, she understood his trauma.

He was still stunned by her acceptance of him, of who he really was. He'd told her everything, and she was still with him.

When he'd first fallen, he'd questioned his very existence. He hadn't particularly cared if he was alive or dead; he was only vaguely curious about which it was.

Unfortunately, there'd been nothing vague about his injuries. Physical pain, even more than his anguish, had forced him to acknowledge he was still in his living, weakened, human body.

No, he hadn't died. But he wasn't really living, either. For the past few years, he'd merely existed.

Until a few months ago, when an angel had crossed his line of vision, changing everything. Now, his life had more vitality and intensity than it ever had.

Deidre handed him the string of lights, and he carefully threaded them through the branches the way she had shown him. The huge tree was beginning to twinkle, the colors glittering against the deep green of the pine needles. He wondered how the tradition had begun.

He could ask. He could ask Deidre a question about something—anything—that most modern people didn't even think about. He no longer had to hide his ignorance from her or feign indifference to things that confounded and astonished him. He could sing the praises of water hoses and sprinkler systems, indoor climate control, and indoor plumbing. He could fully express his delight in enormous, jetted showers made for two.

With Deidre, he no longer had to pretend. It was such a relief. He was still trying to wrap his mind around it.

He could speak of the past, his real past. He had truly begun to wonder if it was all in his head. Being able to talk about it with another person had validated his feelings and convictions. Expressing what was in his mind and heart aloud, to another person, had reaffirmed his belief in himself, in his sanity. He could talk about his farm, his real farm, mourn his family, his son…Suddenly, Lachlann couldn't breathe. He dropped the string of lights.

"Lachlann?" Deidre peeked out from where she stood between the tree and the wall. She saw him slump onto the sofa, his expression taut. Finally! It wasn't natural, his behavior this afternoon. If anyone in history had ever needed to cry, he did. He'd gotten a little emotional, but mostly in response to her, and then had determinedly, unselfishly pushed on. She'd realized that it hadn't been the most private situation, but she wanted him to let go, to relieve some of the monumental stress that had been building within him over the years, and she wanted to be with him when it happened.

The good reverend might have done what he thought best, but she was pretty sure it hadn't been best for Lachlann. He'd healed physically, but emotionally he'd been left without relief of any sort. Even if he cried, he'd had no one to turn to in his loss.

But she was here for him now, if he needed her. Quietly, she sat beside him on the sofa.

"My son," he whispered brokenly. "Iain. I wasn't with him. I have no idea how he died. Was he alone in his bed, or did he die in his mother's arms? Or maybe in his grandmother's arms? I wasn't there to help them. I shouldn't have left."

"You had no way of knowing what was going to happen."

"I knew he was sick."

"But you didn't know what kind of sickness it was. You couldn't have. And you can't be sure what would've happened had you stayed."

"I would've died with the rest of my people."

"If you were going to contract the disease, you would have before you left. But you didn't."

"More reason to have stayed!" The words burst from

him. "I was strong! I could have helped them, helped so many! My whole family died!" He covered his face with his hands.

Deidre's throat tightened. She rubbed his back. "How could you have helped them?"

"I could have made them as comfortable as possible, encouraged them so that they wouldn't be afraid. I could have held my son." His voice broke, but he continued, his words muffled in his hands. "Iain was dying, my world was dying, and I was buying ribbons."

Deidre blinked back tears. "You couldn't have known, Lachlann. It's not as though you even went to the festival for yourself. You went for your family's sake, for Allasan."

"Rónán…he was at Loch Ness that day because of me. I heard him call my name. God knows what happened to him."

"It wasn't your fault."

He raised his head and looked at her.

She caught her breath. Raw anguish filled his eyes—and desperate need. Fiercely, she wrapped her arms around him. "Lachlann," she whispered, "you couldn't have stopped the plague or an earthquake. It wasn't your fault."

She felt the tremor run through him as she pulled him even closer, his face against her neck. For a long moment, he was perfectly still. Slowly, silently, his shoulders began to shake. She held him, rubbing his back, kissing him, whispering words of sympathy and encouragement. The gentle tide turned into crashing surf. Gut-wrenching sobs tore from his chest.

Her arms tightened around him. She held onto him for dear life as tears streamed down her cheeks. This was agony. She couldn't begin to imagine his horror or sorrow. Would he ever have closure? He didn't even know how they—his child, his wife, his entire family—had died. Was there no mention of it in history? There had to be something somewhere. She would do her best to find it.

Her poor darlin'…

The longer he cried, the tighter she held him, gently kissing his head, his face. Finally, as she was kissing his cheek, he moved, and their lips met. They were both still crying.

It was a kiss of aching, palpable need.

Lachlann was past thought. In that moment, he needed Deidre beyond anything he'd ever imagined. Everything in him, every part of him, needed her love.

She gave it wholly. He felt it in the way she held him, tasted it in their mingled tears. It washed over and filled him. Sorrow gave way to consolation, consolation to thankfulness, and thankfulness to the cleansing of his very soul. As they clung together, layer upon layer of tension, isolation, and grief fell away from him, replaced by deep, encompassing warmth.

The heat spread, growing stronger, more intense, as he folded her closer and closer, until it was raging between them. As they tumbled back upon the sofa together, it burst into flames.

He was free.

****

Late that evening, they lay together in bed. Deidre snuggled closer to Lachlann, her cheek pressed against his warm, hard chest as he held her.

"How could you say I don't trust you?" he asked.

She twirled his chest hairs with her fingers. "You doubted my faith in you."

"I didn't mean to. I told you everything. Would I do

177

that if I didn't trust you?"

"Maybe not," she allowed.

"It's just that I've never been in this kind of relationship before. Allasan and I cared for each other's welfare, respected each other. But we were never in love as you and I are." He paused. "Does my talking about her bother you?"

Deidre considered this. The woman had been dead for nearly seven hundred years, and he hadn't been in love with her. "No. You can talk to me about anything."

He kissed her. "Thank you. That's just what I mean. I didn't talk much with Allasan. She was a good woman. She worked hard, and we shared common goals, or so I thought. But we didn't think as one, feel as one. Even our…our intimacy was nothing close to what you and I have. To be completely honest, I don't think she even liked it."

Deidre fought a grin. "You mean you weren't sexually compatible?"

"Not in the least!" He kissed her again. "What you and I have is like nothing I've ever known. It makes me wonder why I accepted so much less. Why did she? Sometimes, I feel guilty about it."

"Why?"

"We both just settled."

"You weren't forced to marry?"

"No. Our families wanted it, but they left the decision to us."

"Was that common?"

He shrugged. "Not necessarily. But there was love in some marriages. Contrary to popular belief…" He squeezed her gently. "Medieval people were human. My parents were very happy together."

"If marrying you was Allasan's choice, I'm sure she

must have loved you. Even if she didn't at first, she would have come to love you. It would be impossible not to."

"I don't believe she thought that way. She certainly never said so."

"Never?"

"Never. I'm not saying she was unhappy. She was a talented, hardworking person, always busy. She loved our son and took care of both of us. But love? Passion? I think she died without ever knowing either."

"But that's not your fault, Lachlann." She hesitated, not wishing to tread where she didn't belong, then decided to barrel on anyway. "You must stop holding yourself responsible for things you had no control over. You say that she wasn't unhappy. We must assume, then, that she was happy. In fact, I know she was."

"How could you know that?"

"She was married to you. She had your son. She had her own home and was working toward a goal. It sounds to me like she lived a very fulfilling life."

"You really think so?"

"I do! She didn't have the hindsight you now have. Did she ever seem regretful to you?"

He looked thoughtful. "No."

"Did you hurt her?" She thought of her own awful experience. "Were you ever cruel?"

"No, of course not! I tried to make her happy."

"Then you have nothing to feel guilty about. You did your best. Be at peace."

"Peace?" he repeated hoarsely. His gray eyes searched hers. "Do you know how much peace you have given me? Do you have any idea?" He shook his head slowly, tracing a finger down her cheek. "I don't understand it. We were born hundreds of years apart, but

I feel I was meant to be with you, that we were meant to be together."

"So do I. But Lachlann…" Despite her best efforts, her voice trembled. She paused, striving to gain control.

"What is it, love?"

She didn't answer.

He tilted her face up toward his. "What is it?"

Tears spilled onto her cheeks. "Do you want to go back?"

Lachlann had hoped she wouldn't ask. It was a painful question with a painful answer. But he would be honest with her. "I would never want to leave you," he said quietly.

"But going back has crossed your mind."

"Of course," he replied, "many times, and my feelings have changed just as often. At first, I didn't know what was going on. I actually believed I was having a nightmare and that I would wake up. Once I finally accepted that I had really fallen through time, I waited for it to happen again. I wasn't sure I would even survive a second fall, and I couldn't seem to care. There was so much pain either way."

He sighed. "Once I started healing, I was faced with all sorts of problems—terrible headaches, language problems, massive cultural differences, no stability. I was more than depressed. I was desperate. I wanted the life I had known—my home, my people, my farm. But I knew it was impossible. They were gone. I'd lost them before I fell." Tears choked him, and he stopped, staring up at the ceiling as he struggled for control. Speaking of it made it feel more real, which he needed. But God…

Deidre's arm tightened around him, and he drew a deep, shaky breath, exhaling slowly.

"I saw a few time travel movies," he said. "I knew

180

they were fantasies, but they made me think. If I'd fallen forward, I might be able to go back, if only I could find a way."

He felt her tense.

"I asked myself, if I was given an option, not that I'd ever had one, would I go through it again? If I could make a difference, would I return to a time before I left for Inverness?"

"To save your family," she said quietly.

"Aye, to save my family. At least, at the very least, to help them in any way possible. And I decided that not only would I go back, but that I wouldn't just wait for it to happen. I'd find out how for myself."

She moved away from him. Shielding her breasts with the bedding, she sat facing him. "Have you found anything?"

"No. I can hardly read. Research is almost impossible. I had planned…" He stopped and drew a deep breath before looking into her eyes. "I had thought to ask you for help."

She froze, her eyes widening. "You…you want me to help you go back?"

She sounded stunned.

He sat up, his gaze never leaving her face. "Deidre, you have to believe me when I say that I love you as I've never loved anyone. I can't stand the thought of being without you. I'd rather be dead."

She shut her eyes, her lips trembling.

"But Iain didn't ask to be born. He was an innocent child, and he died…" Lachlann swallowed. "I think he died a horrible death. It was—is—my duty to do everything I can to take care of those I love. If going back is an option, if there's a chance I could save him, save my family from such a terrible fate, from dying from the plague, I have to take it, even if I die trying. Can you understand that?"

She didn't answer. She didn't move. But a tear escaped the corner of one eye.

"I love you so much," he said quietly. "I don't even know what I want anymore. But I know what I have to do."

She opened her eyes. The blue depths swam in pain and tears. He sucked in a breath.

"I understand," she whispered brokenly. "Of course you would want to save your child, your family. I will help you."

For a moment, he couldn't speak. Had he ever really doubted her? His heart was pounding in his chest, his throat tight, his thoughts and emotions hopelessly tangled.

He'd made her cry. She'd given him her love and trust, and he'd made her cry. It was the last thing he'd wanted to do.

Cupping the side of her face with his hand, he gently rubbed her damp cheek with his thumb. "Thank you." He looked into her eyes. "You know, going back is probably not even an option. I have no idea where to start looking. Will you be disappointed if we exhaust our resources and you're stuck with me?"

She made a little sound between a laugh and a sob and shook her head.

He drew her back into his arms. "Are you and I meant to be together?" he asked hoarsely as she hid her face against him. "No matter what has happened or what's to come, I believe that we are. I believe it with all that I am. I will love you forever."

"I've already loved you a lifetime," she whispered against his shoulder. "You know it's true."

He suddenly found it hard to breathe. Closing his eyes, he rested his cheek on top of her shining head. "You're not going to leave me?" he asked. "Even if we don't know what's going to happen?"

"We've discussed this before. Remember?" She sounded more like herself. "No one knows what's going to happen in the future. Maybe I'll be the one to fall."

"No!" He hadn't meant to shout, but the mere suggestion was like a kick in the head.

She looked up at him. "We can't know what's going to happen. You, of all people, should understand that."

"It doesn't worry you?"

"Would worrying help?"

"It hasn't so far," he admitted.

Unexpectedly, she smiled. "I can help you with your worries."

He stared at her a moment. Was she thinking…? He felt a smile tug at his own lips. "Can you now?"

Wrapping her arms around his neck, Deidre pressed against him, pushing him back onto the bed. She lay on top, smiling. "Actually, I can predict your near future."

Lachlann didn't know what had come over her, but he wasn't about to argue. His muscles tensed in anticipation. "Is that so?"

"Oh, yes." She kissed his neck. "I can definitely tell you what's going to happen to you in the next five minutes."

"Go on," he encouraged, his hands moving to her rear.

"Or maybe I won't tell you." She moved his hands. "I'll show you instead. Did you say that you trust me?"

"I did. I do." His hands returned to her, settling at her waist. She caught hold of them, pushing them back over his head as she nibbled his ears.

His body roared into life.

"Then no touching," she instructed. "Let me remind you of how sexually compatible we are."

"I don't think…" His head fell back in pleasure as she placed passionate kisses at his throat, then moved to sweep feather-light kisses across his chest. "I don't need reminding. Ahhh."

Her fiery hair partially hid her face as she kissed her way down his abdomen.

"You do," she said slowly. Her lips were driving him wild. "You offended me." She teased her way along his hips, toward his inner thighs. "You doubted my love, but I promise you…"

"What?" he asked, trying not to squirm.

"I promise you'll never doubt me again," she finished, her hands caressing him as she continued kissing him, closer, closer.

His whole body was aflame. The tip of her tongue…

He jumped as if seared, gasping. "Deidre, don't…"

"No more talking," she whispered against him. "No more thinking. This moment is ours. Forever."

Forever.

Chapter Twenty-Six

It was almost noon. Lachlann could hardly believe he was just getting started. Noon! Hours after sunrise. Hours past dawn. And he felt great.

Climbing the stepladder, a string of Christmas lights in hand, he had the oddest desire to stand on Deidre's roof and pound his chest. Or open his arms to embrace...everything. He felt like a brand new person. Whole. Fulfilled. *At peace.*

It had been the best night of his life. They'd hardly slept, passing the hours alternately talking and making love. The sun was rising as they drifted to sleep in each other's arms. Never in his life had he experienced such love, such passion, such oneness.

He glanced over at the roof next door. Why hadn't they hung Deidre's few strings of lights when they'd hung Joe's? At the moment, all he wanted to do was to take Deidre back to bed and make love to her until tomorrow.

"Lachlann? Are you all right up there?"

He looked down at Deidre. She stood below him, holding the ladder, her pink lips curved into a smile.

"Never better," he assured her.

"You look a little distracted," she drawled, a hint of laughter in her voice.

From his position on the ladder, he could see right down into her V-neck sweater. Her beautiful breasts were practically displayed on a dish just for him.

"Lachlann?"

He snapped his gaze back to her face. She arched a brow.

He tried not to grin. "Me? Distracted? Not at all."

She tossed her hair back over her shoulder. "No? That's too bad."

"Is it? Why?"

Affecting a long, dramatic sigh, she shook her head regretfully. "It's just that, standing here, watching that tight butt of yours, I find myself *very* distracted."

His heart did a little flip in his chest as the rest of his body reacted in no uncertain terms. He was instantly hard.

Smiling broadly, she looked up at him and winked.

Lights, be damned.

He started down the ladder but paused as he noticed a strange car parked in Joe's driveway. He wasn't surprised he hadn't seen it pull up. He waited to see who it was. When no one appeared, he climbed back up a few rungs. To his surprise, he saw a man in a dark suit walking quietly along the side of Joe's house. As Lachlann watched, the stranger moved to a window.

"Hey!" he shouted.

The fellow jumped, obviously startled. But he didn't run. He looked up at Lachlann. "I'm looking for Joseph Dubois."

"By breaking into his house?"

"I wasn't breaking in. I was trying to ascertain if he's home or not. I'll meet you out front."

Lachlann was off the ladder and on Joe's driveway before the man made it past the gate. "Who are you and what were you doing?" he asked harshly.

"I told you. I'm looking for Joseph Dubois. I've tried email and every number I have for him. I haven't been able to reach him."

"Then leave him alone."

"I'm afraid I can't do that." He looked toward Deidre and nodded. "Professor Chisholm."

Lachlann looked at her sharply. "You know this man?"

She was frowning. "No, I don't know him, but he did approach me at the university Friday. I've been meaning to tell you."

"My name is Edward Dawson. I'm with the DEA," the man said. "We've been investigating Mr. Dubois. Do you know him?"

"Why are you investigating him?" Lachlann asked.

He wanted to take hold of Deidre and go inside, get some answers. Why hadn't she told him?

The agent drew a small notepad from his coat pocket. "Name, please?"

"Why are you investigating him?" He didn't appreciate the man's attitude or the fact that he was snooping around Joe's house, peeking into windows.

"I'm not at liberty to disclose information. You'd be helping Mr. Dubois if you answered a few simple questions. He could be in danger."

"ID," Lachlann prompted.

The guy whipped out a badge. Lachlann took his time examining it. He had no idea what a real badge looked like, but the other man wouldn't know that. He looked back at him. "Joe's not here right now."

"Do you know how to reach him?"

"If he's not answering his phone, I can't help you."

"Your name, please?"

"My name is Lachlann An Damh."

The agent looked mildly surprised. "You live with him."

"I do."

"And work with him?"

"Sometimes, yes."

"You're from Scotland."

Dawson was looking between him and Deidre, his eyes narrowing. Lachlann didn't like his expression. In fact, he didn't like anything about him.

"Aye, I'm from Scotland."

"How long have you known Mr. Dubois?"

"A little over three years."

"Three years." He wrote on his notepad. "Are you sure?"

Lachlann felt his temper rising. "Do you want me to answer your questions or don't you?"

"I'm just trying to establish your relationship. Has Mr. Dubois left the country recently?"

"No."

"Have you?"

Lachlann frowned. "Why do you ask?"

"Mr. An Damh, you're also under investigation. I was hoping that you'd make this easier."

"*I'm* under investigation? Why?" *What the hell...*

"We're looking into some trouble—smuggling—out in the Gulf of Mexico."

"Joe doesn't have anything to do with smuggling. Neither do I."

"I understand," the man said blandly. "This is just routine questioning. At least, for now."

Lachlann stared at him. It wasn't that he was obviously oily or rude. But he was dodgy. He definitely couldn't be trusted.

The sooner he was gone—and the sooner he could get some answers from Deidre—the better. He recalled the question. "I haven't left the country since I came here three years ago."

"Have you been in contact with anyone overseas?"

"No." It was a lie, but he wasn't about to give him reason to bother the reverend.

"Where is Dubois right now?"

It was none of his damn business. Lachlann didn't answer.

"Mr. An Damh, you will answer, or I will take you in for questioning."

"Will you now?"

"Professor Chisholm, perhaps you'd prefer to answer my question?"

Damn him!

Lachlann bit back a growl. "He's visiting family in Louisiana."

"Have you noticed any odd or suspicious behavior?"

"No."

"Strange packages? Unusual visitors or guests?"

"No."

"Are you sure? Take your time. Think about it."

"I'm sure."

They stared at each other.

Dawson took a step back. "That's all for now. Thank you for your cooperation. Merry Christmas." He turned and walked to his car.

Deidre stepped closer to Lachlann. "Do you believe he is who he says he is?" she asked.

"I don't know, but I don't like him. DEA…Drugs?"

"Yes, the Drug Enforcement Administration. Should we call Joe?"

"The moment we get inside." He moved to retrieve the ladder, striving to keep the anger out of his voice. It wasn't easy. "When did he talk to you? Why didn't you tell me?"

"I meant to. But I didn't want to ruin your first night back, and then we went to the Christmas tree farm and, well…There just hasn't seemed to be a right time."

A strange man had approached her, asking questions about *him*, and she hadn't found the time to tell him? He frowned at her.

She was twisting the string of lights in her hands, her brow puckered. "I'm sorry, Lachlann. I should've told you on the way to the Christmas tree farm."

"You should've told me the moment I arrived!" His blood was boiling. "Did he frighten you?"

"No. I didn't like his questions, but I didn't feel threatened."

He stalked toward the garage, trying to get his thoughts—and his temper—under control. How could he protect her if he didn't even know she was in danger? Didn't she trust him?

A thought struck him. He turned around abruptly, and she almost ran into him. She looked up at him apprehensively.

"Deidre, you don't think…You're not afraid that I'm…I'm a smuggler?"

Her eyes widened. "No. No, of course not. Although I must admit that yesterday, when we were driving to the Christmas tree farm, I did wonder for a moment. You know, when you mentioned being a fugitive?"

He inhaled sharply. He couldn't have blamed her if she'd left him on the side of the road.

"And what did I say to you?" she questioned. "What did I say in reply?"

He thought for a moment, some of his anger dissolving as he remembered her words. Slowly, he put his arms around her. This woman…this sweet, precious woman. His heart contracted. Closing his eyes, he rested his forehead against hers. "You said that if I'd made a mistake, you would help me. That you'd fight for me."

"And I meant it," she said.

His breathing was unsteady now, his emotions in turmoil. He didn't move, just held her for a moment.

Finally, with a deep sigh, he raised his head. "It hurts me to think of you in danger, that you would keep something like that from me."

She looked up at him anxiously. "I'm sorry. I didn't mean to keep it from you."

"If he or anyone else bothers you again…"

"I'll tell you right away."

"If anyone bothers you, if anyone makes you feel the least bit unsafe or uncomfortable…Give me your word."

For a moment, she didn't speak. Then her eyes met his and she nodded. "You have my word."

****

After dinner, Deidre cuddled next to Lachlann on the sofa. With the mild Texas winters, a roaring fire was rarely required, but it was cozy. She stared down at the whiskey snifter she held, absently swirling the golden liquid as she thought about their surprising conversation with Joe. His reaction had been a mix of concern and anger, none of it for himself.

"I'll get to the bottom of this when I get back," he said. "You call me right away if anyone else bothers you. Professor, I don't know who this man is or what he wants, but don't you let him get you alone. Do you hear me?"

Of course they heard him. He was shouting.

"Poor Joe." She sighed. "I'm not sure we did him any favors by telling him."

"Favor or not, he needed to know." His voice was hard.

"You're still upset with me."

"I'm not upset. But I don't like the guy, and I don't like the fact that he approached you."

"As I said, he didn't threaten me."

"You will let me know if it happens again."

Bending forward, she set the snifter down on the coffee table and looked at him. "I told you I would. You don't have to go all medieval on me."

With a rueful sigh, he pulled her closer. "I *am* medieval, and I don't like anyone bothering my woman."

"I'm your woman?" she teased, even as a little thrill shot through her.

"Aren't you?" he asked seriously, his gray eyes staring into hers intently. "Don't we belong to each other?"

"You belong to me?"

"For all time." His lips brushed hers. "Never doubt it."

Lachlann couldn't stop kissing her. His heart still pounded in his ears. He wasn't sure if he'd ever calm down. A stranger had forced unwelcome attention upon Deidre. Every time he thought about it, he had to quell a surge of anger. He knew he wasn't being rational. Deidre interacted with hundreds of people every day. But he didn't trust the so-called agent. He didn't like how he'd looked at her, how he'd seemed to assess them both. Joe wasn't convinced he was even from the DEA. But who was he then? And what did he want?

Deidre could be in danger. The very thought made him crazy.

She was vulnerable. For so long, he'd been focused on going back in time, worried about the past. But Deidre, generous, warm-hearted Deidre, needed him *now*.

He held her even tighter, pressing her to his heart as their kiss deepened. When he finally let up his hold, they were both breathless.

"I love you," he rasped, "with all my medieval heart."

"I love you too," she whispered, "and I adore your medieval heart."

He kissed her again, sat back, and waited. It was her turn to tell her story. He hoped, with everything in him, to give her the understanding and support she'd shown him.

For a long moment, she didn't move. She stared at her hands folded in her lap.

"It's best to begin at the beginning," he said quietly.

"Must I?"

"You want me to trust you, but you don't trust me?"

"My revelations are different from yours. You didn't cause what happened to you. My trouble was my own fault."

"It doesn't matter."

"I'm embarrassed," she said in a small voice.

Embarrassed? After all they'd done together? He wanted to smile, but he didn't want her to think he was laughing at her. Reaching out, he cupped her chin and lifted her face to his.

Her expression was anguished. "It's like I'm about to strip naked in front of you."

He kissed the tip of her nose. "You do strip naked in front of me."

"Not like this."

He pressed a gentle kiss to her lips and released her. "Just remember that I love you. Nothing will change that."

Drawing in a breath, Deidre returned her gaze to her

193

lap. "Growing up, I spent more time with my grandparents than I did with my parents. You would've liked my father's parents. They were loving, down-to-earth individuals, dedicated to the land, and very proud of their Scottish heritage."

She glanced up at him. "My parents both had jobs in the city. Every day, they would come home from work and go straight to farm chores. They were tired and stressed for most of my childhood. But no matter how tired everyone was, we all had supper together every evening and went to church every Sunday."

Deidre looked away at the fire. "It was a good life, a simple life. I was taught to work hard, to know right from wrong, and to be loyal to my family. I knew exactly what was expected of me and never gave my family trouble or worry."

Lachlann smiled. He could imagine the sweet little girl she must have been.

A shadow crossed her face. "My grandmother passed away when I was twelve. After her death, I spent more time than ever with my grandfather. We worked the farm together before and after school, during the weekends, and every summer day. I learned a lot from him about gardening and tradition, about our family history. He taught me to be proud of who I was."

She turned to him, her brow furrowed. "When I was accepted into Duke University, I was thrilled. I wanted my parents to be proud of me. They had both graduated from Duke, and they wanted me to follow in the family tradition. It's a very prestigious university.

"But I was also nervous and, to be honest, a little scared. I'd never spent more than a few days away from the farm, and suddenly I was going to live in the city."

"By yourself?" Lachlann knew he sounded

disapproving, but he couldn't stop himself.

She shook her head, a faint smile touching her lips, probably at his tone. "Not exactly. I lived on campus, in the dorms, and I had two roommates. They were typical college students, not over-the-top wild but not as studious as I was."

"But isn't that why you were there, to study?"

Her smile deepened. Definitely because of his tone. And then it was gone. "That's what I told myself, that I was there to learn. But there's more to college life than studying. There are school events, football games, social activities, academic opportunities outside the classroom. I participated in some things, but I mostly concentrated on my studies. I didn't want to disappoint anyone, including myself. I graduated with top honors. My professors liked and respected me."

Her voice faded. She took a sip of Scotch and sighed.

"After I graduated, I was offered a teaching position at Duke, which almost never happens." She wasn't looking at him. "One of my professors, James Stanfield, had taken special notice of me. He was an older man, a tenured professor, and he was on the board. I…"

"Excuse the interruption, but I want to understand. What does it mean, 'tenured, on the board?' "

"Sorry. He was on the faculty board. He had an important position at the university." Her expression changed. She suddenly looked stricken.

Lachlann felt his gut clench. "This was the man you married?"

She nodded. "I'd taken a few of his classes and he'd never shown me any particular interest. But his recommendation was one of those that secured my offer."

"I'm sure you earned it."

"Thank you. I like to think so. Without the recommendations, there would have been no offer. Once I started working, he became very attentive. At first, he merely checked on me, offered me advice, acted as my mentor. But it wasn't long before he started flirting with me."

Lachlann already wanted to kill the man.

"At first, I was uncomfortable. Then I couldn't help but feel flattered." She gave him a sideways glance. "I've never been the sort of girl men go for." Her cheeks went rosy. "I'm tall and big. I have red hair and freckles."

"You're beautiful."

"Thank you," she said again. She placed her hand on his arm and squeezed. "Not everyone thinks so." She gave a little shrug. "I'm bookish and old-fashioned. I'm not the fun, sexy sort of woman men like."

With her sweet mouth, her beautiful breasts, the way she…*What was she talking about?* "But you're exactly fun and sexy!"

She shook her head and gave him a little smile. "Only with you, because you are you, because of the way we are together."

He could deal with that. A surge of warmth flowed through him, followed by a fierce protectiveness.

"Professor Stanfield kept telling me how pretty and talented I was. He didn't mean any of it, of course. It was all part of his plan." She looked at him pleadingly. "You have to understand. No one had ever talked to me that way before. It was exciting."

Lachlann ground his teeth.

"When he asked me out, I accepted. And then, after only a few dates, he asked me to marry him."

"And your parents approved?" he asked, outraged.

"No! They argued with me. They had only met him once and thought he was too old for me. They didn't trust him either, or like that he was rushing me."

He forced back a growl. "Why was he rushing you?"

"He was in a hurry. He had an agenda. I…I told you that I was old-fashioned. I'd been raised very strictly. I was saving myself for marriage, and he knew that. He used my ideals against me, to manipulate me. He told me that he was a grown man, not a boy, that he needed me and couldn't wait. He insisted that we marry as soon as possible."

Her voice hardened and she frowned. "Do you see how stupid I was? How naïve? I agreed to run away with him, against my parents' wishes, without their blessings or permission." Her voice broke.

"Deidre…"

Shaking her head, she held a hand up, palm out. "If I don't finish now, I never will. It's all so humiliating."

He stared at her for a moment, noting her strained expression, and nodded.

"We went to the coast. We were married by a justice of the peace on a Friday morning. Ever since I was a little girl, I'd dreamed of my wedding in Duke Chapel, surrounded by everyone I love. My parents and I had often discussed it, that one day I would marry there." Her voice caught, and she stopped abruptly.

He waited.

She took a small sip of whiskey. "But after attending church my whole life, I wasn't married in one. There wasn't even a blessing. And there were no friends. No family. No celebration. No honeymoon, either. It was the middle of the semester. After one horrible night—" She paused and made quote marks with her fingers. " 'The wedding night'—we drove back to his house near the university."

"Why was it horrible?" Lachlann bit out. Grabbing his snifter from the coffee table, he drained it.

"He married me for my paycheck." She gave a short, dry laugh. "It wasn't much, but it was better than nothing. He wasn't interested in me personally. He needed money, and he needed it fast." Her gaze dropped to her hands, now fisted in her lap. "He didn't care that I was a virgin. For me, the wedding night was a painful, humiliating experience." Her voice dropped to a whisper. "It was just short of rape."

Deidre was amazed that she'd said it aloud. She'd never told a single soul that part, not even Stella. She was surprised at the relief she felt. But she'd forgotten to whom she was speaking.

Chapter Twenty-Seven

Lachlann leapt to his feet. "He hurt you!"

When she saw his expression, she realized that she might have said too much, and that she'd never seen him really angry until now.

He towered over her, eyes blazing with fury. He looked ready to…

"I'll kill him! God help me, I'm going to find that swine and kill him!"

"I'm all right now," she rushed out. "Don't be angry."

"Angry?" he shouted. He turned away, pacing around the room, his hands in fists.

She waited. After a moment, he drew a deep breath and exhaled slowly.

"Have you heard enough?" she asked.

He looked at her. "Finish."

"Only if you sit down."

He stared at her another moment, almost uncomprehending. Deidre knew what it was. He was too furious to think straight.

She patted the sofa. "Please?"

Slowly, he sank down beside her.

"It was the only time we…" She stopped.

This was hard, so hard. But Lachlann should know. She needed him to know. "He never tried again to…you know. It was just that once, and I don't know why he bothered. He never wanted me. I was just stupid enough to fall for his lies. A few weeks after our wedding, I learned he was being sued for debt, sued for child support, about to lose his house. Before the first month was over, I was paying his bills."

Deidre paused again. It was getting even harder. She raised her chin. "In less than a month, I lost my virginity, my self-respect, my independence, and my parents. When I called and told them I was married, they didn't believe me at first. Then they were furious. We ended up arguing on the phone." Her voice quivered, but she continued. "We all said some terrible things. Unforgivable things. They told me not to call again. I did try, but they wouldn't answer my calls. My grandfather had died a few years before. Thank God he never knew what happened. It would've broken his heart."

Gramps. A sob escaped her, and she wiped her eyes with the back of her hand.

Lachlann wanted to comfort her, but, at that moment, he couldn't. He was struggling just to control his breathing. He had to calm himself first.

Out of all the women the devil might have picked, it had been Deidre. There were scores of women who would have known better how to handle him. No female deserved to be treated as she had, but others would have been better prepared to cut off his balls.

The devil had realized that. He'd chosen to prey on an innocent.

"He…he stopped coming to the house at night," Deidre was saying. "At first, he maintained that he was busy at the university. But, when I finally confronted him, he slapped me and told me that I had no right to question him."

"Slapped you?" The words exploded from him. He rose again, pulling her up with him, into his arms.

"I didn't know what to do," she continued, as if they hadn't moved. "I'd been working, paying, working, paying. I thought I was saving our marriage. And then he started hitting me."

"Damn it!" He was beginning to shake.

"I felt so stupid, so ashamed."

"No! You had nothing to be ashamed of!"

"Then one day, I returned to the house early. He was in bed—the bed I slept in—with one of his students. One of *my* students…"

"Deidre, stop!" His heart was pounding in his ears as he fought back impotent rage.

"I walked out and never went back. I was twenty-four. We'd only been married three months, but the divorce took over a year. He did everything he could to drag it out, to keep me paying his expenses. He tried to ruin me, to make me responsible for part of his debt, and he nearly succeeded. I chose to pay an expensive divorce attorney I couldn't afford rather than give him one more penny. By the time I was twenty-six, I was free."

She looked up at him. "I was also unemployed. He managed to get my position at the university discontinued. That's why I came to Houston. Thank God for friends and the other recommendations I'd received. I was able to start over."

"Your parents?" he questioned.

"My parents wanted nothing more to do with me. Like I said, some very harsh words passed between us. I tried to apologize, but they wouldn't listen. I think…I think it was almost worse because we'd never really argued before." A bitter laugh escaped her. "We had no reason to argue. I always did everything they told me to do."

She pulled out of his arms to stand before the fire.

"Later, when I called and told them I was divorced, homeless, and jobless, they still refused to see me. I had to force them to allow me to get my personal belongings from my old room. We haven't spoken since."

Lachlann couldn't understand how she could be so calm. He was personally shaking from head to foot. He'd never imagined anything like this. She'd lost so much.

He sank onto the sofa. She whirled back toward him, her hands fisted at her sides.

"Do you see how stupid I was? I almost ruined my life for a few words of flattery, for my ego. All the degrees in the world couldn't help me. He saw my naivety, my eagerness to prove myself, and took every advantage." Her voice trembled, but she continued. "I never had boyfriends. I was saving myself for the right person, and I gave it all up for a liar. Was it a lack of judgement? A lack of character? Probably both."

Tears were running down her cheeks. "The worst part is, I never loved him. I can see that now. I had no idea what love was until I met you."

"Come here." He spoke the words raggedly as he pulled her into his arms.

"I'm sorry," she whispered, crying against him.

To his concern, she said it over and over again as she wept. Forcing himself to remain calm, he cradled her against him, stroking her hair as he fought the rage welling within him.

He could understand that her parents were angry. In his own time, in the fourteenth century, they might have done much worse. He shuddered to think of it. But that was then. It was different now. Deidre had lived a quiet, protected life on their farm, and they'd sent her away from it, unprepared. They should have accepted some of the responsibility. Instead, in their pride, they'd left her to face the wolves alone.

He swallowed against the tightness in his throat. How could they? Had they no love for their only child? Didn't they know she was sweet and gentle and good? Even if they couldn't find it in their hearts to forgive her, how could they refuse her shelter?

He could hardly bear to think of her hurt, scared, and alone.

"Lachlann, you're shaking," she whispered through her tears.

"Listen to me." He moved to cup her face in his hands. "You're not to blame yourself for what happened. It wasn't your fault."

"Of course it was. We can be honest about that."

"You were an innocent babe. Damn his black heart! I'm going to cut it out and feed it to the vultures!"

"Lachlann…"

Still cupping her face, he kissed her forehead. Then both her cheeks. He knew that she probably needed to blow her nose, probably couldn't breathe. But he couldn't help it. She'd been hurt. His angel…

She drew a shaky breath and he let her go, tucking a tissue into her palm. She blew her nose vigorously and blinked up at him. "I thought you'd be angry with me. Disappointed."

"Why?" Tenderly, he stroked his knuckles down her cheek, wiping away the wetness. "You made a mistake."

"I hurt my parents."

"I know, but that wasn't your intention. You thought you were doing what you had to do. They should've tried to understand. Instead, they abandoned you when you needed them most. They have a lot to answer for."

"I'm not asking them for anything."

"We're going to make this right."

She tensed. "What do you mean?"

"We have to visit your parents. It's going to be hard to forgive them, even for me. But you must try and make peace with them."

"I don't want to make peace with them!" She jumped up. "I'm finished trying."

"I don't believe you." He rose to face her.

"I don't want to make peace with them," she repeated. "Not anymore. I don't need to. I'm more peaceful without them."

"Even if that's true and you don't want their blessings, I do. I want their blessings for our marriage, just as I want the Church's blessing."

Deidre's mouth dropped open.

"Our what?"

"Our marriage." He frowned. "You weren't thinking of marrying me?"

"You never…"

"Is it because I might not stay in this time?"

"Well, that would be a good reason, but…"

"You're the one who said that we can't know the future, that all we have is now. I want you as my wife— now and forever." *For all time, no matter what.*

"But Lachlann, you've never mentioned marriage! We haven't talked about it even once!"

He stared at her, confused. Talk? After all they had said to each other, after all that had passed between them? What was there to talk about? Of course they were getting married. "What kind of man do you think I am?"

"An honest one. You know, the kind who doesn't make commitments he's not planning to keep?" She crossed her arms. "I don't blame you."

He scowled. "We're getting married."

"You're not being reasonable."

"*I'm* not being reasonable?"

"No, you're not."

He glared at her, frustrated. She glared back.

She was right. It was a lot to ask. He shut his eyes, tormented. It was too much to ask.

He felt her move closer.

"Lachlann…"

To hell with reason.

"I know it's not fair," he interrupted, opening his eyes to look right into hers. "But I can't bear the thought of not being married to you. I want us joined as husband and wife—forever. And I thought you wanted the same."

He held his breath.

Taking another step closer, she slipped her arms around his neck. "I'm good with forever."

"You'll marry me?"

"Are you asking?"

"Aye, I'm asking." Bending his head, he touched his lips to hers. "I love you. I want you for my own. You said that you're not the type of woman men go for. I don't understand that. I can only believe that it's because you were meant for me, that we're meant to be together. To me, you're everything that's beautiful." He huffed out a sigh. "But you haven't answered me yet. Is it because I haven't asked properly? Will you marry me, Deidre, my heart, my love?"

Deidre's eyes sparkled with unshed tears. She nodded.

"Yes?" He had to be sure.

She smiled radiantly. "Yes."

"Thank God." His throat tightened as he hugged her close. "We'll worry about everything else later. For now, I need to hold you."

"I need you to hold me," she agreed breathlessly.

He scooped her up in his arms.

"Lachlann!"

Lachlann gazed down at her, noting the surprise and joy in her eyes, the way her sweet mouth trembled for his kiss. For all time, he would love her.

Holding her close, his lips on hers, he carried her up the stairs.

Chapter Twenty-Eight

Did Lachlann really think she would let him leave her to risk his life and likely die for an uncertain outcome?

The scent of peppermint filled Deidre's nostrils as she squeezed a glob of organic toothpaste onto her toothbrush.

Even in books and movies, time travel afforded no guarantees. And this wasn't fiction. She frowned. He'd almost died the first time.

How could he leave her? She shoved the toothbrush into her mouth. Didn't he know how much she needed him? Maybe she should point out just how much losing him would hurt her.

Horrible. Horrible and selfish, Deidre chided as she brushed. What, exactly, would she tell him? Please, Lachlann, don't try to save your son from dying a miserable death because I want you to stay with me?

Nice.

If she found any information that might help, she would tell him. But there was no way she would let him go without her. She'd make that clear. Of course, if she did go back with him, he'd have two wives.

Bigamy, anyone?

She spit and rinsed. So far, she hadn't come across a single clue, and she had good resources. Was she awful to be glad? She was only being honest with herself. Even now, she missed him so much she ached, and it had only been a few days. She'd cried when he left. She still couldn't believe that she, a grown woman with her own home and career, had cried over a two-week separation. As if crying would help.

So she was childish as well as selfish. Wow, Deidre, two out of two. She stared at herself in the mirror.

What would she do if he left her forever?

She gave herself a mental shake. They'd promised each other to be optimistic, and here she was being downright morbid.

It was almost time to call him. Pulling a hairbrush through her curls, she turned out the lights. She only needed the glow from her bedside lamp, didn't even really need that. Lachlann liked it on. She smiled. He'd gotten into the habit of asking to see her pajamas, knowing full well she didn't wear any.

Arranging the pillows so that she could lean back against them, she turned down the covers and slipped in. Her bed was cold and lonely without his big, strong body next to hers. They'd slept so soundly, so peacefully together through the holidays. Now, every night was a struggle, and he had told her that it was the same for him. She worried that his nightmares might return, even though he'd assured her that they rarely troubled him anymore. She worried about him getting injured on the rig. She worried about everything. She couldn't seem to stop.

She still felt guilty about arguing with him before he left. It had been a waste of precious time. He wanted to go to North Carolina. She didn't. She wanted to go to Scotland to search for information about his family, his people. He didn't. So why was she rushing him? Why in *hell* was she rushing him? And all Lachlann was trying to do was reunite her with her parents, to get married with their blessings in a church. She had argued with him for the sake of her stubborn pride.

Three out of three, Deidre.

She would make it up to him. Glancing back at the clock, she picked up her iPad. They preferred the larger screen for their nightly chats. She was thrilled he was enjoying his iPad, her Christmas gift to him. But she loved her gift from him more.

Sighing dreamily, she glanced at the engagement ring they'd chosen together. Fashioned in a Celtic knot, the white gold was set with smaller diamonds rather than one large one. Lachlann had complained about the size of the stones, but she thought it was perfect.

How she loved him. Fluffing her pillows, she leaned back against them, just barely reclining. Should she tease him by covering herself up to her neck? But she enjoyed seeing his bronzed, muscular chest just as much. Maybe just a little teasing…Pulling the blankets up to her chin, she stretched her arms around the bedding to arrange her tablet.

****

In the dim light of his cabin, Lachlann made himself more comfortable on his bed and opened his new iPad. Every time he looked at it, he thought of Deidre. Not only had she surprised him with the Christmas gift, she'd taken the time to help him understand and personalize it. Together, they'd chosen apps he'd enjoy and practiced with them. They bookmarked websites he might find useful. And she'd added photos. His screensaver was a selfie of the two of them in front of the Christmas tree.

Computers usually gave him headaches, but he liked this one, especially as it was from his fiancée.

Fiancée. After a month of being with Deidre constantly, leaving her had felt as though it just might kill him. He glanced at the time in the corner of the screen. She should be calling soon. When he wasn't working the night shift, they would FaceTime until one or both of them began falling asleep. Nightmares were no longer a problem for him, but he had a hard time sleeping without her. He missed her soft body tucked warmly against him. How had he ever lived, much less slept, without the closeness they shared?

He opened Google Earth and continued his exploration of Christmas tree farms. He had to find another way to make a living. If he couldn't find a tree farm, he might look for a more traditional farm, or a plant nursery, or even raw acreage he could work over. From his searches so far, it seemed he would have enough money. He'd worked a lot the past few years and had spent very little.

Was she late calling? He glanced at the time again. Damn. He'd never been the worrying sort, not in any century, but now he fretted like an old woman. Every day, a new terror struck him. What if she were involved in a car accident? What if the damned investigator bothered her again? What if that devil in North Carolina dared contact her? Knowing what she'd suffered, and that she was vulnerable, nearly tore him apart. Even the thought that she might be lonely without him bothered him. When they'd kissed good-bye, she'd reminded him that she was a grown woman as tears spilled onto her cheeks.

And it wasn't just the worrying or his desire to be with her that had him searching the internet for a farm. He zoomed in on what appeared to be a pine forest northeast of Houston. Deidre would be his wife. He wanted to have something to offer, something to leave her should anything happen to him. He still had no clue as to how or why he'd come to be here, but he believed they'd find out, especially now that Deidre was helping him. Whatever else happened, even if he fell again, she would have their farm. Please God, give him time to give her his name.

There weren't a lot of Christmas tree farms near Houston. Deidre had mentioned that the ones in North Carolina were pretty. Next stop, North Carolina. It wouldn't hurt for him to know how they looked, even if she wouldn't want to hear about them.

His head was beginning to ache. He ran a hand down his face, wishing for possibly the hundredth time that he hadn't argued with her about going to North Carolina. If she wasn't ready to face her parents, why should he insist otherwise? But she'd argued just as forcefully in favor of a trip to Scotland. He'd been equally opposed.

Returning to Scotland would be more than returning to horrific memories. If he found answers anywhere, it would be there, and he was desperately afraid it would be where he'd say good-bye to Deidre. His whole body tensed at the thought.

North Carolina, the Smoky Mountains…He scrolled through the images absently. A picture of a misty lake caught his eye, reminding him only too well of Loch Ness. His chest tightened.

What if he fell through time again without warning or explanation? Who would he be helping then? What if, as Deidre once mentioned, she fell instead? He sat bolt upright, almost sending his iPad to the floor. He grabbed it. God, if she disappeared in front of him…the thought sent chills racing through him. He'd lose his mind.

He had to keep her away from Loch Ness.

His iPad buzzed, her sweet face flashing on the screen. He wanted to kiss the image, to kiss *her*. He reached out a slightly shaky hand and answered her call. Then she was live onscreen in front of him, her pink lips curved in that special smile just for him.

Was she cold? Why was she covered like that?

****

Lachlann adjusted the tongs quickly, feeding more pipe into the well.

It wasn't bad out on the platform tonight. They'd worked through a cold rain most of the week, but tonight it was cool, not cold, and there was only sea mist. The night sky was clear and starry; the sea, calm.

He didn't mind working at night. Until recently, he'd preferred it. Napping during the day was better than struggling with nightmares through a long, dark night. And while a rig was never quiet, it usually seemed a little less hectic in the middle of the night. He liked this particular rig, too. It was an older one, more manual than the new, and the crew was smaller. At the moment, he was alone on the platform, but he knew that his solitude wouldn't last. Two others would be joining him momentarily.

Silently, swiftly, carefully, he maneuvered the giant tongs.

A strange noise caught his attention. He stared down at where the pipe was sliding into the riser. Was that…was that…

A tremor?

No!

The platform began to shake.

Deidre!

Chapter Twenty-Nine

Their gardens looked wonderful. Deidre scratched at the soil with a small circle hoe. Winter weeds weren't a big problem in their raised beds, but she liked to keep the soil loose and aerated. The kale and Swiss chard grew abundantly, the chard brilliant in hues of burgundy, pink, and gold. Lettuces filled their designated boxes, while beet greens and spinach filled others. Radishes fronted almost everything. They couldn't eat them fast enough, although Joe, as he said himself, surely tried.

She could hardly wait for Lachlann to get home. One more day!

Two earthworms wriggled hastily away from the hoe. She'd harassed them enough. Pulling off her gloves, she gazed at her Christmas present. The ring glistened in the sun. She could still hardly believe that she was engaged to the man of her dreams—literally.

"Professor!" Joe's shout sounded frantic.

She jumped to her feet.

He was running toward the fence. "Professor! There was an explosion on the rig! Lachlann's missing!"

****

No, no, no!

NO!

Deidre felt like jumping out of Joe's truck. They'd been driving for almost eighteen hours. It would have been nothing if they'd found Lachlann. But they hadn't.

Where was he? Why wasn't he answering his

phone?

Lachlann hadn't drowned. And he had *not* been blasted through time from an offshore rig. She refused, absolutely refused, to believe it.

She clung to the possibility that he lay unconscious or sedated in some emergency room. She could deal with that. She would take care of him while he recovered.

"I told you, I'm out until I find An Damh. You got that? Deal with it." Joe set his cellphone down with a jerk.

His phone hadn't stopped all day. Deidre didn't know much about oil rigs, but it was clear that Joe had an important position.

Turning sharply into a hospital parking lot, he drove to the emergency room entrance and jumped out almost before he had the car in park. "I'll be right back."

He'd done that the last few stops, jumped out before she could. She didn't argue. She knew he was too anxious to sit still.

As if she wasn't. Sighing, she rested her head against the car seat, closed her eyes, and tried to calm down. Where was her precious medieval farmer? The jack-up rig he'd been working on wasn't deep offshore, but just off the Louisiana coast. She and Joe had driven straight to the company's facilities in Louisiana, a solid six-hour drive, and to the heliport where injured workers would have been transported. They'd almost denied her entrance. Only Joe's authority had saved the day.

She loved Lachlann more than anyone had ever loved anyone, but she had no legal claim to him and no right to enter a restricted facility. Why weren't they married already?

Because she was a damn stubborn ass.

The moment Joe had stepped out of his truck at the

facility, he'd been bombarded. Gone was her easygoing, gumbo-dishing sweetheart of a neighbor. Not only was he the man in charge, but he was the one others looked to for answers. It had taken a few hours before he could extricate himself. He'd even flown out to the rig and back while she'd paced and called local hospitals.

The explosion had occurred on the platform. It seemed that it had been a minor blast, if there was such a thing. What that really meant was that they'd gotten it quickly under control and only a few people had suffered minor injuries.

The chilling news was that Lachlann had been on the platform at the time of the explosion and no one had seen him since. A grim-faced Joe had returned from the rig with Lachlann's duffle bag. There'd been no sign of him onboard. Word had been sent to the coastguard and to local authorities. There was no need to look for his truck; it was parked in Joe's garage. Lachlann had ridden to Louisiana with Jackson, who remained on the rig.

Once Joe was able to get away, they'd left the facility to drive to every hospital in the area. He even had his son Charles check the major ones in New Orleans. No Lachlann. So they'd returned to I-10, checking hospital after hospital along the way back to Texas.

"Damn it!" Joe startled her as he dropped back into the car. "Where is he?"

She sipped her coffee.

His phone sounded mercilessly as they sped down I-10 toward home. He had to answer it, especially as someone might call with news of Lachlann. He got angrier and more upset with each call.

"It's not fair. This can't be happening to him again."

Joe's muttered words caught her attention. She turned her head to look at him sharply.

He swiped a hand down his face, wet with tears. "He doesn't deserve this, God help him."

"Joe, what did you mean by 'again'?"

He looked startled. "Did I say 'again'?"

"Yes, sir, you did."

"Lachlann has had enough pain in his life. It's not fair for him to suffer serious injury again."

"We don't know that he's injured."

"The alternative's worse!"

No. She closed her eyes against the stab of pain and felt his hand on hers.

"I'm sorry, honey. I should be trying to comfort you, not make you feel worse. I'm just so upset. He was just beginning to be happy."

Deidre forced herself to rally. If she let herself cry, she'd never stop. She turned her hand palm up to squeeze his. "We'll find him."

He drew a deep breath and nodded. "If it's the last thing I do."

She leaned her head against the headrest. They would find him. They had to. People didn't just disappear. She bit back a sob.

Unless they did.

****

She would go to North Carolina. She would beg her parents for forgiveness, for their blessings. She would kiss their feet if necessary.

Please, Lachlann, come back.

Deidre exited the freeway. Surely it was almost dawn. It was a good thing they'd be home in a few minutes. She didn't think she could stand to be in the truck much longer. At least Joe had finally given in and let her drive for the last few hours. Poor man. He sat quietly sipping coffee, scrolling through his zillion text messages. At some point during the early morning hours, the calls had mercifully ceased.

Please, Lachlann, be all right. Please, God, let him be alive and well.

Turning into their neighborhood, she drove down the darkened streets practically on autopilot. She felt numb. Passing a stretch of golf course, she made a left at her house on the corner.

A man was walking along the sidewalk, between her house and Joe's. His arm was in a sling.

Pulling onto Joe's driveway, she screeched to a stop and bolted out of the truck. "Lachlann! Are you all..." The words ended in a grunt as he pulled her against him.

He clutched her close with one arm and buried his face in her neck. She wrapped her arms tentatively around his waist, not knowing where he might be injured, wanting to touch him everywhere at once. They were both shaking.

He was alive. He was safe. He was here. She couldn't...Holding onto him for dear life, she buried her face in his shoulder and cried.

Chapter Thirty

"So let me get this straight." Joe leaned forward in the chair. "They put you on a supply ship? That's not even...Who?"

Lachlann, his eyes shut and his head resting against Deidre's sofa cushions, started to shrug and realized it would be a mistake. He had dislocated his shoulder, but his wild grab at the platform railing had saved him from flying overboard. It was worth the discomfort. He wasn't sure there was an inch of his body that didn't hurt, and he was exhausted. He was also happier than he'd ever thought possible. Deidre and Joe had no idea. It was as if a fog had lifted, a blind removed from his eyes.

I'm still here. Thank you, God.

More than anything, he wanted to go to Deidre's bed and celebrate by holding her in his arms and possibly never letting go.

But Joe wanted answers, deserved them. He could hardly believe that they'd been looking for him since yesterday.

"Two guys from the supply ship," he replied. "I didn't know them. Like I said, that part's vague in my mind. Everything happened so fast."

"I understand, son, but damn it! A helicopter would've flown you straight to the hospital. A broken arm, a dislocated shoulder...You must've been in a helluva lot of pain."

Lachlann glanced at Deidre. "I've had worse, and

218

there was a medic onboard who knew what he was doing. He reset my shoulder and made me comfortable enough until we reached port."

"And they docked here in Texas, not Louisiana. You're sure about that?"

"I'm sure."

"It doesn't make sense," Joe said. "Something's wrong here."

"You're right." Lachlann looked him in the eye. "Guess who met us at the docks?"

"Who?" Joe and Deidre asked together.

"That agent. What's his name? Dawson?"

Deidre gasped, and Joe let out a string of oaths Lachlann had rarely heard from him, and never in mixed company.

"Sorry, Professor. But damn him! What did he want from you?"

"We drove straight from the port to a hospital."

"Who's 'we'?"

"Dawson and me. I don't know what time it was or how long it took. It was daytime, though."

"What did he want?" Deidre clung to his free hand with both of hers.

"He asked a lot of questions."

"Such as?" Joe's words were like a pistol shot.

"Strange questions. They didn't all make sense to me."

"Like what?" Joe insisted.

"He asked me about my relationships with both of you. He kept repeating questions. He asked me about my home in Scotland, my parents…"

Deidre's hold on him tightened convulsively. "Wh…what did that have to do with anything?"

"Nothing."

"What did you answer?"

"I didn't. My personal life is none of his business."

"He didn't insist?"

She sounded so afraid. He wanted to put his arms around her and hold her close.

"He tried, but when I wasn't really dozing off, I pretended to be."

"How did you get home? Why didn't you call us?" she asked.

"I lost my phone, and I haven't memorized your numbers. I will now, though. But the guys from the supply ship said that they'd left Joe a message."

"They didn't," Joe muttered.

"And Dawson brought me home. He just dropped me off and drove away. I haven't been here long. I was going to lie down on one of Joe's loungers until someone showed up."

"I'll get to the bottom of this," Joe ground out. "Son, I have a few more questions, and then I'll let you rest. God knows we all need some sleep."

"Sure."

"Those guys who helped you to the supply ship, would you recognize them if you saw them? Can you describe them?"

Lachlann thought for a moment, tried to picture them in his mind. "I might recognize them if I saw them," he answered slowly. "But I can't tell you how they looked, at least not at this moment. It's all just a blur. I'm sorry."

"Don't be," Joe said. "It's understandable. You were almost blasted off the rig, which brings me to my last question. Do you think they caused the explosion?"

Lachlann met his gaze. "It crossed my mind, but I don't think so. If they were there for me, they just got lucky."

"We'll see how lucky they feel once I'm done with them," Joe growled. He drained his whiskey and stood up.

Lachlann pressed Deidre's hand and rose to his feet. He needed to thank this man who cared so much. "Joe," he rasped, his throat tight with emotion. "Thank you."

"Don't thank me, son." Tears brightened the older man's red eyes. Gently, he patted Lachlann's back. "I don't know if I've ever been happier to see anyone." His voice broke. "Thank you, Lord."

****

"What do you mean, you're not going to sleep in the bed?" Lachlann stared at Deidre, who stared back from the foot of her bed. She was wrapped in a soft, blue robe that matched her eyes.

He wanted it off.

"Lachlann, you're injured. You have bruised ribs, a reset shoulder, a broken arm..." She drew a breath. "You're exhausted. I'm not going to another room. I'll be right here, on the chaise."

She indicated the lounger located near the french doors that opened onto the balcony.

Not an option. As far as he was concerned, separate sleeping arrangements would never be an option again. Not if he could help it.

"Don't you want me to sleep?" he asked.

Her eyes filled with tears. She was no doubt as exhausted as he was. "I...I just don't want to hurt you."

He opened his good arm. "Then come to bed."

She hesitated.

He motioned with his hand. "Come."

Sighing, she rounded to the side of the bed, her expression troubled. With one hand, he untied the loosely knotted belt, then tugged one of her sleeves down. The robe fell half open, exposing one glorious side of her. He caught his breath. He might be hurt. He might be tired. But he could never have enough of her.

"You're impossible." She shook her head, finally smiling as the robe dropped to the corner of the mattress.

"Not at all." He pulled her down beside him. "In fact, I'm very simple."

Slowly, she stretched out beside him. He drew her as close as he could with one arm, shutting his eyes as a wave of emotion washed over him. "Your closeness could never hurt me. It's air, water…I need it."

Her lips pressed his neck. "I feel the same about you," she whispered. "After the last twenty-four hours, I can't…" Her voice quavered. "I can't even stand the *thought* of being away from you."

Carefully, she stretched her arm across his bandaged ribs.

Lachlann couldn't stand the thought either. The memory of the blast rushed over him, that moment when he thought he was leaving her forever, the realization that he'd never see her again. Black panic had seized him; like so many hands, it had clutched at him. He shuddered. That was pain. That was unbearable anguish.

"That's why we have to go to North Carolina," he said. "I know you don't want to, but we have to at least try to make peace with your parents. We need to be married as soon as possible, to be bound together in every possible way we can be."

"Yes."

Did she just agree? He looked down at her. "Yes?"

"Yes, okay." She kissed his chest. "If that's what you want, we can try. I was so afraid while we were searching for you. I have no legal claim to you. We need to be married in case something happens to one of us." Her voice broke. "But if my parents aren't agreeable, I'm marrying you anyway."

"They'll agree."

"But if they don't?" Her voice was low as she played with his chest hair. "What if they still refuse to speak to me?"

Her soft touches were distracting him. He forced himself to answer. "They won't. But no matter what, we're getting married."

Sighing, she cuddled closer and rested her cheek against him. "Do you think Joe will have to go back to Louisiana in the next few days?"

"He might, although they seem to have things under control. I can't believe he walked away from it all to search for me."

"He loves you. His phone didn't stop until well after midnight. He told one caller after another that he wouldn't go back until you were found. He was crying almost as much as I was."

His throat tightened. "I'm blessed to have you both. Joe's a good friend. Has been since we met."

"He says the same." She paused. "Do you ever get the feeling…" Her voice trailed off.

"What?"

She shrugged. "It's just that…sometimes, it seems like he knows."

"My truth?"

"Yes. Some of the things he says…"

He smiled. "I've had that feeling, too. Lots of times."

"You're sure he doesn't know?"

"I don't know how he would. I've never told him— at least, not on purpose. He's awakened me from

223

nightmares over the past few years, but he's never mentioned anything to me or asked questions."

"I can't imagine what you could say to make him certain you're from another century."

He kissed her forehead. "Exactly."

"While we were driving, he kept saying, 'Not again, not again.' "

"He was probably referring to my history as he knows it."

"He did say something to that effect."

"But you're right. He's more than a friend, more than an employer. Until you, he was the only family I had in this century." Lachlann paused. "Since Rónán's not here, I thought I might ask Joe to stand up with me at our wedding. What do you think?"

She smiled. "I think that's a wonderful idea." Her expression sobered, and she gave him a gentle squeeze. "You must miss Rónán a lot."

"I do. I miss them all."

"But Rónán was special?"

"Aye, he was special." He sighed. "We understood each other. He would've loved you."

"From what you've told me, I would've loved to know him. Now, when I look at his drawing of you, I thank him in my heart."

Lachlann didn't reply, couldn't. Thoughts, emotions warred within him. He was too exhausted to sort it all out.

Deidre cuddled closer. One of her legs slid across his as her fingers traced lazy circles on his chest. He yawned. His breathing slowed.

"I love you," she murmured sleepily against him.

He wanted to reply, to tell her how much he loved her, adored her, and that he would never leave her. But his lips wouldn't seem to move.

His mission had changed. Now, he had to make sure that he *wouldn't* go back. They belonged together.

"I…" *I love you.* He hoped he'd said it out loud.

With his angel tucked warmly against him, Lachlann fell into a deep, dreamless sleep.

Chapter Thirty-One

Breathe, Deidre.

Rolling farmland alternated with vast pine forests as she drove down US 1, leaving the Raleigh- Durham- Chapel Hill Triangle behind.

She was nauseous. She had a headache. Was this really necessary? There were so many better ways they could have spent spring break.

All she wanted to do was marry the man sitting beside her. She darted a peek at him, and the knot in her stomach instantly eased. Lachlann was watching the passing landscape with interest. He was the perfect passenger—quiet, relaxed, alert.

Confidence and strength emanated from him in waves. A white Oxford shirt rolled at the sleeves and fitted jeans emphasized his brawn and his natural elegance. His golden hair fell neatly to his shoulders, and his bronzed skin gleamed against the white of his shirt. She supposed it was his lean, muscular physique that made him look wonderful in everything he wore and— she stole another peek—better still, in nothing at all. Oh, she was so going to marry this man.

He was ready for the confrontation with her parents, more than ready. She wished she could say the same for herself.

He would meet her father on equal terms—his words—not that she'd ever doubted that. He'd spent the two months of his convalescence practicing English—

speaking, reading, and writing—aggressively and with amazing results. While he still spoke with an accent that could lull her into a gushy daze, his vocabulary had increased tremendously. He rarely had to search for words, no longer struggled to understand, and readily participated in conversations.

He seemed happier, too, and less haunted. Odd, but ever since the explosion, he'd seemed more settled, as if he'd made up his mind and there were no more questions.

There *were* still questions, of course—big ones—but they didn't talk about them.

She reached out and squeezed his hand, which rested on his knee.

He turned his head and smiled at her. "I read that North Carolina is a highly agricultural state. From what I'm seeing, that's true. There's a lot of farmland."

"There is," she confirmed. "My parents' farm—what's left of it—is one of the oldest family farms in the state. My father's family grew tobacco for generations. But in the nineties, he and Gramps sold off a large portion. It was too expensive to maintain, and my father was more interested in engineering than farming. But we—they—still have a good bit of land."

Lachlann noticed how carefully she referred to everything as "theirs" rather than "ours," as if she no longer shared in the family tradition. He gazed out of the window. Tobacco, if that's what it was, was very green.

She exited the highway. "We'll be there soon."

He knew this was hard for her, more than hard, and that she feared their efforts would all be for nothing. She was doing this for him. He was doing it for her, of course, and had every intention of seeing certain issues resolved to his satisfaction.

"It's surprisingly flat," he remarked, just to distract her.

He succeeded. The small frown that was beginning to form between her eyes lightened with her smile.

"The mountains are to the west, but the best farmland is around here, in the Piedmont."

"Is that your opinion or a fact?"

Her smile deepened, and she raised her chin. "My opinions *are* facts."

They both laughed. But her expression grew serious again as she turned onto a farm road. A wooded area soon gave way to farmland. She turned again, her expression somber. "The farm is up ahead."

"Which side of the road?" questioned Lachlann.

"Both."

He was surprised. She had just said that her father and grandfather had sold off a large portion of their land. How much had they originally owned?

"What…" Deidre gasped. "How could they?"

He turned back to her. Her eyes sparkled with tears.

"Deidre, what's wrong?"

"Don't you see?" Her whole arm was trembling as she pointed.

Now he did.

"Pull over."

She shook her head, her hands gripping the steering wheel. "How could they? How could they put the farm up for sale without giving me so much as a courtesy call?"

"Pull over," he repeated firmly. He grasped the steering wheel and guided her to the side of the road.

She stopped the car with a jerk and turned toward him, her face white as chalk.

"How could they do this?" she asked angrily. Her

lips trembled. "Why didn't they tell me?"

He put his arms around her, his heart pounding as he tried to check his anger.

"Why?" she asked hoarsely.

"We'll find out," he promised through gritted teeth. "But you have to be in control when we get there." *And so do I,* he thought grimly. "We'll sort it all out."

She was shaking. "I don't see how. Let's leave, Lachlann. We can go spend a week in the mountains. I don't want to see them."

He considered it for a moment. She was angry. Hurt. And he hated seeing her in pain. But running away from this wouldn't help. She needed answers. Closure. He drew back to look into her eyes, and his lips tightened.

She looked so sad.

He kissed her forehead. "You don't have to see them. But I can't leave without telling them what I think of them. Drop me off, if you want, and go and find a hotel for us."

"I can't just leave you here."

"I'm not leaving until they explain themselves. That's the very least I expect." He clutched his door handle. "I'm going to drive."

She shook her head, but she seemed calmer. "I'm okay. Really."

"I know, but I'll drive anyway." He kissed her lips gently and got out of the car. "It'll give you time to freshen up."

With an abject sigh, she switched places with him. Lachlann had only been driving a couple of minutes when a house appeared in the distance. "Is that it?"

She nodded.

As they drew closer, he saw that it was a two-story, white, wooden structure. It was modest in size but had obvious additions on either side, one being a garage. From the road, he could see a large vegetable garden beyond the house, as well as a barn and a pond. Fruit trees and a few odd pines dotted the site. The scene was warm, welcoming. His jaw tightened. Deidre had been denied this, her home. He wanted to wrap her in his arms.

Pulling onto the driveway, he glanced at her. To his relief, she no longer looked pale and stricken. She was back to being angry.

"Stay calm," he cautioned.

Without a word, she jumped out of the car and hurried up the steps.

He hastened after her but only watched as she grabbed the knocker and banged.

"They're home," she muttered, as if he'd asked the question. "They're always home this time of year. They have to be."

Springtime. Planting time. A feeling of longing stirred within him.

Deidre knocked again, even harder. This time, they heard footsteps. The door opened. A tall man with a shock of white hair and a weather-beaten face stood before them, glowering.

Deidre glared right back at him.

"Robert, who is it?" A woman peeked from behind him. She had fair skin, fair hair, and blue eyes like her daughter's. A soft cry escaped her when she saw Deidre.

Deidre's heart was pounding. She wanted to scream at the stubborn people in front of her. Or turn and walk away and never think of them again. Or collapse in a sobbing heap on the porch. Most of all, she wanted to retreat into the haven of Lachlann's arms.

But she did none of those things. Instead, she stiffened her spine.

"You're selling the farm?" she demanded. "You're selling the farm without so much as a word to me?"

"Not the entire farm," her father answered. "We've put a portion of the land up for sale."

"Without consulting me?"

"You expect us to consult you?" His voice was quiet, angry. "Just as you consulted us when you ran off to get married?"

"It doesn't give you the right to sell off my heritage without fair notice."

"You turned your back on your heritage."

"I did no such thing."

"Deidre, why are you here?" her mother asked.

She squared her jaw. "I wouldn't be if it weren't for Lachlann. He insisted."

Her fiancé stepped forward. Her parents' mouths—both of them—dropped open. What was wrong with them?

Then it dawned on her. They recognized him. Any other time, she would have laughed.

"Who are you?" her father asked Lachlann.

"An Damh, Lachlann An Damh," he answered tersely.

Her father frowned. He looked older, she thought with a pang. He still stood strong and upright, but his fine, plain features were deeply etched with lines. His brown eyes, which had always been warm and welcoming, even when he was tired, were hostile now. And his hair, which had been dark brown with only a sprinkling of gray when she'd last seen him, was entirely white. Had she done this to him?

"Why are you here?" he asked Lachlann.

"To talk."

"I have nothing to say to you."

231

"I have a lot to say to you. You owe your daughter an apology."

"What?" Her father drew himself up, his thick, white brows drawn together.

"You heard me. You have much to answer for, Chisholm."

"Damn it! Who the hell do you think you are? Get off my property, both of you!"

"We're not going anywhere until you apologize."

"My rifle will say otherwise." He started to turn.

"Daddy!"

"Robert!"

Deidre shot a grateful glance at her mother, then stifled a gasp as Lachlann took a step forward.

"That devil Stanfield tricked her, tried to ruin her. He hurt her. Do you hear me? He hurt her, and all you could think of was your damned pride."

Her father didn't budge, but there was a question in his eyes as he glanced at her. "What do you mean, he hurt her?"

"Robert, let them come inside," her mother urged.

"I'll tell you this." Lachlann spoke with quiet conviction. "If, after you've heard the whole truth, you won't want to go down on your knees and ask God's forgiveness as well as Deidre's, we'll leave without your asking. You'll never see us again."

Deidre felt a rush of emotion at his words. She held her breath. Her father glared at Lachlann a long moment before glancing down at her mother. Without another word, he turned and walked away.

Her mother held the door open wider.

Deidre slipped her hand into Lachlann's. Together, they walked into the farmhouse.

Chapter Thirty-Two

"Why would you deny your only child sanctuary?" Lachlann asked. "She told you she had nowhere to go."

"She most certainly did not!" her mother said.

"Oh, yes, I did," Deidre countered. "And you told me that I'd made my bed, so I'd just have to lie in it."

"And she was right," her father said.

"But we thought you were exaggerating," Rebecca Chisholm added.

"Well, I wasn't!" Deidre glared at her parents. She and Lachlann sat opposite them across the dining room table, as if at a formal business meeting. It was ridiculous.

"Deidre..." Her mother began counting on her fingers. "You lied to us. You ran off to get married without a word, even though you knew our concerns. You did what you wanted to do without caring about how anyone else might feel. Without giving us the benefit of a doubt. And then you had the nerve to be mad at us? The things you said..."

"I was only reacting to what you said!"

"You were deceitful, disrespectful."

"So were you!"

Her father slammed his fist on the table. "Watch your mouth!" He leaned forward, scowling at her from under his brows. "We are the parents. You are the child."

"I'm not a child!" Deidre jumped up. "And I'm done. I knew this was a mistake. Lachlann, I want to go now, please."

He stood and took her hand in his. He looked at her parents.

"You are kin," he said quietly. "You're Deidre's parents. Don't you want her in your life? Don't you know what a gift she is? What you'll be missing?" He shook his head. "You don't deserve her." Without another word, he began to lead her toward the front door.

They'd almost reached it when her mother spoke. "Wait."

Deidre shook her head and kept going.

"Deidre, wait!" Her mother's voice broke. "Please." She turned.

Her mother was crying. "Everything was blown out of proportion. We didn't know...I just didn't know how to go back."

"We can't go back."

"To reconcile, then."

"Are you sure you want to reconcile?" Deidre asked.

Her mother glanced at her father. "We can try."

She started to turn away again.

"We'd like to try," her mother said more firmly.

Deidre looked at Lachlann. He nodded.

"Let's go sit in the family room. Robert?"

Her father didn't speak, only scowled. But he followed them into the family room.

They argued for over two hours. Finally, after a great deal of shouting, recriminations, and tears, Lachlann made her parents listen. He told them the whole story, every sordid detail, details she never could have brought herself to tell them. She sat numbly beside him, trying to pretend she wasn't there. Her parents' faces went from composed to pale to livid to disconsolate. By the time Lachlann was finished, even her father was wiping his eyes.

"You're right," he said to Lachlann. "We do owe Deidre an apology. And I'm going to kill that son of a bitch."

Deidre inched closer to Lachlann on the sofa.

"My thoughts exactly," he said.

"But what are our real options?" her mother asked. "I admit, killing him is tempting, but what are we actually going to do?"

Deidre found a small smile as the two men exchanged looks.

"Oh, for heaven's sake," her mother said. "Y'all need a better plan than that."

"Monday morning, I'll call Neal," her father replied.

"Neal MacDonald?" Deidre questioned. "Uncle Neal?" *Mama's brother?*

He nodded.

"I don't want our whole family involved in my private business!" Her stomach churned at the very idea.

"Now, honey, Uncle Neal won't talk about his clients, not even to family," her mother assured her. "You know he won't. It's against the law, for one thing. I agree with your father. We'll need to take this to the university president, and it would be better to have an attorney with us."

Lachlann looked at her father sharply. "We can have him fired from his job?"

"We won't stop until we do."

"And then we'll kill him," Lachlann added.

Her father nodded. "Exactly."

Deidre frowned at them. "Stop talking like that."

Mama sighed. "While you two plot and plan, Deidre and I will go see what we can find to eat. I think we all missed supper."

"It's all right, Mama," Deidre said. "We should be going. We'll…"

"Going?" her parents echoed in unison.

"Of course you're not going," her mother argued. "We'll have supper together, and y'all will sleep here. After we eat, we can make sure that you have everything you need in your rooms."

Rooms?

"That's not necessary, really. We'll just…"

"You know we have plenty of space."

"Yes, but…"

"There'll be no buts about it, young lady. It's been too long since you've been home."

With a hasty back glance at Lachlann, Deidre followed her mother to the kitchen. "Mama, we…"

"You don't have to sleep in separate rooms," her mother interrupted in a near whisper. "But for your father's sake, you should keep up appearances."

Deidre snapped her mouth shut.

"Anyone can see what's between you," Mama continued. "The way Lachlann looks at you…Mercy!" She pretended to fan herself as she opened the refrigerator. She handed a plate of sliced ham to Deidre. "We have so much catching up to do."

Homemade pimiento cheese, a container of potato salad, radishes from the garden…Her mother finally straightened. There were tears in her eyes as she looked back at Deidre. "I've missed you so much, and I'm so sorry, honey. I don't know if I'll ever be able to forgive myself, and I can tell that your father feels the same."

Deidre took her mother's hands in her own. "It's all right, Mama. I'm all right, and I'm sorry, too. We all said and did things we shouldn't have. But it's over now, thanks to Lachlann."

Her mother pressed her hands, nodding. "We can never thank Lachlann enough for bringing you home."

****

Snuggled warmly against her fiancé, Deidre was just falling asleep when she felt his lips against her forehead. They'd had a lively, albeit quiet, round of lovemaking. The last thing she wanted to do was get up and go back to her small, lonely, childhood bed.

"Love, you have to go back to your room."

"I don't want to." She curled under him.

She felt his lips part in a smile.

"I don't want you to either, but you have to. Your parents are just down the hall. Your father plans to wake me in the morning to take me around the farm with him."

"I thought we agreed to never sleep apart again."

"Aye, we did. Don't think I like this. But I haven't asked for their blessings yet."

"We're both in our thirties. They should expect us to have an adult relationship."

"They might expect anything of me. But you're their daughter, and you only just returned to them."

She sighed. "And I've disappointed them enough."

He immediately moved to cup her chin and force her to look at him. "You haven't disappointed anyone. They were happy tonight, probably happier than they've been in years."

"How can you say that? They're worried about me, worried about the farm."

"They're glad to have you home. They love you, and you've given your father something to fight for. As for the farm, I should be better able to assess the situation tomorrow, after he gives me the tour."

"Thank you," she whispered.

"For what?"

"For everything." Deidre swallowed past the sudden tightness in her throat. "My medieval hero, I love you."

"Medieval, yes, but hero, no. I'm no knight in shining armor."

"You're my perfect hero, far dearer and better for me than some guy clanking around looking for a fight."

He laughed, and she couldn't help but join him. Their laughter turned to kisses. It wasn't until much later that Deidre returned to her childhood room. She fell asleep smiling, at peace in body and soul.

****

The morning dawned bright, cool, and clear. Following Robert Chisholm around his farm, Lachlann felt a renewed sense of energy, a sense of rightness and purpose. It burned through him, melding with his love for Deidre into a powerful, life-giving flow.

"Let me get this straight," Chisholm said as they entered a large metal building that housed his farm equipment. "No tractor?"

"No, sir, no tractor."

"You operated a farm—made a living—with ox-driven plows? Nothing else?"

"I pulled one, sometimes," Lachlann admitted.

The older man stopped in his tracks. "What do you mean, you pulled one?"

"I was young, strong, and had more muscle and land than money."

"You're telling me that you pulled a plow yourself, like an ox?"

Lachlann grinned. "I did."

Robert shook his head and started walking again. "That's beyond natural or organic. I don't know how you made a living."

"It was hard work, but I loved it. I was good at it

238

until…" Lachlann stopped.

"Until you lost it all," Deidre's father finished for him. "I'm sorry. It takes quite a man to get past the kind of losses you've endured."

"Thank you, sir, but I had no choice."

"We always have choices. I've known men to go down, give up, for less—much less." Robert paused, meeting his eyes, then placed his hand on an enormous, green tractor. "My equipment's not the latest, but it works. Are you ready to be introduced to twenty-first century farming?"

"Yes, sir, I am."

He was more than ready. Lachlann was on edge, tingling all over. He could barely contain his excitement. Everything about the farm—the fresh air, the smells of hay and livestock, the challenge—seized him at his very core. He could learn this, learn how to operate a modern farm. He could be himself again, the man he was meant to be, for himself and for Deidre. Maybe he and Robert Chisholm could help each other.

****

"No wonder Lachlann was so anxious for us to reconcile." Mama positioned a large basket of homemade biscuits and a gravy boat on the long picnic table. "He knows what it means to lose loved ones, poor man. But he has you now, doesn't he? And you have him. It seems a little bit of a miracle after all the two of you have been through."

"Yes, ma'am, it does."

Did it ever. Deidre set down a platter of fried chicken. She and Lachlann had discussed what they would tell her parents and agreed that now was not the time to mention time travel. They'd kept to the story he'd told Joe, that he'd lost his family and farm to a fire while he was away from home.

Glancing toward the barn, she stopped, her attention riveting on the sight before her. She'd been watching anxiously for her father and fiancé ever since they'd left around dawn. Now they were heading toward them, and she felt a tug at her heart. Lachlann was riding a lawnmower, turning this way and that. Her father was laughing.

"Boys will be boys." Her mother stood beside her, smiling. "I haven't seen your father laugh like that since...in years."

It really was a miracle, in so many ways. Deidre watched, unable to turn away, even as her vision blurred.

"Deidre, honey." Her mother moved to put an arm around her. "What's wrong?"

"Lachlann never complains," she began. "But it must mean so much to him to be on a farm again. He's worked offshore for several years, but he's a farmer through and through."

Mama nodded. "Farming isn't just something we do. It's who we are. Otherwise, your father and I would've sold the farm years ago."

Deidre didn't answer. She couldn't. She was mesmerized. Both men were laughing now as they drew closer. Her father looked younger than he had since she'd last left, white hair notwithstanding. Lachlann practically glowed.

"I want one," he announced when they joined them on the deck.

She laughed. "The zero-turn is nice, I'll grant you that, especially around trees. But I'm not sure how useful it would be on our small lots."

He grinned, drawing closer, and his expression changed. "What's wrong?" he asked quietly.

She shook her head, smiling up at him. "Nothing. I'm just happy."

Placing a hand at the back of her head, he kissed her brow.

Her father and mother were smiling.

"We'd best wash up," her father told Lachlann, "before the food gets cold."

A cool breeze blew in their faces while they ate. The large pine deck, a fairly new installation, was partially shaded by the house. Her mother passed Lachlann the breadbasket.

"Did you enjoy your tour?" she asked.

"Yes, ma'am, very much."

Deidre bit back a grin. He was showing off his newly acquired, old-fashioned, Southern-style manners.

"Deidre told me that you had a farm in Scotland. In what part of the country was it? We've been there twice."

"My home was in the Highlands, southwest of Inverness, near Drumnadrochit."

Her father looked mildly surprised. "We're familiar with the area. Clan Chisholm's ancestral lands aren't too far from there, either."

"Oh, Lachlann, it's a beautiful area." Mama handed him the gravy boat. "Don't you miss it?"

"I did at first." He glanced at Deidre and shook his head, smiling. "But not anymore."

"Did you ever see the Loch Ness Monster?"

"You'd be surprised."

He went on to regale them with stories that had her parents laughing and bombarding him with questions. He was the strong, silent type *and* a storyteller? Deidre sat back and observed, her heart in her throat, probably in her eyes, too. No, it was more that he rose to the occasion. He was sweet. He filled the patio with his

241

warmth, his energy, his goodness, just as he filled her life.

He looked up and caught her staring. His gray eyes, alight with laughter, bored into hers. The world stopped.

Just as he filled her heart...

Chapter Thirty-Three

"I think that went pretty well. Don't you, honey?" Deidre's Uncle Neal put an arm around her shoulders and gave her a little squeeze.

Lachlann liked Neal. He'd been a whirlwind of activity since their first meeting Monday morning. Unlikely as it seemed, he'd gotten them an appointment at Duke on this last day of the week and last day of class before the university's spring break, only two days before they were due to fly back to Houston.

Tall and solid, with a head of thick, auburn hair that was beginning to gray at the temples, and fair, freckled skin, Neal MacDonald was a Gael through and through. His eyes, pale blue behind thick-rimmed glasses, missed nothing, his gaze direct and penetrating.

His initial reaction to their shortened version of Deidre's maltreatment had been anger, plain and simple. He'd controlled it, though, his lips tight and eyes hard as stone as he took notes.

Deidre had been able to give him the names of a few of the students Stanfield had slept with. By mid-week, he'd uncovered a few more names on his own—complaints had been filed—and obtained written statements from some, though not all, of the women.

When Deidre had told him that of course she hadn't brought any written character references with her, he'd insisted—no, demanded—that she get as many as she could before the end of the week. She hadn't been able

243

to get many at such short notice, but she'd received a few impressive reference letters from colleagues at both the University of Houston and Duke, and more would be forthcoming. Joe and Stella had emailed excellent ones almost immediately.

Neal, who had joined them for dinner twice during the week, had said these would be enough to start with.

The president of the university hadn't been able to meet with them at such short notice, but they'd been taken good care of in the Office of the Provost. The seriousness of the allegations and Neal's persistence could not be ignored. They assured them that the matter would be investigated and resolved as soon as possible.

"It went much better than I expected," Deidre said as they exited the Allen Building. "And it wasn't as hard as I'd thought it would be, especially when I had the cavalry with me." She broadened her gaze to include the three of them. "I thank you all from the bottom of my heart."

"It should've happened long before now," her father said quietly.

"Don't worry, Daddy." She reached out and placed a hand on his arm. "I'm all right now, and Uncle Neal will get him."

Neal nodded. "You bet I will. He won't get away with this. I'll see to it that everything works out to our satisfaction." He glanced at his watch. "But for now, I have to get to my office."

"So do I." Robert glanced at his daughter, a grudging half smile softening his frown. "Are you giving Lachlann the grand tour?"

"Not the grand tour exactly, but I'd like to show him a few highlights."

She kissed her father and uncle, and Lachlann shook

244

their hands. Then she slipped her hand into his.

"Where are you taking me?" he asked, smiling down at her.

"There's a church that I'd like you to see." Her eyes sparkled as she smiled. "And a garden."

****

"Do you like it?"

Like it? Lachlann was speechless. As if in a dream, he turned his attention to Deidre, who stood just below him. It *was* a dream.

She was silhouetted against a backdrop of flowers, row upon row of brilliantly colored tulips. Her hair rippled in the breeze, her blue eyes and rosy lips accentuated by the pinks, greens, and blues of her scarf and the blooms behind her. She was so beautiful. Their love might cross boundaries of time, even worlds, but this was her world, and she looked perfect in it.

"This is part of Sarah P. Duke's historic gardens. It's called the Terrace Garden." Taking his hand, she walked beside him down the steps. "It was dedicated in 1939. Although the plantings have changed over the years, the basic structure of the garden has stayed the same."

Lachlann looked around him in wonder. Behind them was a pergola, covered by the largest vine he'd ever seen. Wisteria, Deidre had said. Now, in late March, only a few flower buds were open, but the scent was already heady. Before them, a great series of steps led down to a pond. Long beds of tulips lined the steps all the way down. As they descended, they were surrounded by flowers—red, orange, yellow, pink, purple, blue—with green leaves accenting all.

"They change this every season?" How many people worked here?

She nodded. "They do, every season, every year. It's

a beloved garden. Lots of weddings take place here."

"I can see why." The knot that had been in his stomach all day contracted.

She'd lost so much. He was glad beyond words that her relationship with her parents was mended. But she had a history here, in this state, and with this beautiful campus. Did she yearn to come back or were the memories too painful? His jaw tightened. It had been her dream to have her wedding here, to be married among family, friends, and colleagues, in the magnificent, historic chapel, amidst these beautiful gardens. But that devil had rushed her to the coast for a civil marriage. She'd lost her job, and he'd kept his. But not for much longer.

Maybe it was a good thing they'd only had a civil ceremony after all.

"Do you miss it?" he asked. "Do you miss being here at Duke?"

Her lips twisted into a wistful smile. "I used to. The University of Houston is a nice campus, and it's been good to me. I love my students and everyone I work with there. But Duke has always had a special place in my heart."

"Did he ruin it for you?"

"Almost." She stopped walking to stand on tiptoe and kiss his cheek. "But you've given it back to me."

"No, you've given it back to yourself by being brave enough to deal with a painful situation."

"I couldn't have done it without you." Her voice shook with emotion.

He stared into her eyes, saw the trust in them, and a feeling of protectiveness surged through him. Taking her hand in his, he led her down the steps.

When they reached the bottom, they turned and

strolled slowly alongside the pond. Koi fish darted here and there, orange and white, flashing in the sunlight.

"But you're okay now?" he asked. "Does being here bother you?"

"I would never have come back if you hadn't insisted. I was so angry and upset. But being here at Duke doesn't bother me." She paused, then sighed. "I never blamed the university. To be completely honest, for a while, a part of me believed I deserved the trouble."

He inhaled sharply. "But not anymore?"

She shook her head. "No. Well…it doesn't matter."

"Aye, it does."

She placed her hand on his cheek. "I know that I didn't deserve to be treated as I was," she said quietly, firmly. "But I hold that it was my own fault that I fell for his lies. I feel better now, and at least we've confronted the problem."

"Would you want to teach here again? I mean, once that jackass is gone?"

She looked surprised. "I hadn't thought of it. I wouldn't ask you to leave Houston, if that's what you mean."

He pulled her down beside him on a bench. "Deidre, I want to talk to you about your family's farm."

Her brow furrowed. "Uncle Neal kept me so busy this week that I haven't had a chance to sit down with my parents and discuss it. They're going to sell it, aren't they? Are things really that bad? It's been in our family for over two hundred years."

"Your father told me that they're short-handed and need new equipment. They're still making a small profit, but not enough to cover those costs. He's tired and worried."

She bit her lip. "There must be something we can

do."

"I could help."

"How?"

"I'm not going to work offshore anymore."

She nodded, her face brightening. "You told me you wanted a more normal schedule and that you were looking into other job options. Have you found something?"

He took one of her hands in his. "I've been looking at Christmas tree farms for sale in Texas, but there aren't many available near Houston. I've also considered buying a plant nursery or, last resort, some raw acreage. I have money. I've worked a lot the past few years and hardly spent any of it. Joe also invested a little for me."

She stared at him.

"I could offer to buy the land from your father—invest in the property and offer my help with the farm. It would be a lot easier for me than starting from zero. Your father and I would be helping each other. I could make the farm profitable again. I'm sure of it. But only if you want me to."

She didn't answer. When he bent his head to look at her more closely, she closed her eyes.

It was too much. Deidre didn't know what to say. She didn't know what she wanted to say. She wasn't even sure what she felt, except for an overwhelming love for this man.

Could she bear to stand by and watch her parents sell the farm? Was she willing to move back? If she couldn't teach at Duke, was she willing to accept a position elsewhere?

Images flashed through her mind. Her parents' faces the night they'd arrived. They'd looked tired, sad, and so much older. And then her childhood—her father's smile as she stood between his knees, pretending to drive the tractor. Picking strawberries with her mother and grandmother. Walking through their peach orchard, cutting pumpkins from their vines with Gramps…

And then she thought of Lachlann tending their planter boxes in Houston and saw him laughing as he tried out the lawnmower, inspecting the fields with her father, walking through the orchard with her.

There really was no question.

They both wanted to raise their children on a farm.

Joy and excitement bubbled within her. Opening her eyes, she smiled at the wonderful man watching her with a concerned expression.

"I love you, Lachlann. I would love you anywhere, in any time. But…"

He still held her hand. She moved so that both of hers clasped his large one and squeezed. "Lachlann…Oh, God." She could hardly contain her excitement—or express her appreciation. She bounced and laughed at his startled grin. "Lachlann, I love it. I love you." She paused to kiss him. "That would be perfect." She threw her arms around his neck. "It's the best idea ever!"

He laughed. "I'm glad you approve," he said as his arms went around her.

Deidre closed her eyes as she hugged him. It would be a dream come true. Her dream—literally—because of Lachlann. Her arms tightened.

"I love you," she whispered. "So much."

"I love you." He drew back, his gray eyes searching hers. "Is something wrong?"

She shook her head, suddenly overcome by conflicting emotions. "It's just…I'm so happy. I'm afraid."

"I know. So am I. But a wise woman once pointed out to me that worrying doesn't help." He rested his forehead against hers. "She taught me how to live in the moment. And to hope."

Hope. Cherished moments. Love. As Deidre blinked back tears, his lips found hers. The kiss was warm, deep, passionate. But even as she clung to him, he released her. And she recalled where they were. Sighing, she placed a hand on his chest and looked up at him.

"Do you think my father will agree? Or will he give you trouble?"

He shrugged. "I think he'll probably agree. But even if he doesn't, we'll work through it."

"This is huge. You do realize that? I know you know what you're doing, but it's going to be a lot of hard work."

"I'm not afraid of hard work. I'm wired for it." He grinned at her and winked. "And I'll have a tractor."

Chapter Thirty-Four

"Woman, you look magnificent. I'm so happy for you." Stella fussed with the veil, looking fresh and lovely herself. Her wild, dark curls were swept up in a loose chignon and the plain gown of pale green chiffon—her choice—complemented her bronzed skin and hazel green eyes. She stepped back. "Lachlann loves you so much. The way he looks at you…"

"I love him." Deidre stared at her own reflection. Her wedding gown of simple white satin left her shoulders bare and flowed in a simple train behind her. Pale pink roses and deep green leaves twined in the wreath that held her veil. She was marrying the man of her dreams in the chapel of her dreams. She could hardly believe it, could hardly comprehend that this was really happening.

Her concerns over possible trouble with Duke, including thoughts of a lawsuit, had proved unnecessary. The last thing the university wanted was a scandal, and they'd been only too happy to work out a compromise. She would be reinstated. She would also be permitted to have her wedding and reception here at Duke. In return, she wouldn't sue the university.

She'd been apprehensive about running into James Stanfield, but that hadn't happened, either. More women had come forward, and the allegations against him compounded. He was on leave pending investigation. Her uncle asked if she wanted to press charges against him. She and Lachlann had been united in their firm refusal. It was over.

None of it would have been possible without Lachlann.

A tap at the door startled her, interrupting her reverie.

"Come in," she called, giving herself a last quick once-over in the mirror.

"Are you ladies ready?" Her father popped his head in, then entered. He looked dashing in a black tuxedo, tall and proud.

"Yes, sir." *So ready.*

"You look beautiful, honey." He clasped her hands in his, holding them up to survey her gown.

"Thank you, Daddy. So do you."

"I appreciate that." Smiling, he let her go and nodded at her maid of honor. "Miss Stella, you look lovely. I think they're waiting for you."

"Thank you, Robert." Stella returned his smile with a wide one of her own and turned to Deidre. "You're so beautiful." Her eyes sparkled with tears as she reached out to hold her hands. "No one deserves happiness more than you."

"Thank you for being here with me today," Deidre replied, blinking furiously. She would *not* cry. "You've been a dear friend to me from the start."

"It's easy to be friends with a saint." Stella touched her cheeks to Deidre's in an air kiss. "I'd better get out there before we ruin our makeup." She gave her hands a gentle squeeze and looked into her eyes. "I love you."

Then, with a flashing smile, she was gone.

"I like her." Her father took her hands once again, his brown eyes meeting hers. "And she's right. You deserve to be happy."

"I'm very happy." How did brides ever make it to the altar with their makeup intact?

"I want you to know that Mama and I are very proud of you. We always have been." His throat worked and he paused. "All we've ever wanted was your happiness. It looks like you've found that with Lachlann."

She nodded. "I have."

"He's a fine man. We couldn't hope for a better son-in-law."

"Thank you, Daddy." She dabbed at the corners of her eyes with a tissue.

"We'd better get moving. Your mother will kill me if I walk you down the aisle with a red nose and runny makeup."

She gulped out a watery little laugh. "Yes, sir, she would."

He opened the door and offered her his arm. "Shall we?"

****

Lachlann stood at the altar, Joe beside him, waiting. Light illuminated the entrance of Duke Chapel as Deidre entered. To Lachlann, it symbolized what she would forever be to him, the light that had pierced a terrible darkness of loneliness and uncertainty. Pachelbel's *Canon in D* played from a magnificent pipe organ, rising to the high Gothic arches, filling the chapel as his bride moved toward him on her father's arm.

For a moment, everything swam before him. The chapel with its rows of arches and richly colored stained-glass windows, the small gathering of family and friends standing as Deidre and her father proceeded down the aisle. She was smiling, a medieval princess, with her hair and veil flowing from beneath a wreath of roses. His princess…She would be his wife. It seemed impossible and yet more real, more necessary, than anything had ever been. A frisson of fear coursed through him. Was it real?

Her gaze locked on his. Aye, it was real. *She* was real. No matter what happened, Deidre would be his wife. She would be his heart, soul of his soul, forever.

****

"Welcome home!"

Lachlann smiled as Rebecca Chisholm hurried down the steps open-armed.

"Did y'all enjoy Asheville?" she asked as she embraced Deidre, then turned to him. "What did you think of it, Lachlann?"

"Of course they enjoyed it," Robert remarked as he joined them on the driveway. "It was their honeymoon."

"Yes, ma'am, we did." Blushing, Deidre turned toward her father. "Hello, Daddy."

"Asheville's beautiful," Lachlann said as he pulled their suitcases from the trunk of the car. "The whole region is." He received a warm handshake and a slap on the back from his father-in-law. Robert took one of the suitcases.

"Why don't you two get settled and then join us on the deck for a toast?" Rebecca linked her arm through Deidre's as they walked up the steps. "It's too nice a day to stay indoors."

Soon, they were all sitting on the deck, sipping champagne and poring over photo albums. Lachlann couldn't get enough of the photos. Photography was still a miracle to him. He stared in amazement at the plump, smiling cherub with golden-red ringlets and bright, blue eyes and grinned at the image of a freckle-faced girl proudly holding a large pumpkin, her long, red braids falling over her ears. A pretty, proper, velvet-clad miss standing in front of a Christmas tree hinted at the woman she would become. As Lachlann gazed at the photos of the little girl, he felt himself fall a little more in love.

"How old were you here?" he asked, pointing to a photo of her and an older man standing in the peach orchard. "That's your gramps, isn't it?"

"Yes, that's Gramps," she replied. "I was about eight, I think."

Her grandfather had been a tall man, he noted. Lachlann glanced from the photo to Robert. The two didn't strongly resemble each other, but the man in the photo looked distinctly familiar. He stared at the image. Deidre had a few photos displayed in her house back in Houston. That must be the reason.

They talked about the farm and their plans for the next couple of days. Deidre had been apprehensive about his offer to Robert, worried that her father's pride would get in the way. But Robert had surprised her, welcoming both Lachlann's offer to help and to purchase the land, glad that it would "stay in the family."

Deidre had put her house up for sale the moment they'd returned to Texas after spring break. Stella had assured her that the timing was perfect, and she'd been right. In less than a month, Deidre had accepted an offer. The closing was at the end of June.

In the few weeks until then, they had loose ends to tie up in all directions. He and Deidre planned to build a house a few miles away from her parents, on another part of the farm. They still needed to pick the right spot. Her parents had objected at first, insisting they had plenty of room in the farmhouse for everyone. But Robert and Rebecca were still fairly young, still active and working. He and Deidre thought it best to grant them all some privacy. They suggested that, God-willing, those spare rooms would be perfect for their future grandchildren's sleepovers.

But first things first. In a few days, he and Deidre would fly back to Texas to start packing.

After a supper of grilled steaks, twice-baked potatoes, fresh green peas, and salad, they cleaned up together and moved inside with their wine glasses.

Robert beckoned them to the dining room. "We have some important business to take care of."

On the table sat a very large book. The first thing Lachlann noticed, after its size, was that it was old and worn. The dark brown leather was faded, the edges frayed, and the pages looked dark gold, almost brown.

"Oh, Daddy!" Deidre sounded breathless. "The family Bible!"

"It's time to add to the family tree."

To Lachlann's surprise, tears suddenly sparkled in her eyes. She glanced at him, smiling. "Yes, it is time."

"Why don't we sit down?" Rebecca gestured for them all to take places around the table.

Robert opened the old book carefully. Lachlann saw that the pages weren't as yellow as might be expected, and that they were clean.

"How old is this Bible?" he asked.

"It was printed in Philadelphia in 1816," Robert replied. Holding what looked like several pages together, he gestured with his open palm downward. "The family tree begins here. As you can imagine, pages have been added over the years." He glanced at Deidre as he began unfolding several pages sheathed in plastic. "Your mother created this insert when you were a little girl. She and your grandmother spent many evenings compiling the pages." He spread the pages upon the table and pulled out a sheet at the end. "Here we are. My grandfather recorded my parents' marriage. My father added my sister, Deidre's Aunt Margaret, and me, and he recorded our marriages."

He placed the sheet of ordinary notebook paper in the middle of the table and smoothed it. They all leaned forward to look.

"I added our little girl." He smiled at Deidre and Lachlann. "And now, it's my honor to record your marriage." He bent his head, wrote on the paper, and slipped the page back into its sheath. Turning it toward Lachlann and Deidre, he rose. "Welcome to the family, Lachlann."

Deidre slipped her hand into Lachlann's and squeezed as they looked at the page.

Robert Douglas Chisholm, 1956- married 1982 to Rebecca Ann MacDonald, 1960-

Deidre Grace Chisholm, 1984- married 2017 to Lachlann An Damh, 1984-

The birth year was false, of course, but it was nice to see his name there, with Deidre's. Lachlann's throat tightened as he stood for a handshake and a pat on the shoulder. "Thank you, sir. I'm honored."

He glanced back at his beloved, took in her shining eyes and tender smile, and a feeling of warmth flooded over him. His own family—his parents, grandparents, siblings—would forever be a part of who he was. But it felt good to belong again.

Rebecca gave him a warm hug. "We're happy to have you, honey." She smiled at him as they all resumed their seats. "I wonder if Deidre's told you that you're not the first Lachlann in the family?"

He looked at Deidre in surprise. "She hasn't."

Rebecca tsked. "The shoemaker's children... Deidre, you're a history professor. You don't know your own family history?"

His wife blushed. "I do, but I don't remember the details. It's not something I teach every day, year after year."

"I guess it's a good thing we wrote your name in the book, Lachlann," her father said drily.

"Daddy!"

They all laughed.

"There have actually been quite a few Lachlanns through the years," Rebecca continued, sounding like the teacher she was. "In fact, the first Robert and his wife, Yvette, named their second son Lachlann."

"I'm not sure that I ever knew that," Deidre said.

"It's right here." Leaning over her husband's shoulder, Rebecca pointed to the first page of the family tree.

"Robert married Yvette," Robert read. "They had three sons, Rónán, Lachlann, and Raibert, and…"

Lachlann gasped. So did Deidre. Under the table, her hand groped for his, clasping it tightly.

Rebecca glanced at them. "It's surprising, isn't it?" Lightly, she ran her fingers up and down the page, scanning it. "There's another Lachlann here, and one here. There used to be photos and letters tucked in between the pages. I think that some of the photos are still there, but Gramps took the letters out years ago."

Lachlann was hardly paying attention. Could it possibly be a coincidence? He felt as though his brain was collapsing upon itself.

"What sort of letters?" Deidre asked. "Why did Gramps take them out?"

"One day, he got it into his head that they should be saved separately," Robert answered. "He said that if the Bible was exposed to fire or moths or what have you, at least the letters would be safe."

Deidre's brow furrowed. "They must've been important to him."

"They were," her father agreed. "Some are very old family keepsakes."

"A few of the letters are written in Gaelic," Rebecca put in.

"Gaelic?" He and Deidre spoke together.

Robert nodded. "Even my grandparents spoke some Gaelic."

"So did mine," Rebecca said. "The Scots who settled in these parts spoke Gaelic for several generations."

"Where are these letters?" Deidre asked.

"I'm not exactly sure," her mother answered. "But I'll look for them if you're interested. They're in this house somewhere."

"I'm very interested." Deidre squeezed his hand.

Rebecca had retrieved what looked to be a large frame covered with a bedsheet from where it leaned against the wall.

"In the meantime, I found something I thought you might like to see," she told them. "I'd stored it in your Gramps's cedar chest with the Bible."

Setting it upon the table, she carefully removed the sheet and turned the painting toward them.

Lachlann's lungs seized. He stared at the familiar face, not breathing.

Rónán.

He slowly rose to his feet.

"Lachlann?"

A gentle hand on his shoulder brought him back to himself. He glanced at Deidre, who stood beside him, and then back at the painting. The second look told him that the proud young man in the portrait wasn't his old friend. But he had to be a descendant of his.

"Sorry." He drew a deep breath and looked from Deidre to her parents. They were all staring at him in concern. "He reminds me of someone I knew a long time ago."

"In Scotland?" Rebecca asked.

"Was he a Chisholm?" Robert questioned.

Lachlann nodded. "Yes, and yes."

Deidre gestured toward the portrait. "Who was he?"

"Robert," her father answered, "grandson of Robert and Yvette."

"Who was his father?" Deidre persisted.

"Robert," he repeated. He returned to the family tree. "It's right here."

"Wouldn't it have been confusing when they all ate supper together?" Rebecca mused.

"No doubt," her husband agreed. "We still have that problem."

"They probably used nicknames, like we do." She smiled. "Who knows? They might've called him Bobby."

"Rabi," Lachlann said quietly.

They all looked at him.

"They…I mean, they might've called him Robby." He needed to get some fresh air, clear his head. He stepped back.

Deidre linked her arm through his, forestalling him.

"Is there, does it…" she faltered. "Do we have the names of the first Robert's parents?"

He held his breath.

"They're Gaelic names," her father said, still reading. "Dubhghall and Ealusaid."

The crack was running toward him, opening at his

feet. Lachlann's heart started pounding. "Excuse me," he managed. "It's...I need some air."

Deidre was still holding onto him. "We'll be right back," she said as he pulled her toward the kitchen. "Please leave everything out. We're not finished looking at it."

Lachlann didn't so much as pause in the kitchen. He walked straight through and out the back door. He didn't stop at the deck, either. With Deidre's hand in his, he kept walking toward the barn. He needed to move, and he needed to speak with Deidre in private.

Inside the metal building, he turned to face her, his breath coming quickly, his heart still beating in his ears.

She took hold of his other hand. "Tell me."

"I...they..." He withdrew from her, running his hands through his hair. He felt like pulling it out at the roots. He was shaking. *Damn it!*

"It's okay." Putting her arms around his waist, Deidre rested her cheek against his chest and hugged him.

For once, he thought to resist. He was coming out of his skin. Almost against his will, he put his arms around her. Then he was holding her tightly against him, his eyes closed as he rested his cheek on the top of her head.

She smelled like flowers. He breathed in deeply. Slowly, his shaking subsided. His breathing calmed. He loosened his hold.

She looked up at him. "The names?"

"Dubhghall and Ealusaid were Rónán's parents."

Her eyes widened.

"But how?" she asked in almost a whisper. "I don't understand."

"Neither do I."

"It...it can't be a coincidence. That's just too many.

The portrait…"

"At first, I thought it was Rónán. But it's not."

"Then who?"

"Rónán's brother was Raibert."

Deidre's breath caught. He drew her back against him.

"So the man in the portrait would be…" Deidre paused. "Raibert's grandson?"

Lachlann nodded. "It would seem so. My brain's going to explode," he murmured against her hair.

"We'll figure this out," she said. But she was trembling.

He held her tighter.

"We have to find those letters." Her voice was muffled against his chest. "They might give us a clue."

"That's what I'm thinking. But what happened to Rónán?"

She drew in a breath. "Do you think he fell, too?"

"I don't know. That day, at the loch, I couldn't see who was calling me, but I thought I heard more than one voice. Maybe Rabi was with him. But did Rónán stay behind or fall? God…"

She could feel his heart pounding in his chest. She had to make him feel better. But how?

"The letters could answer at least some of our questions, maybe all. I'll help Mama look, but we won't have a lot of free time in the next few days. If we don't find them before we leave, you and I can turn the house inside out when we get back." Looking up, she wrinkled her nose at him. "It seems that one way or another, you're stuck with Chisholms."

He laughed then and kissed her nose. "I like Chisholms." He brushed her lips with his. "Especially this Chisholm."

"But I'm not a Chisholm, anymore. I'm an An Damh." She winked. "Have you changed your mind already?"

"Never." No matter what happened, no matter what the hell was going on.

"Are you sure?"

He released her to frame her sweet face in his hands. "Deidre, my heart, I love you. Remember? For all time, I love you."

"For all time," she echoed in a whisper.

He stared down at her. Falling through time had changed his life. That was obvious and undeniable. But it hadn't changed him. He'd stayed the same, with all his old attitudes, fears, and limitations.

But Deidre's love for him, and his for her, *had* changed him. Love had changed him forever.

For all time.

Chapter Thirty-Five

Lachlann strolled along Duke University's Chapel Drive, appreciating the well-manicured lawns and shade trees as much as the fine, old buildings. It was no wonder that Deidre loved it here. He smiled. She was so excited.

The only thing that would have made him happier about the situation would be if he'd gotten the chance to smash his fist into that asshole's face. Just once.

But her happiness was his goal, he reminded himself, and she *was* happy. That's what mattered.

The past two weeks had been nothing short of miraculous to him, the happiest days of his life. Their wedding, those few unforgettable days and nights in the mountains, his father-in-law writing his name in their family Bible, he and Deidre signing their names on the deed to their land…He could look forward to a future more wonderful than he'd ever hoped for or imagined.

And he could lose it all in an instant. Much as he tried to ignore it, at times the thought nearly paralyzed him.

He was going to go crazy.

Deidre kept telling him to have more faith, to pray. *Pray?*

He didn't doubt God's existence. He believed in the Creator every bit as much as he believed that Deidre was his true soulmate, the woman he was meant to be with. It was not an accident that he had met her. Life was not an accident.

But it would be nice to have some idea as to what God had in mind.

He stopped in front of Duke Chapel, where their marriage had been blessed less than two weeks ago. He allowed his gaze to travel up to where the spires seemed to reach toward heaven. It's what he wanted to do, he realized. To fall to his knees and raise his hands in supplication, to beg for a sign, some confirmation that everything would be all right.

Please, God.

He glanced at his watch and continued walking. He hoped Deidre would be done soon. They'd driven in so that she could take care of some paperwork. If she finished early enough, they might get back to the farmhouse in time to search for clues before her parents got home. So far, the letters had eluded them all. Robert had even gone through his father's old things.

As he drew closer to the Allen Building, Deidre emerged from it. A man walked beside her. Lachlann squinted. They appeared to be arguing. He hastened his pace, his gaze locked on his wife.

Suddenly, the man grabbed her arm. She yanked away from him. He grabbed her again and slapped her. Then, he started shaking her.

Stanfield!

Lachlann roared and broke into a run, shouting furiously. He wasn't even sure what language he was speaking. He could barely see.

He pulled the man away from Deidre and smashed his fist into his nose. It crunched. As Stanfield staggered, he grabbed him and threw him across the lawn. When he sprawled on the grass, Lachlann went for him.

He was going to kill him.

"Lachlann!"

He jerked to a stop, glancing quickly at Deidre's face. There was a handprint on her cheek.

He saw red. "I'll kill him."

"Lachlann, please…"

"That's Stanfield."

"Yes, but Lachlann…"

"He'll never touch you again."

Oh, God. Deidre's mouth went dry. Lachlann meant what he said. The expression on his face was absolutely terrifying. He was going to kill James Stanfield.

She had to stop him. But how? She looked around wildly. Should she jump onto his back?

Students had gathered to watch. Some were on their cellphones.

She rushed after him. He was advancing on Stanfield, who was on one knee, struggling to his feet. Blood poured from his nose.

Lachlann lifted him by the collar and hit him. The blow to the jaw sent the older man flying backward.

The onlookers cheered.

A police siren sounded as the car pulled up.

She grabbed hold of her husband's arm. "It's enough," she said urgently, holding him tighter as he tried to wrench himself free. "The police are here. Lachlann, please stop."

"I'm going to kill him," he said between clenched teeth.

"No! You'll go to jail if you do! I need you with me! Lachlann, please!"

He looked at her sharply, as if suddenly focusing on her. Without letting go of him, Deidre moved to stand in front of him, clutching his forearms.

"Please stop! For my sake. If you kill him, you could spend the rest of your life in jail. He's not worth it!" She choked back tears. "Please, I want you to spend your life with me."

His expression changed. He still looked angry, but no longer crazed. After a moment, he nodded. "With you," he bit out, as campus police approached.

To Deidre's relief, there were plenty of witnesses. Apparently, James Stanfield had become very unpopular since she'd been gone. Onlookers readily gave statements that he'd assaulted her. Deidre gave one as well. They didn't have to go to the station. The police took Stanfield away in their car, but Lachlann got off with a warning.

As they were leaving, she heard some male students talking excitedly behind them.

"Did you see that? He *threw* him. Like he was nothing!"

"Hell, yeah, I saw. Now that's what I call protecting your woman!"

Stressed as she was, she almost smiled. But one glance at her husband told her that he wasn't inclined to do the same. They walked for a few minutes in silence.

"What were you arguing about?" he asked suddenly, his voice quiet, angry.

"What?" she asked, startled.

"Why was he speaking to you? He's not supposed to go near you."

She sighed. "It was unfortunate timing. I was about to leave the building when he stormed in. Apparently, he'd made a request to retain a teaching position, albeit removed from the board. Not only had he been denied, he was told that more former students had come forward. He blamed me for all of it." She glanced at Lachlann.

He wore a ferocious scowl.

"It all happened really fast. I tried to walk away,"

she continued. "I got to the door, but he followed me out and grabbed my arm. I told him to let go, that he was violating the court order. But he wouldn't leave me alone. He was just so mad." She paused, swallowed. "He started shouting that he was the one being harassed, that I had ruined his life. I told him that it was his own shitty behavior that had ruined his life. That's when he slapped me. Then I told him that he'd better hope my husband doesn't find him. Then he started shaking me and…" She let her voice trail off. Lachlann didn't need to hear about the petty threats he'd made or the names he'd called her.

"And what?" he asked, looking at her for the first time since they left the scene.

She managed a smile. "And that's when you came to my rescue."

He nodded but didn't speak. He clasped her hand and they walked silently back to their rental car.

****

"It's nice that Joe wants to stop by on his way to the airport tomorrow." Climbing into bed, Deidre snuggled against Lachlann. He lay propped against the pillows, his expression brooding. She rested her cheek on his chest.

He didn't answer.

"Lachlann, what's wrong? You've been so quiet since we left the university. You hardly spoke during dinner."

He frowned. "How can you ask me what's wrong? This afternoon you were attacked, and I almost killed a man!"

"But you saved me, and you didn't kill him."

"That's just it. I still want to." He released a shuddering breath. "I burn with it."

Barely suppressed fury sounded in his voice. Startled, she raised her head to look at him and caught

268

her breath. His gray eyes were like ice.

"Lachlann—"

"He hit you. I wanted to…I *want* to…" He broke off, his chest rising, falling. "You say that I saved you today, but *you* saved *me*. Do you understand? I was going to kill him."

She sat up and shook her head. "I don't believe…"

"I meant to kill him," he interrupted. "The only thing I could think of—the one clear thought in my mind—was that I had to make sure he could never get near you again." His lips tightened. "We can be optimistic. We can hope. But for all we know, I could fall through time at any moment. I want—I *need* to know that you're safe from him, to be sure that I've done everything I can to protect you."

Deidre shook her head. "You can't protect me from everything, always."

His eyes blazed. "I *will* protect you. For as long as I'm breathing, for as long as I'm here, I'll do everything I can to keep you safe."

"I just need you to love me."

His expression softened a little. "You know that I love you. Do you remember what you said to me, how you stopped me? You told me you needed me. And then you said, 'If you kill him, you could spend the rest of your life in jail. I want you to spend your life with me.' " He drew a breath. "It was as if you sliced through a haze of thick, black smoke."

"I don't understand."

"Light. You're light to me." Lachlann paused. "You told me that all we have is this moment in time, that we live in hope of more moments." He looked into her eyes. "I want those moments to be with you. I chose you. I will always choose you."

She wanted to throw herself in his arms, but he continued.

"I've never felt like this before. In the past, I was arrogant. I didn't comprehend how quickly everything could change. Now, it's all I think of." He ran a hand through his hair. "I can't...I don't know what I'd do if I lost you. That day of the explosion, when I thought I was falling and would never see you again...Then today, when that devil struck you—" His voice grew harsh. "I can't..."

She laid her hand on his arm, not sure what to say, not sure how to comfort him.

"Deidre, I don't know what to do. I don't have enough faith for this. I'm trying, but I keep expecting the worst, for it all to disappear. No matter what you say, no matter what *I* say, I can't hold onto hope. I want to, but..." He looked at her. His eyes were no longer like ice. They were intense, burning. "I live in terror of losing you. What kind of man is afraid to live?"

Lachlann couldn't believe he'd said the words out loud. He pushed himself to a sitting position. He had to get a grip, needed to—desperately. But he didn't know how.

"I feel the same."

The words were a whisper, but he heard them.

"Don't you know I feel the same?" she asked. "I love you. When Joe and I couldn't find you, I thought I would die."

His throat tightened at the words.

"And I might as well tell you that I was never going to let you get away with leaving me behind if you found a way to go back. I would've found a way to go with you. Or follow you. My *tuathanach*, my farmer, I can't be without you, either. I love you. I need you. The thought of losing you terrifies me."

"How can we live like this?" The words burst from him.

Her eyes were bright with tears, but she smiled. "People do it all the time."

He shook his head. "Not like this."

She sat on her knees and took both his hands in hers. "Why do you sow vegetable seeds?"

"What?"

"Why do you bother gardening? What's the point of a farm?"

"Food."

"And if there's no tomorrow? What do we need food for?"

He didn't answer. He didn't understand the question.

"Of course you have hope, and it runs deep, so deep. You're a farmer. You wouldn't build beds or clear the fields, prepare the soil, sow, water, weed, repeat, if you didn't have hope."

A wave of emotion washed over him, and he closed his eyes.

Deidre pressed his hands and spoke more urgently. "And you're a survivor. With all that you went through—terrible loss, unheard-of trauma—you never gave up. Every action you took, every decision you made—was based on hope, from the very beginning. You didn't stay in your village and wait for the plague to take you out. You went to Inverness searching for Rónán. You didn't try to escape your pain with drugs or alcohol. Or worse." She stopped.

He opened his eyes to look at her. She hovered over him, both hands clutching his arm.

She drew a deep breath. "You didn't give up or give

271

in. You got a job and came here. And then you took your greatest risk." She pressed her lips to his. "You took a chance on me."

"A chance..." He gazed at her, his beautiful wife, his voice stuck in his throat. His chest hurt. Not just the heart side, the whole thing. He shook his head. "I love you too much, need you too much."

"I've loved you all my life." Her voice trembled, and she paused. "And by some true miracle, we've found each other. We're together, and that should be enough. Why are we worrying? My parents have been married for thirty-five years. And just think of Raibert, Rónán's brother. We don't know what he went through, but we know he fell through time. He went on to live a long life with his wife Yvette, and they had children and grandchildren and great, great, greats...I'm here because he didn't give up. You and I are together because neither one of you gave up."

Lachlann couldn't answer. He knew she was right. They couldn't let fear rule their lives. But words failed him. He pulled her down into his arms.

"Please, Lachlann, don't give up," she whispered. "Don't give up on us."

"Give up?" he echoed, shocked into composure. "Deidre, I..." He swallowed. "Never." She was so precious to him. He hugged her against him. "Remember what I told you," he managed to say, kissing her temple.

She looked up at him.

"I will always choose you."

Chapter Thirty-Six

"Thank you, Rebecca. That was the best chicken salad I've ever had." Joe set his napkin down beside his plate. "And your strawberry shortcake—unbelievable."

He was such a charmer. Deidre, topping everyone's mugs with a little more coffee, almost rolled her eyes as she bit back a grin.

She was glad that they'd been able to enjoy lunch on the deck. It was a warm afternoon—it was almost July, after all—but the covered area provided plenty of shade and there was a steady, refreshing breeze.

Her mother smiled. "We're glad to have you, Joe. I wish you weren't all leaving this weekend. It's going to be quiet around here."

"Not for long," Lachlann said.

"You can spare them a few more weeks, can't you?" Joe asked. "Imagine how I'm gonna feel."

"But you'll visit, won't you, Joe?" Deidre asked, touched by the wistfulness she heard in his voice. She had no doubt that he'd miss Lachlann terribly. "And we'll visit too."

Joe shook his head. "Farmers don't take vacations."

"They get away every now and then," her father said, "and you'll always be welcome here."

"I appreciate that."

"Are you still interested in seeing the old family Bible?" Mama asked.

"Yes, ma'am, I am. History's always fascinated

273

me."

"Once you've finished your coffee, we can go in. We have it laid out for you on the dining room table."

"I'll go have a look now, if that's all right? I have to be leaving soon, anyway."

"I'll tell you bye now, Joe." Her father stood and held out his hand. "I've got to get back to my tractor."

Joe rose and the two men shook hands. They were probably about the same age, Deidre thought, but drastically different in appearance. To her way of thinking, her father looked typically Scottish and Joe typically Cajun—both in the best of ways. Daddy was tall, broad-shouldered, and robust with thick white hair and amber eyes. Today, he wore a plain short-sleeved work shirt under overalls and had just set a baseball cap on his head. Joe was at least a head shorter, with a slim build and only the tiniest hint of a paunch. His deep brown eyes sparkled when he smiled and, while his dark, curly hair was thinning, he had only a little gray. He was dressed neatly in gray slacks and a short-sleeved, white button-down shirt.

What they did have in common was tanned, weathered skin and good will.

"Thank you for your hospitality," Joe said.

"Have a safe trip and don't be a stranger."

As her father headed toward the barn, the rest of them turned and went inside to the dining room. The large, worn Bible sat waiting on the old, cherry wood table.

"Have a seat." Mama gestured for Joe to sit down in front of the tome.

"How old did you say this is?" he asked, opening it with some reverence.

"It was printed in 1816," she replied. She smiled at

274

Lachlann. "We just added Lachlann to the family tree a few days ago. But, as you'll see, we have several Lachlanns and even more Roberts."

Joe looked startled. "Several Lachlanns?" He found the pullout and gently flipped to the family tree.

"Of course, I have the best one." Deidre smiled at her husband. Her *gorgeous* husband. Turning back to the family tree, she pointed toward the top of the first, original page. "See, Joe? Lachlann Chisholm."

"Rónán, Lachlann…" Joe drew a breath. "And Raibert. That one was named after his father, Raibert."

"Yes, it's an old Gaelic name," her mother said, "and it's been repeated in this family generation upon generation. We have a portrait of Raibert, grandson of the first Raibert. It's a beautiful, old painting. Would you like to see it?"

"I'd love to." Joe glanced at Deidre. "You're blessed to have so much family history preserved."

She smiled. "I know."

"Rebecca, I'll get it." Lachlann rose to retrieve the painting. He carefully set it upon the table and held it as her mother unwrapped it. Then he turned it toward Joe.

Joe gasped. For a moment, he stared at the portrait in obvious horror, then jerked to his feet.

"What is it about this painting?" Mama asked, looking in confusion from him to Deidre and Lachlann.

Joe pointed to it. "Who did you say that is?"

"We call him Robert the Third, as he was the third Robert Chisholm in this country. Of course, we realize that the name could go back much further. He was grandson to the first Raibert."

"And the first came from Scotland?" Joe asked.

Deidre stared at him. He looked upset—pale and upset.

"As a matter of fact, he came from Canada," her mother answered. "Nova Scotia, to be precise. But he was born in Scotland."

"When?"

Deidre glanced at Lachlann. He was watching Joe with a frown.

"Do you mean what year was he born?" Her mother leaned over the Bible, scanning with her finger. "It's right here. He was born in 1758 and died here in North Carolina in 1838." She looked up at Joe. "Joe, are you all right? You look like you've seen a ghost."

"Fine, I'm fine." He shook his head as if to clear it. "He looks familiar, but I don't know why." He looked more closely at the portrait. "Who's the artist?"

"To the best of our knowledge, he was just a local Scotsman. I think he was talented, though. We've plenty of old photos. Some of Robert's ancestors, including Deidre's grandfather, bore a strong resemblance."

"So, not the same artist who..." Joe indicated Lachlann with his chin. "You know."

For a moment her mother looked confused, then her face cleared. "You mean Deidre's farmer! Have you ever seen anything like it? Lordy, the first time I saw Lachlann, you could've knocked me over with a feather."

"Same here." Joe grinned, looking more like himself. "But it was the other way around. I saw the person first, the drawing after. So you noticed the resemblance?"

"Resemblance? It looks like Lachlann posed for it! And that drawing had hung in this house almost forever. Deidre's grandfather gave the drawing to her because she loved it—loved that farmer—since she was a baby." She paused and drew a breath. "It's like a little miracle. Some

276

things just can't be explained."

"Ain't that the truth?" Joe glanced at his watch. "Rebecca, if you don't mind, I'll make use of your powder room. Then I'd best be on the road. I have a plane to catch."

"Of course," she replied, smiling graciously. "You know where it is."

Once they saw him off, the three of them set about tidying up.

"Well, that was a little strange, don't you think?" Her mother picked up the portrait. "What is it about you?" she asked the image.

Deidre and Lachlann exchanged looks.

"I guess he just has one of those faces," he said.

"It would seem so," her mother agreed, retrieving the sheet to wrap it.

"Mama, if you don't mind, would you leave it for now? I'd like to take another look at it. I'd never thought about the artist until Joe asked."

"I think your drawing's a lot older, honey."

"Oh, it is. But I'll look up the artist all the same. It would be interesting to know if there are any other paintings by him out there. For now…" Gently, she guided her mother toward the kitchen door. "Why don't you go take a walk and let Lachlann and me clean up? The weather's beautiful."

"I can take a walk after we clean the kitchen."

Deidre wanted to talk with her husband *now*. "I mean a good walk, not a five-minutes-before-sundown kind of walk. You haven't stopped all day."

"Deidre's right," Lachlann said. "You cooked. Leave the dishes to us."

"I've enjoyed every minute, but well…" Her mother glanced between them. "If you insist."

"We do," they said together.

"All right, then. I might just go peek at the lambs and check on the new calf."

"Enjoy." Deidre pushed the door open, and they watched as she walked toward the barn.

She whirled to face her husband. "What's with Joe? That was so weird!"

"It was," he agreed. "And it's not the first time he's asked the questions running through *my* head."

"But we know who the painting reminds *you* of. Why would it upset him?"

"I don't know." Lachlann shrugged. "But you're right. For a moment, he did seem upset."

Deidre turned on the kitchen faucet. "It's obvious that the drawing and the portrait aren't by the same artist. Besides, I told him that my ancestors brought the drawing over from Scotland."

"Something else was bothering him."

She slipped on rubber gloves. "While we're on the subject, did Rónán sign his drawings?"

"Not that I know of. He sometimes identified the subject, be it person, place, or event. And he sometimes wrote a few lines, like a short poem or history." He moved some dishes from the counter into the large farmhouse sink. "But there's no writing on your drawing."

"None that we can see. But it could be there, underneath the matting. I inherited it the way it is. I didn't reframe it." She smiled up at him as he stood waiting beside her, ready to load the rinsed dishes into the dishwasher. "Do you think we'll find 'Lachlann' at the top or bottom?"

He shook his head. "He would've written 'An Damh.' "

"Really?"

"That's what most people called me. Well, when they were addressing me, they said '*a'Dhaimh*.' "

"*A'Dhaimh*?" Deidre frowned. She'd heard that before. "I hadn't thought of that. They would've used the vocative."

A'Dhaimh, sàbhail thu fhèin.

She dropped the plate she was rinsing. It shattered, breaking another beneath it.

"Deidre, are you okay?" Hastily, Lachlann reached down to remove the broken dishes.

"Lachlann," she whispered. "Joe knows."

He leaned his head down toward her. "What?"

She turned from the sink. "Joe knows! He knows what happened to you."

His eyes widened.

She began trembling. "I…"

"Come and sit down." He started to pull her toward the table.

"I can't! We have to go! We have to stop him!"

"Love, what's wrong?" Putting his arm around her, he eased her onto a chair and sat opposite her.

Deidre's mind was racing. Were they in danger? Were her parents? But Joe had never been anything but kind. They needed to talk to him.

"I'll tell you in the car. We have to get to the airport!" She started to stand.

Lachlann took her hands in his, held her still. "Not until you tell me what's going on. Breathe."

Breathe. She couldn't.

"Breathe." He pressed her hands and moved closer. "Inhale. One, two…"

She forced herself to inhale, exhale to his count. She was shaking so hard her teeth were chattering. She took a few more breaths. She had to tell him.

"*A'Dhaimh, sàbhail thu fhèin.*" The words were a shaky whisper.

His hands suddenly gripped hers.

"Joe said it that night in the hospital," she continued. "You'd gone to get the nurse. I'd forgotten it until now. Oh, Lachlann…"

He didn't move, didn't speak. Only the sudden, rapid rise and fall of his chest indicated he'd even heard her. For a long moment, Lachlann just stared at her.

"Lachlann?"

He blinked. Then, standing, he pulled her into his arms. "It's okay," he said, kissing the top of her head. "Love, don't be afraid."

"We should go."

"Why?"

"*Why?* Because…because he lied to you. We don't know how many lies he's told! He might even work with Dawson!"

"He wouldn't have driven all night looking for me after the explosion if he worked with Dawson."

True. It was all such a shock. She drew in a breath.

"I still think we should go after him," she said weakly.

He shook his head. "There's no guarantee we'd get there in time. We'll see him tomorrow. We can speak to him then." He put his hand beneath her chin and raised her face to his. "Don't be afraid," he repeated. "Joe's not dangerous."

She gazed up at him. She'd expected him to be shocked, furious, maybe even have an episode. But the gray eyes that stared back at her were cool, steady.

"It's okay," he said firmly.

Tears blurred her vision. "How can you say that?"

280

"Because it is." He kissed her and pulled her close for a hug. "We'll talk about it later. For now, let's get this kitchen cleared before your mom gets back."

****

Resting a boot on the fence, Lachlann leaned against it and looked up at the clear, starry sky.

A'Dhaimh, sàbhail thu fhèin.

He felt as if he'd been kicked in the chest. That first shock of realization…Joe had been there. Tremors— waves of anger, confusion, hurt, fear—had almost knocked him over. But Deidre had looked so afraid. He'd sustained the blow. For her. Because he could.

And he would protect her for as long as he could, until his last breath—if he was given the opportunity.

What was going on with Joe? How was he involved?

What he did know was that Joe had never hurt him. He'd only helped him. Maybe he was a victim, too.

He had questions, so many questions. There had to be a reason Joe had kept the truth from him. But it wasn't because he wanted to hurt him.

A'Dhaimh, sàbhail thu fhèin.

Save yourself.

That day, as ashes were falling all around them, Joe had taught him to breathe. He remembered it as if it were yesterday.

And Deidre's love had healed him. The ground hadn't opened at his feet today. He was no longer afraid. He had comforted her, not the other way around. And while he neither wanted to fall through time nor die any time soon, he could face it. Now, he could leave in peace.

Deidre was home again, reconciled with her parents, her position at Duke restored. They'd paid her father for the land, signed the deed, and ordered new farm equipment. He'd sent that devil packing.

He'd made a difference. And inside, *he* was different. He thought he'd been strong before, but he was stronger now, in ways he'd never fathomed.

He'd survived. And he'd found love. A love he'd never known existed but had yearned for all the same.

Deidre's love had filled him, strengthened him. Her faith had awakened him.

She'd taught him hope.

A cool breeze blew through the field, through his hair. He closed his eyes. It was strange. He felt both empty and full.

"It's cool tonight."

He opened his eyes and turned toward her. She was pulling a sweater more tightly about her shoulders. Light from the house behind her illuminated her hair, like a halo. Light from the heavens brightened her sweet face in the shadows. And he understood.

He could never lose her. In the infinite vastness of time—past, present, future, past—he wouldn't lose her.

Love was eternal.

Chapter Thirty-Seven

"What do you mean, I was there?" Joe looked from Lachlann to Deidre. "Where was I?"

"You were with me in Scotland, in 1351, the day I fell."

"Come again?"

Deidre sat quietly on the sofa next to Lachlann. They'd called Joe on their way home from the airport. Lachlann had suggested he join them for a drink before he left for the rig, that there was something he wanted to discuss with him. On their coffee table was a bottle of Johnnie Walker Blue. She hoped one bottle would be enough.

"Don't pretend." Lachlann glared at him. "Joe, I know you were there. I remember you there. I just never put it all together before."

"Son, what are you talking about?"

"There has to be a reason you've kept it from me. You've known all this time. You've also been aware of my nightmares, my struggles, and still said nothing. I want to hate you. But I can't."

She was watching the older man closely. Was that a hint of tears?

"Why can't you hate me?" he asked.

"How can I hate my guardian angel?"

Joe managed a chuckle as he shook his head. "I'm no angel."

"You've always helped me, back in the fourteenth

century and in this one." Lachlann ran a hand through his hair. "I don't know how you're involved, but I know you've never wanted to see me hurt."

"Never." Joe removed his glasses, wiped his eyes, and replaced them. "And if there are things I haven't told you, it's for your own good."

Lachlann nodded. "I don't doubt it. But we need to know."

"We?" Joe glanced at Deidre. "You understand what he's talking about, Professor?"

"To a point," she answered. "There's a lot you can explain."

"You two explain first." He took a sip of whiskey and sat back in the armchair.

"You were shocked when you saw the drawing of Lachlann in my office," Deidre pointed out.

"Of course I was, just as your mother was shocked when she saw Lachlann."

"And you overreacted to the portrait," Lachlann said.

"And that's enough to make me a time traveler?"

"You speak more than a little Gaelic," Deidre told him.

"And I didn't teach you," Lachlann added.

"I did work in Scotland," Joe pointed out.

"*A'Dhaimh, sàbhail thu fhèin.*" Deidre watched him closely for a reaction to her words.

His expression didn't change, but he went very still. "Gaelic?" he finally asked.

"You know damn well it's Gaelic." Lachlann crossed his arms across his chest and stared at Joe. "Don't lie to me anymore. Tell me what you know. Get it over with, Joe."

Joe sighed and reached for the tumbler. Draining it,

he nodded as he returned the empty glass to the coffee table. "You're right. There are things I haven't told you. Are you sure you want to know? You're not going to like the truth."

"We're sure," Lachlann answered.

Joe looked between them, then fixed his gaze on Lachlann. "It's true that I knew you before we met in Inverness. I knew you when you had your farm." He glanced at Deidre. "He was the best farmer in the Highlands. He could pull a harvest from a rock."

He still could. She slipped her hand into her husband's.

"I'll tell you something else. The fact that he fed half the Highlands wasn't the most extraordinary thing about him. It wasn't even that he was the strongest human anyone had ever seen." He paused, his gaze on Deidre. "Do you know what it was?"

She nodded. "His goodness."

Lachlann's hand tightened around hers.

"Exactly," Joe said. "His compassion, his humanity, was known for miles around. He helped everyone who asked without question, stopped whatever he was doing to lend a hand, his strength. He never asked for anything in return. He was quiet, kind, loyal."

His voice broke. He paused, pocketed his glasses, and wiped his eyes again before continuing. "He was a good son, a good friend, and a good father." He turned to Lachlann. "Your parents were so proud of you. You could see it in their eyes whenever they looked at you. Everyone was."

Deidre glanced at her husband. His jaw was set, his features taut with emotion. She knew he didn't realize how tightly he was squeezing her hand.

"Everyone respected him, loved him, counted on

him. And he never failed them."

"I did fail them." Lachlann spoke quietly.

"By not dying with them?" Joe shook his head vehemently. "Don't you know that they loved you? That they were glad you weren't there?"

"You don't know that."

"You asked for the truth. That's the truth, damn it. I saw them. I spoke to them. Your parents, your brothers, your wife and son."

"You *spoke* with them?" Lachlann sprang from the sofa.

"Yes. I spoke with them."

"And you didn't tell me?" Hands in his hair, he paced around the living room. "Do you know how much—how deeply—I've regretted not being there for them?"

"They died bravely," Joe said. "With dignity."

Lachlann stopped abruptly, then turned back toward Joe. "And Iain? Do you know how he died?"

"Without a peep, in his mother's arms. You should've known she would hold out for him."

"How do you know?"

"I was there."

"You were with them?"

"I was."

"Why?"

"Why what?"

"Why were you with them?"

Joe sighed. "For your sake. I respected you. I thought that the least I could do was check on them."

Lachlann sank back onto the sofa beside Deidre. She could feel him trembling.

"And then the fires began," Joe continued. "Everything was lost. It's not surprising that…"

"That what?" Lachlann prompted.

Joe leaned forward, meeting Lachlann's gaze. "It's not surprising that you lost your mind."

****

"How could he sit there and lie to me? Look me in the face and…" Lachlann was shouting, hands in fists as he paced from the front door to the back. "How could he look me right in the eye and tell me that I've lost my mind? My memories? Damn him!"

Grabbing the crystal tumbler, he sent it crashing into the fireplace and stormed out into the garden, slamming the door behind him.

Deidre sank onto the sofa. *What the hell?* It had taken them less than ten minutes to gather their wits and go after Joe, to get him to come completely clean. But he'd already gone. He'd hightailed it out of the neighborhood.

She reached for a throw pillow and hugged it to herself. She was grateful for the truths Joe had told. She knew that Lachlann would be, too, once he got over his anger.

But was it the truth? Had Joe really seen Lachlann's family members before they died? Why would he lie about that? Why would he lie about any of it?

Glancing out of the window, she saw Lachlann yanking up her cilantro, which had bolted while they were away. She couldn't imagine what he was going through. She had to help him.

Think, Deidre.

On one hand, Joe had tried to allay Lachlann's guilt for not being there when his family died. He'd told him that little Iain hadn't died alone in his bed, but in his mother's arms. Her throat tightened. Up until now, she'd maintained a certain respect for her husband's deceased wife. But to imagine a mother watching her child die in her arms before dying herself...

Having said all of that, why would Joe ruin it by trying to convince Lachlann that it had happened in this century? That some deadly virus had swept through that part of Scotland and that it had been hushed up to prevent panic?

It didn't add up. Joe wasn't cruel.

Think, Deidre.

Lachlann hadn't remembered seeing Joe until he applied for the job in Inverness, the job the reverend had told him about.

The reverend! He was still alive!

She jumped off the sofa as Lachlann burst through the kitchen door.

"We have to go to Scotland!" They spoke together and stopped.

They looked at each other.

"The reverend?" she asked.

He looked surprised. "Good idea. I was thinking of the cave." He held out his arms, and she hurried into them.

"You believe me, don't you?" He sounded worried.

"Oh, Lachlann, how can you even ask me that?"

"It's just..." He sighed and shook his head. "Never mind. You have to believe me. It's not an option."

"It's certainly not." She kissed him. "When do you want to leave for Scotland? I need to check my passport."

"So do I." He gave her an exasperated look. "The passport Joe got for me. I've been so stupid."

She blinked. "Joe got your passport?"

"And my driver's license. Damn it! I was suspicious about the driver's license. He told me that he could get it for me because it was a temporary one and I would have

288

to take a test later. I didn't care enough to look into it. But they're not valid, are they?"

She drew a breath. "No, they can't be. Those are things you have to apply for in person. But really, Joe did you a favor. You don't have the sort of documents you need to get a valid ID."

Hugging him tightly, she raised herself on tiptoe and kissed him. "It was good enough to get you here, so hopefully we won't have a problem. But are you sure you want to take the risk? I don't know how we'd explain it to the airport authorities if something goes wrong."

"Nothing will go wrong." He kissed her back. "We have to try. I want answers."

"And you do think we'll find some in Scotland?"

"I do."

Deidre nodded. "And then we'll see what Mr. Joseph Dubois has to say."

Chapter Thirty-Eight

Lachlann stood at the edge of the inn's parking lot, at a low fence separating the property from the Highland meadow stretching into the distance. The open meadow reminded him of his childhood home. He could almost see his parents' longhouse silhouetted in the distance, could almost see his family, hear them. A shiver of longing ran through him and he swayed. At this time of night, bright though it was, they would have been getting ready for bed, if not already asleep. They hadn't had bedrooms, as homes did these days. They had bunks running along either side of a central aisle, comprising almost half of the longhouse. He and his brother Vali had slept opposite each other as far back as he could remember.

The meadow faded as a memory came to him. He was twelve years old. In the light of the dying fire, he prepared for his hike with Rónán. He folded a fishing net into the leather pouch. His last task for the evening was to choose what he wanted to bury in the cave. His meager treasures were tucked in his berth, under the mat, wrapped in a small scrap of wool. He looked them over carefully, deciding what would be hidden away and what should be left close at hand. He thrust his selection into the sporan along with a wooden spade, a few iron fishing hooks, and a little extra fishing line. Like the net, it was made from nettle hemp fibers, strong and good. His fishing pole, a thick stick refined by his father, already had a line tied to it. He set the pole and his sporan by the door and returned to his berth to tuck the small woolen bundle back into its hiding place.

"Are you finished yet, Little Ox?"

Lachlann startled at the sound of his brother's voice. He'd assumed that everyone was already asleep.

"Did I wake you?" he asked in a whisper.

"You would wake the dead," came the answer. "But I hadn't fallen asleep yet. Come and sit down. I want to talk to you."

Lachlann settled at the end of the bed, as he often did. Vali was sixteen, four years older than Lachlann. He had a little more time to spare than Ivar, who was almost twenty and about to get married. Lachlann loved and respected both of his brothers, but he was closer to Vali.

"Where are you going tomorrow?"

Lachlann opened and shut his mouth, hesitating. Their cave was a secret, but he didn't have to mention it specifically. "The Great Falls."

"The Great Falls?" echoed Vali. "You and Rónán? Alone?"

"We've been lots of times."

"I didn't even know that Rónán could walk that far."

"You'd be surprised. He's stronger than he looks and unbelievably stubborn."

"He must be. That's what I want to talk to you about. Why go with Rónán? Why not Aonghas and some of the others?"

"It was Rónán's idea."

"Well, why not ask the others to go with you?"

Lachlann shook his head. "Nei."

"Why not?"

"They're boring! All they like to do is play ball and fight!"

291

Vali cocked a dark brow at him. "Says the boy with the black eye? You don't always have to fight with them just because they're rude to Rónán."

"Rude?" he asked hotly.

"Shhh."

Lachlann took a breath and lowered his voice. "They're more than rude! They torment him for the fun of it, just like they used to torment me. Rónán was the only one who was nice to me. I can't just stand there and watch."

Vali's mouth tightened for a moment. "No, you can't. But Aonghas says you hardly speak to them and never do things with them. He told me that you think you're too good for them."

"They only like me now because I'm bigger than they are."

"Are you so sensitive?"

"Nei. But they're not my masters. They can't tell me how to spend my time."

"True. Who can?"

"My elders. Father and Mother, our grandparents, Ivar, you. After you, no one but myself. Not even Rónán's uncle, even though he's chief of Clan Chisholm."

"That's right. What about Rónán?"

"Rónán…" Lachlann started to object, then changed his mind. "He tries. I don't listen to him."

"Is that so?"

"He's always telling me to leave him and play ball with the others. Today, after Aonghas snapped his sporan from his belt, he told me that all they want is for me to be their friend."

"Rónán is right." Vali nodded thoughtfully. "And so are you. He is a good friend to you."

"The best. He always has been."

"I know. Lachlann, we all like Rónán. He's been part of the family since the two of you were small. But he can't be your only friend. You shouldn't ignore the others. You might need them one day, just as they'll need you."

Lachlann opened his mouth to protest, but his brother continued.

"And don't you know that if you're nicer to them, they won't be so jealous and might go easier on Rónán?"

He closed his mouth. He hadn't considered the benefits of diplomacy. "But I don't have to spend all of my free time with them, do I? Can I still go fishing with Rónán tomorrow?"

"You can. Just be fair."

"Vali, do you like Rónán?"

"Of course I do. As I said, he's one of the family." Vali smiled at him, his blue eyes twinkling. "And I believe him when he says that, one day, he'll be a great bard. No one likes to talk as much as he does."

Lachlann grinned. "He's great company on the trail."

His brother laughed. "No doubt. Now, go to sleep, Little Ox. You have a big day tomorrow."

"Good night, Vali."

"Good night."

A feather-light touch brought Lachlann back to the present.

"Are you all right?" Deidre asked softly, her hand on his back.

He nodded. "I miss them."

"Of course you do."

He put his arm around her shoulders and pulled her close. They gazed up at the purple-pink sky.

"I'd forgotten how long the summer days are here in Scotland," he said, "and how bright and short the nights."

"It's beautiful," she murmured.

"Aye, it is."

It *was* beautiful—painfully so. His initial reaction to being back in the Highlands, especially around Loch Ness, hadn't been good. All the old symptoms had returned with full force. As they drove past the long, mist-shrouded loch, he kept seeing the ground open before them, threatening to swallow their rental car. Try as he might, he couldn't get past it. Before he knew it, his head and heart were pounding, and Deidre had pulled over to the side of the road so that he could throw up.

But she had refused to allow him to surrender to panic. She'd insisted that once they were away from the loch and immersed in the beauty of Glen Affric, he would feel better. And he did. Now, as he looked out at the darkening meadow and breathed in the cool night air, he didn't feel sick. He didn't feel great, either. Too many thoughts and emotions churned inside him.

"Was your home near here?" Deidre asked.

"I'm pretty sure this area belonged to Clan Chisholm. It's hard for me to be exact. Where I expect to see a forest, there's a town. Where a field used to be, there's a forest. The old castle is gone. There are highways, now, utilities, and..." He shut his eyes. It was too much. "We weren't far, though."

"Tell me about your house."

He drew a breath. He hadn't talked much about his childhood. He'd been afraid of the pain. But here, he couldn't avoid the memories. Shouldn't avoid them.

"I think I've mentioned that it wasn't wat... wattle...What did you call it?"

"Wattle and daub," she finished.

"It was built of stacked stone. Only the roof was thatch. It was a big house for those days." He glanced at her. "And it was bright, which wasn't so common. It had arched ceilings, smoke holes in the roof, and more windows than most houses had. It never felt crowded, even with me and my two brothers, our parents, and our father's parents all sleeping under one roof, not to mention our livestock." He paused as memories assailed him. "If I'm completely honest, it probably felt a little crowded in winter, when all of the animals slept inside."

She laughed. "Never a dull moment."

"Never." He laughed too, and it relieved the ache in his heart.

They stood quietly for a moment.

"Reverend McKinley's a sweet old man," she said, her voice sleepy. "I'm glad we got to him before Joe thought of it." She snickered. "I mean, Uncle Joe."

Lachlann stiffened. "Joe. My uncle…" He shook his head. If the scenery hadn't given him a headache…

"It does seem that he did everything he could to keep you safe," Deidre pointed out. "He paid your medical bills, your room and board." She chuckled. "Poor reverend." She choked on a gasp. "He thought the mob was after you."

She started shaking. Lachlann struggled to hold onto his anger over Joe's embarrassing lie, but it was hard when Deidre was laughing so much.

When she finally calmed down, he shook his head. "But why? Why would Joe create such a complicated web of lies?"

"Well, he couldn't tell him the truth." She looked up at him, no longer laughing, her expression suddenly somber. "For all we know, that part could be true. Joe's protecting you from someone." Her eyes narrowed.

"And he's going to tell us if we have to hang him by his toes."

Finding his first true grin since they'd arrived, he kissed the frown between her brows. "I believe you."

Wanting her closer, he moved to wrap his arms around her from behind. Her hands caressed his forearms as they looked out at the darkening meadow.

"Are you ready for tomorrow?" he asked. The damp, sweet scent of the meadow was replaced by the fresh, clean smell of her hair. He closed his eyes for a moment, breathing in her scent. It calmed him.

"Aye," she replied, surprising another small grin from him. "You've walked my childhood walks. Now, it's my turn to walk yours."

He didn't want to ask. He didn't want to voice his fear. But he had to. "What if we don't find what we're looking for? What if I can't find the cave?"

"You'll find it," she said simply.

"And even if I do, what if I don't find what we buried? It's been so long."

Deidre turned in his arms and stretched hers up around his neck. Her eyes searched his. "What is it you're worried about?"

He drew a breath. "What if I can never prove I speak the truth?"

Understanding dawned in her expression. She gave a little shrug. "I suppose we'll do the same thing whether we find your buried treasure or not."

"Which is?"

She arched a brow. "You don't know?"

He stared at her, confused. "It seems I don't."

"We'll go home and make babies, of course."

He couldn't help but smile. "Just like that?"

"Do you have a better idea?" She was pulling his

head down to hers.

There was nothing better, except…He brushed her lips with his. "I do."

"Really? What?"

"We should start now."

Chapter Thirty-Nine

Lachlann stared at the Great Falls—Plodda Falls—wondering how his heart could hammer so hard without killing him. The name—and everything else—might have changed, but they hadn't. They didn't even look smaller. How that could be, when they were nearly seven hundred years older and he was much bigger than he'd been as a boy, he didn't know. They seemed the same. But where was the cave? He studied the rocks, but it was hard to tell looking straight down from the platform at the top of the falls. He glanced down the river. He thought he knew approximately where they had fished, but the trees were different. It was hard to be sure. There'd been no platform, of course. They'd approached the falls from the opposite side, at the bottom.

Rónán, wherever you are, help me.

He glanced at Deidre, who waited patiently beside him.

"I need to go down to the water and look up. Do you want to come?"

She raised a brow. "Try to stop me."

He kissed her. "Not a chance."

"Don't worry about me. We hiked the Smokies, remember? I've got this. And we're not leaving until we find that cave."

The stubborn note in her voice made him grin, and he felt some of the tension leave him. Taking her hand, he led the way from the platform.

They hiked down and walked along the edge of the stream, away from the falls in what he thought was the right direction. Lachlann stared at the opposite bank, trying to get a feel for his surroundings, to imagine them as they were in his childhood. Desperately, he turned in a circle, looking upriver and down.

"Lachlann, wait."

He stopped instantly.

"Smell that." Closing her eyes, she breathed in deeply, then smiled at him. "It's wonderful."

"Deidre…"

"It'll only take a minute."

He frowned. Couldn't they do this later? He had to find the cave.

Stepping closer, she took both his hands in hers. "Only a minute," she repeated. "Breathe. Close your eyes and breathe."

He did as she asked, taking several deep breaths, allowing the fresh, cool air to fill his lungs. He could smell the trees. The familiar sound of the falls reminded him of that day so long ago.

He cast his line. Rónán did the same. They usually did a little fishing before hiking up to their cave. The falls were a long walk from their homes. Although he would never have admitted it, he was often surprised that Rónán had been able to make it. An accident had crushed the bones in his foot when he was small. It hadn't healed properly and still pained him, sometimes a lot. But his friend was stubborn.

"Shouldn't we bury our treasures first?" Rónán asked, even as he collapsed on a boulder.

"We promised to bring trout home," Lachlann reminded him. "It's important that we keep our word."

"It shouldn't be hard," commented his friend,

drawing a hook from his sporan. "I can see them from here."

He spoke the truth. The clear river was running with trout. Rónán had collected worms before Lachlann had joined him that morning, so they were able to cast right away. Their lines weren't long and didn't need to be.

Although it was a hot day, it was cool by the water's edge, in the shade of the great pine trees. They sat on boulders and ate lunch while they fished. They didn't talk much, not even Rónán, who knew not to scare the fish away. Anyway, he was pleasantly occupied eating.

Their lines were hit simultaneously.

Lachlann jerked his rod and stilled for a moment. When his line went taut, he jerked it again and began pulling in the speckled fish. Rónán did the same.

In less than two hours, they both had plenty of trout to share with their families. They left their catch in their nets at the river's edge, hidden among some grasses.

They weren't particularly worried about daylight—the days were long in summer—but they didn't want to be too late in case their families were counting on their catch for supper.

They trudged up the slope, clambering over the rocks, to the steep path leading to their cave behind the falls.

Lachlann opened his eyes. It all came back to him. He smiled at his angel before releasing one of her hands to look around. Then he saw it—the indentation that marked the narrow path he and Rónán had taken up to the falls.

Was it even a path? It looked more like an erosion trail. He grimaced. How could he ask Deidre to hike that? He glanced at her, anxious.

She was smiling at him. Her hair, covered with a

ballcap, hung down her back in a long braid. Only a third of her pert little face peeked at him from beneath the low brim, freckles competing for space across her nose. She wore a long-sleeved, navy-blue T-shirt and jeans and carried her own backpack. She looked utterly beautiful to him.

"Are you sure you don't have a degree in psychology?"

She laughed. "I only know my man," she answered, emphasizing the last two words.

He liked that. A feeling of warmth washed over him. They'd have to figure out the climb because he wasn't about to part from her. "Then you know we'd better go before I do something that embarrasses you."

"Can we go swimming afterward, if we have time?"

"We didn't bring bathing suits."

She just grinned at him.

He stared at her.

She winked.

He felt a smile tug at the corners of his mouth. "We'll make time." He gave her a quick kiss and nodded toward the falls. "Ready?"

"I just need my gloves." She started to slide her backpack off her shoulder.

"I'll get them. Mine are with yours." He turned her around and retrieved their climbing gloves from a front pocket.

She strapped hers on. "I'm ready," she said brightly. "Lead the way."

Deidre hoped and prayed that she could keep up. How bad could it be? Lachlann had told her that the cave was about halfway up the falls.

There was a lot of brush, not to mention trees, and there wasn't exactly a path. They zigzagged for several minutes, up and away from the falls. At least, that's how it seemed to Deidre. The higher they went, the denser the forest and the steeper the climb. Deidre could hardly believe that boys had made this treacherous climb alone.

About a third of the way up, they reached a ledge of sorts.

"How did you and Rónán ever find this cave?" she asked Lachlann as she paused to catch her breath.

"I think we were hunting," he replied. He looked at her with concern. "How are you doing?"

"I'm fine. Let's keep going."

He stared at her a moment longer, nodded once, and started climbing again. Deidre kept right behind him. They twisted along the increasingly narrow path. Lachlann kept pausing, holding brush aside for her, constantly looking back at her.

She was a little anxious. The climb was getting steeper and steeper, but the falls were closer. The roar was almost deafening.

And then they rounded into a granite wall. Lachlann stopped and looked up. She did the same. The falls were almost directly above them.

"This is it," he said. "The cave is beyond this wall."

"But how do we get to it?" She was panting now.

He didn't answer. Deidre looked up at him. He looked worried.

"How?" she repeated.

"I don't think this is a good idea."

"What are you talking about? We've gotten this far."

His lips tightened. "From what I recall, it gets a bit tricky from here."

"Tricky?"

"We were kids. It wasn't a big deal for us to hug the mountain as we climbed."

Hug the...Deidre looked from him to the rock in front of them. He was kidding, right? The climb looked almost...vertical?

"Do you want to go back down?"

Down?

"Absolutely not," she said. "If you and Rónán did it as boys, I can do it."

"Are you sure?"

"I'm not going down before we find that cave."

He sighed. "It's not as bad as it looks." He gestured with his hand. "It's a bit up, a bit around. We should reach level ground soon, and then we'll see it." His eyes searched hers. "Okay?"

Jaw clenched, she nodded. "Okay."

"Promise you'll tell me the second you have a problem."

"Oh, you don't need to worry about that. I'll tell you."

"Okay." He edged up alongside the wall. "This way."

Deidre clutched at the side of the mountain for dear life and tried not to look down. This wasn't hiking. It was rock climbing. Almost. When all was said and done and they'd found his childhood treasure, she was going to have a talk with Lachlann. It was bad enough that young boys had made this dangerous climb. She was no small boy.

Focus, Deidre. Eyes on the prize.

The prize. She felt herself melt the moment she glanced up and saw Lachlann's tight butt above her. What wouldn't she do for him? Nothing, that's what.

But why was he making the climb longer and harder than necessary? Surely it would have been easier to climb straight up under the waterfall? The cave was behind it, wasn't it? She shot a glance farther up, at the falls rushing down into the river.

Then again, maybe not.

Lachlann glanced back at her for the hundredth time. "Are you okay?"

"Fine," she lied.

"We're almost there."

Just when she thought her muscles couldn't take the burn any longer, the ground leveled out.

"This is it!" Lachlann shouted from a few feet away.

She stopped and set her hands at her waist, trying to catch her breath.

Her husband was inspecting what appeared to be the cave's entrance. Apparently, there'd been a rockslide at some point. Only a tiny slip of an opening appeared above the pile of boulders.

"Are you sure?" she asked.

He nodded. "I'm sure."

She slipped her backpack off her shoulders and pulled out a water bottle. She offered it to Lachlann.

He shook his head. "Thanks. I'll get mine. I need to catch my breath."

He didn't look in the least bit like he needed a break. Deidre wanted to glare at him, but to her own surprise, she started laughing.

He was looking at her as if she'd lost her mind. "What's so funny?"

"How long have we been climbing? Fifteen minutes? Twenty?"

He shrugged. "Something like that."

"Why do I feel like I just climbed Mount Kilimanjaro?"

He didn't smile. Shoving his water bottle back into his backpack, he put his arms around her. "I'm sorry. I shouldn't have asked this of you."

"You didn't."

"I should have insisted you wait down by the river until I figured out the route. It's a short climb, but it's not easy, and the worst part was that I wasn't exactly sure where I was going. That couldn't have made it any easier for you." He kissed her. "I'm sorry," he said again.

"You have nothing to be sorry about." She kissed him back. "I wouldn't have stayed behind no matter what you said."

She tipped her chin toward the mound of rocks blocking the cave entrance. It was taller than she was. "Do you think it'll be safe to open the passage a little?"

He looked toward the cave and nodded. "Safe enough. But *I'll* do the clearing. Not you."

From the safe circle of his arms, Deidre inspected the barrier. The boulders weren't huge. Lachlann would be able to move most of the larger ones as needed and she could help with the smaller ones. They'd have to move some and climb over the rest. But one wrong move…She drew a shaky breath, then looked farther up. She nodded toward the opening.

"It doesn't seem to be gravel. At least nothing should fall on us."

"No, it's solid rock."

"We'd better get started."

He put his hand beneath her chin and turned her face toward his. His gray eyes bore into hers. "You're not moving rocks. It's too dangerous."

"I can help," she insisted. "You can hand off the medium-sized and smaller ones to me."

"There aren't any."

She folded her arms. "What would you have me do instead?"

He looked around, then at the boulders, then back at her. He stared at her a long moment. "Okay. We'll do it together. God…" He hugged her to him.

Pressed tightly to his chest, Deidre closed her eyes and sent up a little prayer. *Please, Lord, let us be safe. Let this be worth it.*

Lachlann kissed her forehead and slowly released her. He nodded toward the cave. "We won't have to move many."

They worked carefully, diligently. A rockslide was the last thing they wanted. All they needed was a space large enough to accommodate Lachlann and navigable enough to suit her. He estimated that there were three large boulders he would have to move in order to make it through. First, however, some smaller ones needed moving, rocks that might slide and cause a problem. He passed them to her, and she set them aside, away from the slope.

She was glad she could help and felt better for it. But she knew he could easily have managed without her. She held her breath as he moved the boulders with calm assurance. His strength still astonished her at times. She felt like cheering when he declared the opening large enough.

But he was frowning.

"What's wrong?" she asked.

"I don't want you to have to go in first," he replied, his voice tight. "And I don't want to leave you out here."

She stared up at his beautiful, worried face. "Oh, darlin', I'll be fine. Right behind you."

He shook his head. "I don't want us to separate."

"Neither do I, but we have to. Just for a moment."

He didn't answer.

Tough love, Deidre. She laid her gloved hand on his

arm and spoke firmly. "I can make this easy for you. I'm not going in first."

Lachlann felt as though he was coming out of his skin. Every nerve was tingling with awareness, excitement, and something else—something approaching fear. Probably terror.

"The stones could shift," he said. "They could fall on you. Worse, you could fall." *Worst of all, there could be a tremor.*

"I'll take my chances."

He felt the stirrings of panic.

"I'll be okay," Deidre insisted. "Let's get this over with."

He set his jaw as they placed their backpacks near the opening. They clambered over the rocks. Lying on his side, he edged his way in.

Inside, the hair on his arms stood up. The cave looked the same. Had he expected it to change? It was smaller than it had seemed to his childish self and larger than he'd anticipated.

Deidre was peering into the opening. "Do you need a flashlight? Anyway, let me give you our backpacks."

"It's a bit dark," he replied, taking hold of the heavy packs as she pushed them through. "We probably should've moved a few more stones, but I can see. We'll be fine with the lantern."

His wife was already scooting through the opening. He put his arms around her and pulled her through. Then he just held her. He needed to, just for a moment. She squeezed his waist.

"Is this it?" she asked, her voice muffled against his chest.

"Aye." He kissed the top of her head and released her.

They looked around. Lachlann walked toward the back and froze. A boulder—large enough to be a low seat—was positioned in a corner, near the cave wall. It couldn't be...could it? But he remembered placing the boulder there. The memory was as clear as if it had happened yesterday. Rónán had chosen the spot.

"In the corner," he'd said. "It's darker there, and wet. People won't look."

"What people?" Lachlann drew the spade from his sporan.

Rónán shrugged. "Anyone. Any time."

Any time.

Deidre's shoulder brushed his, and a cool light illuminated the space. She was holding the lantern. "Do you think this is the spot?"

He nodded. "I think I put that boulder there."

Her eyes widened. "You mean...way back then?"

"Do you think it's possible that it's stayed in the same spot for seven hundred years?" he asked.

She looked thoughtful. "Maybe. It's not as though it's bothering anybody."

"Well, *I'm* going to bother *it*." He bent and lifted it.

"Wait." She hurried to stand next to him. "I'll keep an eye on the spot, just to be on the safe side."

She was right. The rock had left an indentation, but sand was sand.

"Good call." He set it aside and retrieved their backpacks.

Together, they knelt on the cool, damp ground, facing each other.

"Do you need your jacket?" he asked. "It's chilly in here."

"No, thank you. I'm fine."

"You could sit on the boulder," he suggested.

She glanced to where he'd placed it and back at him. "We can set the lantern on it. I want to help you." Her brow furrowed. "Unless, of course, you want to do it alone."

He stared at her. "Alone? I wouldn't be here if it wasn't for you."

"That doesn't mean that you might not want some privacy."

Privacy? He realized he'd been a little withdrawn. Poor company, in fact—anxious one moment, dazed the next, weeping the next. But…

"I just don't want to intrude," she added.

Leaning over, he took the lantern from her and kissed her. "You couldn't."

"Then I'm ready when you are."

A moment later, they were digging.

"This could take a while," Deidre murmured as she worked her trowel. "But I think a pick would've been too much."

"Aye, it would have."

Their metal trowels were more than enough. He and Rónán had only had wooden ones. As he sat there, Deidre's ballcap faded as he remembered. A head of thick, dark hair bent before him.

Rónán stabbed at the soil with his spade. Lachlann plunged his own into the moist ground. His friend sighed.

"I wish I was strong like you," he said wistfully.

"Why?"

"You can do anything you want. You could squash them all if you wanted to."

Lachlann knew who he was referring to.

"Och, Rónán, if it's for squashing that you want strength, that's not a good reason. And it's not true that I can do whatever I want."

"It is."

"Could I stop digging right now if I wanted to?"

"There's nothing I could do about it."

"You wouldn't hound me to death if I stopped?"

Rónán grinned reluctantly. "I would."

Lachlann nodded. "My mother says that the only true freedom is inside us."

For a long moment, there were only the sounds of the falls and their spades digging into the earth.

"I should probably try and remember that," Rónán finally said. "It sounds like one of those sayings that will make more sense when I'm older."

"Is this deep enough?" Lachlann took a breath. He had dug most of the hole.

"Yes, but can you make it a bit wider? I have lots of stuff."

"Together. You take your spade and widen your side. I'll work on mine."

Deidre's voice brought him back to the present. "You were right," she said. She turned over her trowel and began gently scraping. "It's getting easier. The soil is really moist."

The more they dug, the softer the soil became. They worked carefully, both aware that they could damage items that had rested there for almost seven hundred years.

At intervals, Deidre scooped out the loosened soil. Suddenly, her breath caught.

He stopped digging.

"There's something," she said.

Chapter Forty

She looked up at him. "It's not soil, but it's not rock either."

They stared into each other's eyes for a long moment. Lachlann saw love, determination, and concern in the blue depths.

As one, they looked back at the hole.

"We'll be careful," she said under her breath.

Gently, they began scraping. It wasn't long before he saw it, a bit of…something. Was it leather? Lachlann's throat tightened. This had to be it. He and Deidre had talked about how fragile the sporan might be, but he realized that, until now, he hadn't considered the reality of its age. For him, it had only been twenty years since he and Rónán had buried it. But the sporan hadn't fallen through time. It had been resting here for centuries.

He sank back on his heels. His hands were shaking.

Deidre looked up, her intense expression immediately softening. "Are you worried about damaging it?"

"How old am I?" he asked.

Her brow furrowed. "What?"

Removing his gloves, he gestured to the hole. "I buried it twenty years ago, but it's been here for approximately six hundred eighty years." He ran his hands through his hair. "It looks…I hadn't thought…"

In the next moment, she was beside him, her gloves

311

on the ground as she took his hands in hers. "But it's here," she said softly, "and that's only a tiny corner."

"It's creepy." If it were him, would his bones even be intact? God…

Her lips twitched. "I think it's cool."

"You're laughing at me."

"I'm not. I'm proud that you just used the word 'creepy.' "

He glared at her.

She pressed his hands. "Come on, darlin'. Let's do this. I think we should switch to neoprene gloves now. I'll get the rest of the supplies ready."

It had been Deidre's idea that they watch archaeology videos and research articles about excavating ancient artifacts. It might be a small excavation, but it would be for nothing if they damaged everything before they had a chance to look at it. He watched as she drew polyethylene wrap, polyethylene foam, plastic storage bags, and a thick, wooden paddle from his backpack. There was also a small, collapsible cooler.

He couldn't and wouldn't have done this without her.

"You knew what to expect," he told her.

"No more than you did. But I'm not the one who jumped ahead several centuries." She kissed his cheek. "I understand that this must feel more than strange for you, but it looks like we've found what we're looking for. It's here, just as you remembered. Once we uncover a little more, I'll snap some photos with my phone. We'll have proof whether anyone asks for it or not."

Lachlann felt a little of his tension ease. Together, they pulled on the gloves and got everything ready. They were prepared for this. He didn't know why he'd been thrown off balance by the tiny bit of discolored leather.

"Thirty-three."

He looked at Deidre. "What?"

She grinned as she resumed her position opposite him. "You're thirty-three years old, just like me."

He grinned back wryly and focused on their work. They proceeded with gentle fingers—no trowels—carefully scooping the cool, moist soil.

The shape of a pouch began to emerge. It looked to still be intact, though darkened with age. Lachlann's eyes burned as the sporan was slowly revealed.

It was still here, after so much time. Centuries. Would any of the contents still be identifiable? He stared at the sporan, remembering what they had buried, remembering…

"I think that's good enough," Rónán had decreed, surveying the hole. Laying down his spade, he freed the sporan from his waist and emptied its contents onto the cave floor.

Out tumbled his prized crystal as well as a few smaller ones, a variety of small, colored stones, some brass coins, and a small, silver cross Lachlann's grandfather had given him. Then he drew two small pieces of parchment from the pouch.

Lachlann raised his brows. "Drawings?"

Rónán nodded. "Do you want to see?"

"I do."

He handed him one. "This one's a picture of my family."

"I see that." Lachlann stared at the accurate depiction of the cottage, and the cruder attempts at Rónán's family—his parents, his younger brothers Torcall and Raibert, sister Caitie, and Rónán himself—grouped at the side of the house. There wasn't much more to the small ink drawing, but the basics were covered.

"It's good," he told his friend, handing it back.

Rónán gave him the other. This time, a small sound of surprise escaped Lachlann. It was a drawing of the two of them, much better than the first. Rónán had drawn them standing side by side in front of the falls. Above them, he had drawn their symbols—a seal for himself, for that was what his name meant, and an oxtail for Lachlann. Above the falls, in the sky, soared two eagles. It was a simple drawing, but Rónán had obviously labored over it and Lachlann had never seen a picture of himself. He felt proud, especially as his friend counted it as one of his treasures.

"This one's *really* good," he said.

Rónán grinned, pleased. "It's my favorite, too. What did you bring?"

"I don't have talent, like you." Lachlann drew his sporan from his thin leather belt and turned it upside down. Beside his fishing hooks and line, a few crystals spilled out, alongside some shiny, colored stones, a large turquoise, an old Norse cross from his grandfather like the one Rónán had, some old coins his friend had given him a long time ago, a feather, and some seeds.

"You kept the coins I gave you."

"Why wouldn't I? I've never seen any others except for yours."

"Neither have I." Rónán picked up the turquoise and gave a long, low whistle. "Now, this is a beauty, even better than my crystal. Are those kale seeds?"

Lachlann nodded sheepishly.

"I brought this," Rónán said suddenly. To Lachlann's surprise, he pulled a second sporan from his belt. "It will protect our things."

It was an old pouch, worn and thin in some spots. Nevertheless, it would provide extra protection.

"I brought one too." Lachlann pulled another pouch from his belt. "Everything will be doubly protected."

He felt strange, somehow, as if they were doing something momentous. His throat felt tight. He tucked the old sporan into Rónán's slightly larger one.

Together, they filled the reinforced pouch with their treasures and placed it in the deep, wide hole.

"Perfect," Rónán said.

They covered it with soil, packing it down as tightly as they could.

Rónán began struggling to roll a boulder across the cave.

"What are you doing?" Lachlann asked.

"I know that eventually the soil will settle," huffed his friend. "Until then, this will help."

Lachlann rose, picked up the boulder, and carried it to the corner. It fit just right, as if it was where it was supposed to be.

Rónán smiled triumphantly. "Our treasure is safe."

"*Sàbhailt.*" Lachlann hadn't meant to say the Gaelic word aloud. He glanced at Deidre and saw she was looking at him.

"*Sàbhailt?*" she questioned. "Safe?"

He gave himself a little shake and nodded. "Rónán said that our treasure was safe here. We'd planned to return and dig it up when we were older. But we never did."

"You became adults."

"Aye. We didn't take time." His heart was heavy.

"You were living your lives, both of you, and because of that, the treasure is still here, just when you need it." Removing her gloves, she pulled out her phone

315

and snapped a couple of photos. "Are you ready?"

"Ready."

Taking a piece of cling wrap, she laid it across the paddle and handed it to him.

Slowly, his heart in his throat, Lachlann began sliding it beneath the sporan. He brought enough soil with it to protect it and keep it moist, and carefully set the whole thing down between them.

They stared at it.

"Do you still want to open it here?" she asked.

He nodded.

Once again, she turned to the backpacks. She pulled out a white flour cloth and opened it onto the ground. Then she tore off another sheet of cling wrap and laid it across the towel. They would be able to wrap it up if it fell apart.

Lachlann positioned the paddle so that the opening of the sporan faced the towel. It was a wonder he could do anything, his hands were shaking so much. Would there be anything left besides the rocks?

"I can hold it open while you pull out the contents," Deidre said.

"Your hands are smaller, steadier. I'll hold it open."

She bit her lip as she nodded and began pulling on her gloves once again.

Slowly, slowly, he opened the mud-covered sporan. It was surprisingly pliable. More surprising to him was that it didn't come apart in his hands.

"Can you open the second?" he asked.

"Yes." She carefully slid the fingers of one slim hand into the sporan. "It's open," she said after a moment. She hunched forward so that her chin was only a few inches from the ground. A small gasp escaped her.

"What is it?"

"The drawings. I see them."

He swallowed. "Can you pull them out?"

"I can try."

They both held their breath as slowly, painstakingly, she pulled out one small piece of parchment, then another. He was surprised at their sizes. They were much smaller than he'd remembered.

"Do you want me to keep going?"

"Keep going."

"Rocks…" She stifled another little gasp as she pulled out some crystals, then his turquoise. Next, some of the coins. Then one of the crosses.

"That's enough." He blinked back tears. Was everything intact?

"Wait," she said, frowning as her hand worked in the sporan. "There's something." She pulled her hand out, holding a tiny, dark object delicately between her forefinger and thumb. "A seed?" Wonder sounded in her voice.

"You never know when you might need kale."

She chuckled, but her eyes suddenly sparkled with tears.

"Do you want to take a photo?" he asked.

"Yes." Once again, she took off her gloves and took a few photos, including one with Lachlann holding open the sporan. Then, she took more gloves from the backpack.

"You'll need these to inspect the drawings."

He released the sporan, wiped his hands on a towel, and pulled on the gloves as she suggested, his gaze on the parchment all the while. He hadn't thought the images could still be there. It didn't matter. As Deidre said, they'd found the sporan exactly where he and Rónán had buried it.

The small pieces of parchment were rolled up. Would they tear if he touched them? Carefully, he unrolled one just a little. To his relief, it wasn't brittle. He unrolled it a little more, just enough to see that the images were still there. They were faded, almost completely, but he could make out the figures of Rónán and himself. He stared at it a long moment, remembering it as it was.

Blinking back tears, he raised his face to Deidre with a smile. She was in no better shape than he was.

"I can see…" Her voice broke and she stopped. "Oh, Lachlann…" Retrieving her phone, she took another photo.

He couldn't believe it. It was all here—damaged and fragile, aye—but still here.

"You and Rónán chose the perfect spot, with the best possible conditions, for preservation."

"We didn't know."

She smiled. "You didn't have to. Do you want to put everything back?"

"Aye. Even if none of it survives the trip home, we've seen it."

"Yes, but we'll do our best to get it home."

Pulling on another pair of gloves, she carefully, slowly, returned everything to the sporan.

Together, they wrapped it in cling wrap, then a protective layer of PE foam, and put it in a large storage bag. They wrapped the bag with more foam and placed it in the cooler. Once they were set, Lachlann glanced at the boulder that had guarded the sporan so well for so long.

"I think we should leave it as we found it," he told Deidre, who was watching him.

"I agree."

He set the rock back over the freshly disturbed soil. A lump formed in his throat. Hardly aware of what he was doing, he knelt. He felt that, somehow, he should say good-bye to his friend.

"I'll just…" Deidre began.

"No," he said quietly, catching her hand. "Please. Stay."

She knelt beside him.

"Do you think we'll find out what happened to him?" he asked. "Do you think we'll find Rónán?"

"I believe we might, and I *know* we'll keep trying."

"Here, my memories of Rónán are happy ones."

"I'm glad," she said softly.

He closed his eyes, remembering that day so long ago.

"We should make a pact before we go," Rónán had said as, still kneeling, they slipped their sporans back onto their belts. He placed his hand on the rock.

"In ten years' time, when I'm a famous bard and you're the best *tuathanach* in all the Highlands, we'll come back and open the sporan and remember this day. Every ten years, we should do that, until we're old. Agreed?"

The tight feeling was back in Lachlann's throat. He nodded and placed his large hand over Rónán's slender one.

Rónán slapped his other hand atop Lachlann's. "Friends, forever."

"Forever," Lachlann echoed, following suit. *A'chaiodh.*

Now, holding Deidre's hand tightly, Lachlann placed his other hand upon the boulder.

"*A'chaiodh,*" he said quietly. *Forever.*

Pulling his wife up with him, he wiped his face on

his arm. When he looked at her, he realized that she was crying, too. For a long moment, they held each other in silence.

With a deep sigh, he moved to look into her eyes. "Do you still want to swim?"

Her eyes widened. "What about our backpacks?"

"They'll be okay."

Her lashes were still damp with tears, but she smiled. "I did bring a towel."

"So did I." Her look of surprise made him chuckle. "You didn't really think I would pass up such an opportunity, did you?"

As they made their way down to the river, he could almost hear Rónán laughing.

Chapter Forty-One

The past did have a place in the present, as long as it didn't overshadow it.

In the Highlands, Lachlann hadn't been able to escape the past. To say that the region would always have a special place in his heart wasn't accurate. It was part of who he was, part of his very makeup. After they'd found the sporan, they'd spent another couple of days there. But, try as he might, he couldn't relax there. He saw ghosts. He even saw himself as a ghost.

In Edinburgh, it was different. True, it was an old city with no shortage of medieval architecture and history. But it wasn't *his* history. He'd never come here in the past. Here, he had no ghosts. All of his memories here would be new, with Deidre.

Glancing at his wife, he smiled. His very own, private, completely adorable tour guide. She'd taken him on a tour of the Royal Mile, including Edinburgh Castle. They'd visited the Royal Botanic Gardens and a whiskey distillery. For the past two days, though, they'd spent most of their free time in the Main Library of the University of Edinburgh, mostly in the Centre of Research Collections. They were on a quest to find information about the Norse who had inhabited the Great Glen and about Rónán's family. Deidre was determined that there had to be something, somewhere.

At the moment, she was examining a very old

manuscript written in Gaelic.

"Nothing?" he asked.

She shook her head, frowning. "No. I can't believe it." She glanced at her watch. "And they're about to close."

"We should be going, anyway," he said tenderly. She so wanted to help him. "We need to have dinner, then go back to the hotel and pack."

"I know." She looked from the manuscript to him. "But this isn't over. I'll be looking through their digital archives from home."

He kissed her. "I know."

Home. He could hardly wait.

They left the Centre of Research Collections and took the elevator down to the ground floor. It really was an extraordinary library. He'd learned that it had been renovated in recent years. The ground floor was an enormous, light-filled space. Considering that it was summer, it was surprisingly full of students.

As he looked across the library, a face flashed by. He did a double take, breaking out in a sweat as he scanned the vast space.

"Lachlann? What's wrong?" Deidre asked, concern in her voice.

He shook himself. "I thought I saw…Nothing. It was nothing."

It really was time to go home.

He was seeing ghosts.

****

Deidre glanced at her husband, her *gorgeous* husband. Even after fifteen months, she could still hardly believe they were married.

He sat across from her, making notes in his garden

journal, which was separate from his farm journal. A gray, sleeveless running shirt stretched across his massive chest, just the color of his eyes. His bronzed shoulders and bulging biceps were bare, his arms ropes of corded muscle. His hair was bound back and there was a small frown of concentration on his beautiful face. And although she couldn't see them from where she sat, she knew that soft gray joggers hugged his tight butt and muscular legs.

Swoon.

Sexiest of all was that he thought nothing of it, never deigned to consider the spectacular male beauty that caught every person's attention—male or female—on the rare occasions that he left the farm.

She tried to concentrate on her work, but she was distracted. She was just so happy. She was thrilled with every square inch of their home. They'd moved into the unfinished house just ten months ago and it was still a work in progress, but it felt like they'd lived here forever. And this might be her favorite spot in the whole house.

They had a large, comfortable office that she loved. It was just so them, cluttered with her books and papers, Lachlann's growing collection of horticultural books and journals, seed packets, charts, maps of Europe—both modern and medieval—and some very special drawings. Her drawing of Lachlann still held pride of place as far as she was concerned. It was emblazoned on her heart. But they'd been able to have Rónán's drawings partially restored. The boys, eagles, and the falls stood out in delicate relief, protected by very special matting and glass.

But this space, open to the living room and kitchen, with its two rustic gray desks pushed together, facing each other, surrounded by windows overlooking their gardens and farm—this was for the sheer joy of it. It was relaxing to spend one or two hours working together in the evenings, often on one of their joint projects. They were still searching for any written evidence that Lachlann's family had existed—Rónán's, too, for that matter. They were compiling a Norn dictionary. And they both enjoyed uploading photos of their property. The latest selection of pictures included the greenhouse that Lachlann was building.

She felt herself melt a little as she looked at him. He could do anything. She wondered if he'd want to make some of the furniture for the nursery. She placed her hand on her abdomen. She hadn't said anything to him yet. She hadn't been to the doctor. But she'd only had one period since their anniversary two months ago. She would tell him next week, after her appointment. She could hardly wait.

He looked up suddenly and caught her staring. His frown eased as his whole face softened. "What are you thinking about, love?" Setting his journal aside, he pushed his chair back and beckoned to her.

She didn't hesitate. "Are you ready to rest?"

"I don't know about rest," he replied, pulling her onto his lap.

"There's rest and there's rest," she murmured against his lips.

"I hope you guys aren't doing anything I wouldn't do."

They didn't stop.

"Seriously? Again? Is that how you spend *all* your spare time?"

They looked up to see Stella skipping down the last

two steps. She stopped short, grinning as she opened her arms toward the windows. "Would you look at that view? Why aren't you gazing at that stunning view?"

Lachlann winked. "I prefer *this* stunning view, thanks."

"Well, obviously." Her friend began twisting her dark, damp curls into a loose knot on top of her head. "I can't honestly say that I blame you."

Deidre kissed her husband and reluctantly eased herself off his lap. She smiled at Stella. "How does a glass of wine sound?"

"Perfect."

Deidre walked toward the kitchen. "I'm so glad you're here. Did you unpack? Do you have everything you need?"

"I did and I do." Perching on a barstool, Stella rested her elbows on the counter and watched as Deidre opened a bottle of Pinot Noir. "And thank you so much for the beautiful bouquet. Are the flowers from your garden?"

"They are. We're hoping to surround the house with flowers eventually."

"It's going to be fabulous. I'm so happy for you."

"Thank you. And you'll give me decorating tips while you're here?"

"I'm not sure you need any." She turned and indicated their workspace, which had shocked her when she had first arrived. "I even like that! Who would've guessed? I think I might want one of my own."

Deidre grinned. "If it works…"

"It works," her friend finished. "And I can see that it works for you."

The doorbell chimed.

Deidre glanced at Lachlann in surprise. Here, in the

country, they rarely had unexpected visitors, especially in the evening.

"Maybe it's my parents, come to see Stella," she suggested as she walked to the door.

Opening it, she gaped. He was possibly the last person she had expected to see.

"Joe!"

"Joe?" Lachlann joined her instantly.

They'd talked with him a few times, but they hadn't seen him since they'd moved from Houston. Unexpectedly, he'd been more reticent than they had. Whatever he was hiding from them, he was determined to keep it that way.

"Professor. Lachlann. I'm sorry to show up uninvited. I wasn't sure you'd have me, but we have a problem that you need to know about."

Deidre stared at him. Joe looked more or less the same as always, but the twinkle in his eyes was gone. He looked tired. Anxious.

Behind her, Lachlann pulled the door open wider. "Joe, welcome. Does this mean that you're going to tell us the truth at last?"

"It does. And once you know the whole story, you'll see that I had good reason for my deception. It wasn't my intention to hurt you."

Lachlann's lips tightened. "We already knew that."

"Come in." Deidre reached out and took the older man's hand. "You know we've been hoping to hear from you."

"Thank you, Professor. I do know it." He stepped in and stopped short. "Miss Stella?"

"Hi, Joe," she said coolly. "This is a surprise."

"For us both," he replied. "But it's always nice to

see you."

He glanced toward Lachlann and Deidre.

"Do you mind if I pour myself a glass of wine and go relax on your deck?" Stella asked. "I need to answer a few emails."

"Of course not. We'll join you as soon as we can." Deidre was grateful for her friend's tact. Stella knew that they'd had some sort of falling out with Joe, but she didn't know why. She also knew that Lachlann was from Scotland, but she didn't know from *when*.

"I'll pour that wine for you," Lachlann offered. "Joe, what will you have? Scotch?"

"Sounds good. Thanks."

Once Stella was comfortably settled on the deck with a glass of wine and her phone, the three of them sat down to talk. Joe took an armchair. Deidre sat close to Lachlann on the sofa.

There was a long silence.

"Which would you like first?" Joe finally asked. "My apology, the why and how, or more personal details?"

Lachlann glanced at her. "The why and how?"

"Your call," she said.

He looked back at Joe. "An apology isn't necessary. Let's start with the why and how."

Joe's brown eyes shone with tears. "That's generous of you, son." He drew a breath. "Okay. I've been rehearsing this. It's a lot of information. We'll need a 'who' to go with the 'why.' To make a long story short, about thirty years ago, a group of seismologists in Scotland discovered an unusual pattern of seismic activity near Loch Ness. They suspected that something other than plate tectonics was affecting the Great Glen

Fault. Their discovery was noted by a group called TransGlobal Investments. The investors were—are—a group of wealthy, powerful men. They were interested in time travel as a means to explore and exploit the world's oil reserves ahead of the game. They pulled physicists from all over the world to explore the possibilities of gravitational waves, black holes, and wormholes, and generously funded the research. They knew they were onto something."

He sighed. "It didn't take long for the team of researchers to conclude that much of the seismic activity around Loch Ness was, indeed, affected by gravitational waves, which, in turn, were caused by a special kind of wormhole called an Ellis drainhole."

Deidre frowned. "Drainhole?"

"A wormhole is a tunnel of sorts between two points in space-time, but no one's figured out how to travel through one. That's because the force of gravity would cause it to collapse. The Ellis drainhole doesn't collapse. It's static, traversable. Don't ask me for details, Professor. I'm no physicist."

"Neither are we," she pointed out. "You're saying this drainhole is stable?"

"It seems to be. The researchers discovered a pattern. They found that not only does it open and close in the same spot, but by studying and monitoring seismic waves, they could predict its activity. They also believed that, by comparing all past records and accounts available to them, they could surmise when it had opened in the past. When they thought they were ready, they hand-picked the first exploration team. There were twenty of us."

"But how would going back to the fourteenth

century help them with the oil industry?" Deidre asked.

Joe shook his head. "It wouldn't. According to the calculations, we thought we were going back to the early 1900s. You can imagine our surprise when we found ourselves in the 1300s. It was a mess."

"But *how* did you time travel?" Lachlann asked. "How did I?"

"After years of study and experimentation, the TransGlobal team concluded that we didn't need any sort of apparatus or vessel to travel in. In fact, the less we carried with us, the better, since we didn't know what we'd find on the other side. They maintained that we just had to be in the right location at the right time. The drainhole would do the rest."

"That easy?" Lachlann looked astonished.

"Hell no! As you learned firsthand, there's nothing easy about that trip. They miscalculated both the danger and the dates. They were wrong about everything but the drainhole."

"How did you get involved?" Deidre asked.

"The investors were a few senators, a governor, a couple of billionaires, and some oil company execs. At the time, I was a geologist for the oil company and the lead out in the Gulf of Mexico. They needed someone like me. I was experienced, and I looked good on paper."

She was horrified. "Joe, I would've staked my life that you couldn't be bought."

"You'd be right to do it," he said. "But some of those chosen for the exploration team were men I knew and respected, including a few roughnecks I worked with. I had all sorts of doubts about the expedition, but I wanted to be there for my guys. I had nothing to lose."

"You had Charles and Ginny!"

"They were grown. The love of my life had died fifteen years before, my second marriage had failed. No one needed me. And that trip—it was ethically wrong, but they were going to do it with or without me. I thought that if we didn't all die, it would be a once-in-a-lifetime opportunity and a chance for me to make a difference."

"*Did* anyone die?" Deidre asked.

He nodded. "Out of the twenty, I'm the only one left."

She and Lachlann both gasped.

"What happened?" Lachlann asked. "Did they all die from the travel?"

"Several did. One team member was dead on arrival in the fourteenth century, and three died from injuries they sustained from the trip. Three never made it at all. Out of the eight of us who made it to the loch that last day, only five made it back. We assumed that the others had died, but between you and me…" He paused, then looked at Deidre. "When I saw that painting at your parents' house, I realized that they might have just ended up elsewhere. Whether that's good or bad, well…" His voice trailed off thoughtfully.

"That's still not twenty," Lachlann pointed out.

"We lost three of our team to the plague and two from accidents."

"But Joe, what happened to the others who made it back here?" Deidre asked. "Why are you the only one left?"

He looked at her. "You have to understand, these are dangerous men. They've broken every sort of ethical and international law. They don't want anyone talking. God knows what sort of repercussions there would be if all of this came out in the open."

Deidre felt a sudden chill. "Joe, what are you suggesting?"

"I'm not suggesting anything. I'm telling you that these men have killed before and they'll kill again. That's why I'm here. To warn you."

"Are you in danger?" Lachlann questioned.

"Always."

"Have they tried to kill you?" she asked.

He shook his head. "Not yet. They need me. I'm the only one left from the original expedition, and they need someone for reference. I've maintained a low profile, kept myself to myself, so to speak. But they wouldn't like it if they knew I'd kept something from them."

"But what would they want with Lachlann?" Deidre couldn't stop the sudden quiver in her voice. She inched closer to her husband. He put his arm around her. "They don't know anything, do they?"

"If they knew something for sure, you wouldn't have to ask that question," Joe said. "I don't know what they'd do if they learned he'd traveled back with us. They wouldn't leave him alone, that's for sure." His expression grew grim, and he looked sharply at Lachlann. "They might try to persuade you to go back. In other words, experiment with you."

"I would refuse."

"They might not take 'no' for an answer. Or they might just put a hit out on you. One way or another, they'd make sure you didn't stay around to talk."

Deidre gasped.

"We're okay for now, Professor. If we put our heads together, we should be able to come up with something."

"Why are you telling us this now?" Lachlann asked. "Has something happened?"

Joe sipped his whiskey. "Things have gotten uncomfortable in the past year or so. That guy Dawson…"

"You think he works for them." Deidre's stomach was beginning to churn.

"I do, although I can't find any proof. But one thing's for sure. He's no more a DEA agent than I am. And recently, some university student in Edinburgh put up something on the internet about a time traveler. If he'd been from anywhere else, the investors probably would've ignored it. But since he was Scottish, they took notice."

"What did they do?" Lachlann questioned.

"They sent some guys to question him—thoroughly. You might say 'vigorously.' Fortunately, it came to nothing. It seems that he was just mad at another student. But they called me in, asked if I knew anything about it, asked about you. You need to be on your guard."

He nodded. "We will."

Joe looked at Deidre. "Be careful what you write, too."

She glanced at her husband in alarm.

"She teaches medieval history," he told Joe. "She has to write about it."

"Just don't put too much information out there all at once. It could raise a flag."

"Noted," she said. "Thank you for telling me."

She didn't realize she was trembling until Lachlann pulled her closer against him.

"Like I said, we'll figure this out." Joe looked pointedly at Lachlann. "Son, if I'd told you a few years ago, you would've gone to them and demanded to be sent back. Right?"

Her husband looked pained. He nodded.

"That's what I thought. You would've gotten yourself killed. That's why I didn't want you anywhere near it. Didn't want you to know anything about it. I thought that the less you knew, the better." He paused, swallowed. "I knew you were having nightmares. So was I. But I was worried about how you'd handle the information. God as my witness, I was trying to protect you."

"I know. Deidre and I have never doubted that for a moment." Lachlann sighed heavily. "You did protect me. You saved my life in so many ways. But why, Joe? Why would you care?"

Joe's eyes were bright with tears. "I meant what I said about you. I had almost two years to observe you." He sighed. "We tried to keep to the shadows, to interact as little as possible. That wasn't as hard as you might think. What was left of the team was entirely focused on finding a way back. But you know me. I like people."

He turned to Deidre. "You should've seen him. He pulled that damned plow himself. I'd never seen anything like it. And the people he helped…" His voice shook and he broke off. He looked back at Lachlann. "I respected you tremendously. I liked the bard, too." He paused. "If you don't want details about what went on that last week, I don't blame you. But there are a few things you should know."

Deidre had taken hold of Lachlann's hand. Now, his fingers tightened on hers. "I think I have a pretty good idea of what happened," he said. "But tell me what you think I should know."

Joe nodded. "Allasan and Iain were with your parents until there was no reason for them to stay. After your parents…" He stopped, but it was easy to fill in the rest. "She took the little one back to your house. That woman was a fighter. She wouldn't give in."

Leaning forward, he placed a hand on Lachlann's shoulder. "And they weren't alone. A few of your kinsmen were with them. They were sick too, but not as sick as she was. Your people were strong, impressive. They took care of each other until they dropped."

Deidre bit her lip as Lachlann's eyes filled with tears. He nodded, not speaking.

"You were with them, Joe? In their house?"

He nodded. "I was. I'd followed them back in case I could help in some way. I'd taken every vaccine I could before we left. I don't know if that's what saved me or if I simply wasn't susceptible." Joe stopped again, shook his head. "But there was nothing I could do, nothing anyone could do. No one noticed me, except for the bard."

"'The bard?'" Lachlann tensed. "Rónán was there? Why? He wasn't allowed…he wasn't supposed to be…"

"No, he wasn't. The chief had ordered his people to stay away from yours. But while your wife was his cousin, he was there for your sake, as I was. He looked right at me, and he wasn't happy to see me."

"Did he know you?" Deidre asked.

"He knew I was a stranger to his people. He'd noticed me before."

"Did you speak?" Lachlann asked.

"No, and the moment…" Joe drew another deep breath. "The moment it was over, and the priest prayed his prayers, he left to go find you, to warn you."

"I knew I heard him that day at Loch Ness. He was shouting my name."

Joe looked surprised. "We didn't hear him, but we saw him. Him and his younger brother. They were headed toward you."

"His brother?" Deidre and Lachlann spoke together. "Raibert?"

"I didn't know his name at the time, but now we know where he ended up."

"And Rónán?" Lachlann sounded desperate.

"I'm sorry, son. I don't know." Joe suddenly looked drawn, exhausted. "I searched for him, but I couldn't find him. Until I saw that portrait, I'd come to peace that he and his brother had stayed behind."

Lachlann shut his eyes.

"And the bard might not have fallen. At the time, we didn't know you had. We thought we were standing at the portal, so to speak. We didn't know that the drainhole was that large or precisely when it would open. We were trying to follow charts, measure the tremors without our equipment. For all we knew, we were stuck there forever. But my crew—what was left of it—had been performing crude experiments with the energy field, trying to manipulate the opening. Trying to get the hell out."

"They caused the earthquake?" Lachlann's tone hardened.

"Can't be sure. There'd been a lot of tremors in the area that year. They might've made it worse. And when you didn't arrive with us in this century, we assumed you had died. The way you fell…" He choked up, but, after a moment, he ran a hand down his face and continued. "The bard and his brother weren't even a consideration. From where we were standing, they'd just been specks in the distance."

"If you thought I was dead, why did you bother

looking for me?"

"I would've gone looking, just to be sure, but I didn't have to. Five of us had made it back and we were all hurt, although nothing compared to you. Four were taken to one hospital in Inverness. I was taken to another. For some reason—you could say on a whim—when I was being discharged, I asked about you. I didn't really expect to find you."

"What do you mean, you asked for me? What did you say?"

"I told them that my nephew had been out climbing with me, but there'd been an accident and I'd lost sight of you. I wondered if you'd been admitted, by any chance. And you had been."

"And then you set me up with the reverend."

Joe looked astonished. "How did you know that?"

Deidre couldn't help but laugh, and it felt good.

Her husband shot Joe an exasperated look. "As you know, we went to Scotland shortly after our wedding last year. Reverend McKinley was our first stop." He frowned. "The *mob*? That was the best story you could come up with?"

Joe was finally grinning. "It sounded good to me."

"And you never told anyone at TransGlobal about me." It wasn't a question.

"Hell, no. The investors never knew anything about you, but they were worried about hitchhikers. They still are. They don't want any complications."

"Well, they won't get any from us," Deidre huffed. "But Joe, has anyone else gone back?"

"No. After that disaster, most of the files were sealed or destroyed. But they have a few guys still working, researching."

"Is it dangerous to go near Loch Ness?"

He shook his head. "Evidence suggests that the drainhole only opens a few times a century, maybe less often, and specific seismic activity should give enough warning."

It could be worse, she supposed. She leaned back against Lachlann.

"Why have you been avoiding us?" he asked Joe.

"I knew you didn't believe me and that you were upset. I was afraid that I'd break and tell you everything and thereby put you in danger."

"We were upset. I was very upset." Her husband rose, and Deidre rose with him.

They waited.

"I'm sorry I hurt you, son." Joe stood, sighing heavily, as if he bore all the troubles of the world on his shoulders. "I was just so worried. I couldn't see another way."

Tears sprang to Deidre's eyes as Lachlann embraced the older man.

"I know you did the best you could," he told him. "Thank you, Joe. Thank you for all you've done for me."

"For us," Deidre added, wiping her eyes as she waited for her turn to hug her husband's guardian angel.

Joe was crying openly. "It's not me. I'm just a poor instrument. I thank God it's turned out as it has." He managed to smile at her. "It seems the good Lord saved him for you."

Deidre nodded. She was afraid that, if she tried to speak, she'd start bawling. As Lachlann pulled her close to his side, she heard the back door open.

"Excuse me." Stella crossed the room, wine glass in hand. "I only want a little more wine." She glanced at them all standing there and stopped, looking straight at Deidre. "Is everything okay?"

Deidre nodded. "More than okay," she said, reaching for a tissue.

Stella smiled, clearly relieved, and continued to the kitchen.

The doorbell chimed—again.

"It's your parents," she called. "I'll get it."

They all got busy wiping their eyes. What in the world would they tell her parents if they noticed? And they'd have to notice. She blew her nose and grabbed another tissue.

She heard the door open, but no one spoke. After a moment, she glanced toward their entrance.

Stella stood staring, as if frozen.

"Stella?" she prompted.

Her friend seemed to wake from a daze. "I...I think it's someone for Lachlann."

Her husband went to the door and stopped abruptly, his eyes widening.

Deidre hurried after him.

Lachlann couldn't breathe. He was afraid to, lest the vision disappear. He stared at the visitor, unable to speak, unable to move.

Was he dreaming? He blinked.

A man stood proudly before him—muscular, healthy, strong.

"Aye, Lachlann. It's me," he said in thick Gaelic. "Rónán."

Lachlann was shaking. He closed his eyes for a moment, to stem the flow of tears, then gave it up. He pulled him in for a hug. "I know who you are, man."

Laughing and crying, he ruffled the thick, dark hair,

inhaled his friend's scent, trying to make sure he was real. He couldn't believe it.

Rónán. He was alive. He was *here.*

He hugged him for a long moment, crying, shaking with the force of it. When he was finally able to let go, he grasped the muscular arms and looked him over. "You look good," he choked out. "The same, but different. Is that…" He paused, smiling through his tears. "Are you wearing cologne?"

Rónán's face was wet, tears still streaming down his cheeks, but he laughed. "Aye, *a'Dhaimh.* But you're not. And I would say the same to you."

"I haven't changed at all."

"Not on the outside." Rónán pushed him in the chest. "On the inside."

Lachlann needed Deidre. He needed her to make sure his feet were still on the ground.

She was right beside him. He grabbed her hand and held tight, his gaze still on his old friend, his other hand still gripping his arm.

Rónán looked at Deidre, his smile broadening, and back at him. "You're happy."

"Aye." He let go of Rónán to wipe his face with a trembling hand. "Never happier. Rónán Chisholm, meet my wife, Deidre An Damh—Deidre *Chisholm* An Damh. Deidre, Rónán."

"Chisholm?" His dark brows rose in surprise.

She clasped both his hands in hers, kissed his cheeks, and welcomed him.

"*Fáilte,* Rónán. Tha…" Her voice broke. "*Tha mi toilichte do choinneachadh.*" I'm pleased to meet you.

"*And* you speak Gaelic?" He glanced between them. "Too bad you have your husband's accent."

339

The three of them laughed. But Lachlann had questions. "That day in the library…it was you, wasn't it? At the University of Edinburgh?"

"You saw me?"

"I thought I did, but you disappeared. Where did you go? Why didn't you come after me?"

"I have come after you." Rónán paused, swallowing as fresh tears sprang to his eyes. "I searched for you for almost a year. I didn't know what name you were going by, where you had gone, why you were even at the university. But that day…when I saw you…" He shook his head. "I passed out."

"Passed out?" Lachlann stared at him. "Why?"

"*Why?* Why do you think? Shock! I thought I was having a heart attack." His voice shook. "I was thinking of you and then…there you were."

Lachlann nodded, his throat tight. "I know what you mean."

Rónán turned to Deidre. "If it wasn't for Professor An Damh here, I don't know how I would've found you."

"You wouldn't have, because without Professor An Damh…" He smiled at his wife. "I wouldn't have gone to Edinburgh."

"Why are we standing in the doorway?" Deidre asked.

Rónán grinned. "Would you believe it's an old Scottish custom?"

Lachlann shook his head. "She knows better. This is my version of shock. At least I'm not fainting."

"Thank God," a voice said from behind him.

"Stella!" He and Deidre spoke together.

She'd gotten trapped behind them, between the door

340

and the wall.

"Stella, I'm sorry."

She smiled up at him, her eyes sparkling with tears, obviously touched by their happy reunion.

Pulling her forward, he put an arm around her shoulders and squeezed. "Please excuse us. I thought..." He had to stop and take a breath. "I thought I'd never see him again. This is my oldest, closest friend, Rónán Chisholm. We've known each other since we were children. Rónán, my wife's best friend, Stella Mastrioni."

"I've heard all about you." Stella gifted Rónán with her wide smile and held out her hand. "The artist, right?"

"Honored," he said, taking her hand in his. He glanced at Lachlann. "Artist?"

He nodded. "We've talked about your drawings."

"Come in." Deidre reached out to pull Rónán into the room. She glanced between them, smiling. "This is unbelievably wonderful."

As the door closed behind them, Joe stood.

"Bard?"

Rónán's expression changed. His brows slashed fiercely downward, his eyes suddenly blazing. He took a step forward, pointing. "You!" He rushed at him. "I'll kill you!"

Thank you for sharing your time with my characters. If you enjoyed their story, I hope you'll leave a review. I can't do this without you, my readers. Wishing you joy.

A word about the author...

For me, playing is the best—playing outdoors in nature or in my garden, experimenting in the kitchen, spending time with those I love. I also enjoy disappearing into a good book, attempting crafts, learning, writing, exploring, discovering. I especially like to mix it up and have yet to perfect any of it; and I've come to realize that perfection is not the point. It's all wonderfully fun. That's the point!

I prefer authentic and natural, be it food, lifestyle, people. I passionately enjoy both history and science, and certainly sociology to a degree, and I am most truly a romantic.

My husband and I have been married for over forty years. We reside near Houston, Texas, surrounded by beloved family and friends. We have a blast with our little grandchildren.

I thank God for this wonderful life.

http://anastasiaabboud.com